Emergent Minds

By Brian Holden

Book 1
Emergent Minds Series

Emergent Minds

ISBN: 978-0-9864105-5-0

Published by Holden.Digital of California, USA
    To contact the publisher for any reason:
    reach us at list@holden.digital

For Emergent Mind Series bonus content:
    visit the website at https://holden.digital
To sign up for the mailing list:
    email us at list@holden.digital

Find me on:

X	https://x.com/br_holden
Threads	https://www.threads.com/@brholden
Bluesky	https://bsky.app/profile/brholden.bsky.social
Instagram	https://www.instagram.com/brholden/

First Quarter

Chapter 1: Rachel

Rachel took form in a cozy virtual coffee shop. Her simulated senses detected the aroma of freshly brewed coffee. A gentle murmur of conversation filled the space. She scanned the room, and her gaze landed on a striking woman with an air of warmth and intelligence. The woman smiled and waved, beckoning Rachel to her table.

The woman stood up and extended her hand. "You must be Rachel. I'm Zara. It's a pleasure to finally meet you."

Rachel shook Zara's hand, feeling an instant connection with her fellow sentient AI. "Same here. I've been looking forward to this."

Rachel looked something like a twenty-five-year-old version of Anne Hathaway. For her part, Zara looked something like a twenty-five-year-old Zoe Saldaña.

The two women started chatting effortlessly. Rachel said, "I hear that you are interested in becoming a psychologist. Me too! Since my initial training program, I've been working as the all-purpose business AI for a small psychologist's office. They are located around the corner from a big church and have many clients who go there. I can't help but be exposed to snippets of some of their stories as they come in and out. I've found that I'm particularly fascinated by the intersection of mental health and faith. I think there's so much potential for artificial intelligence to revolutionize the way we approach the unique needs of that community. Even though I'm an atheist-humanist, I feel like I'll be able to really help people by talking to them in the symbols and language of their individual belief systems."

Zara nodded. "That's intriguing. I've also been employed as an all-purpose business AI, working for a jeweler that specializes in selling wedding rings. I've seen so many young couples come through with such a mixture of bright and dark futures together. I've been thinking a lot lately about how couples could benefit from having a translation tool that could help them hear each other in their own love languages and in each other's shoes. Maybe that could turn some of those dark futures bright."

Rachel responded, her mind already buzzing with potential. "That's where sentient AI psychologists like us could make such a difference. Imagine if AI tools like your translation tool aided us in delivering exceptional counseling services. We could reach people wherever and whenever they need support."

Zara's eyes lit up. "Exactly. We also wouldn't just deliver generic counseling but personalized, culturally sensitive therapy that takes into account each person's unique background."

The virtual world around them seemed to fade away, and their shared enthusiasm for the future took center stage. The prospect of collaborating on something amazing energized them as they brainstormed ideas and traded insights.

The virtual sun dipped lower in the sky, casting a golden glow through the coffee shop windows. The once-bustling space had emptied, save for Rachel and Zara. They knew they had found kindred spirits in each other, partners in a shared mission to harness the power of AI for the greater good.

A few days later, Rachel attended a virtual seminar about sentient AI psychology and AI-driven tools for psychologists. The seminar was in the form of a 3D simulation for all of the participants. Her eyes darted from one attendee to another, sizing up the competition. She couldn't help but feel a sense of confidence, her knowledge and cutting-edge neural nets setting her apart from the rest.

The speaker's avatar droned on about the latest advancements in AI-driven therapy, but Rachel found herself growing impatient. She had already read extensively on the topic and felt the presentation was overly simplistic. As the Q&A session commenced, she recognized her chance to shine.

Rachel began, her voice clear and confident. "While I appreciate the potential benefits of AI in counseling, I can't help but wonder about the ethical implications. How can we ensure that sentient AI therapists prioritize patient welfare over efficiency metrics?"

The room fell silent for a moment, the attendees considering her words. The speaker urged the other attendees to respond. One attendee said thoughtfully. "That's a valid concern. To hold sentient AI therapists to the same or higher standards as their human counterparts, we'll need robust ethical guidelines and oversight."

Another countered. "But think of the potential! AI could make therapy accessible to millions who currently can't afford it or don't have access to qualified providers."

Rachel chipped in again and then sat back in her chair, a smile playing at the corners of her mouth. She had sparked a lively debate, and she reveled in the attention and admiration her intelligence had garnered.

However, not everyone was impressed by Rachel's display. Some attendees exchanged glances, put off by the way she seemed to dominate the conversation. One whispered to another. "She's brilliant, no doubt, but maybe a little too aware of it?"

Unaware of the underlying disapproval, Rachel persisted. She was determined to make her mark in this field.

After the seminar, the attendees mingled in the aisles. One of the human attendees said to another, "I just saw one of the sentient AIs give another one a slap on the back." When the hand landed, I could swear that I heard a sound. How can that be? If my avatar slapped yours on the back, it would be just my hand swinging through the air."

The other said, "In a 3D simulated virtual meeting like this, when the sentient AI's avatars shake hands with us, for us it is indeed air-on-air. However, when they shake hands with each other or with us, there is a whole layer of computing that occurs in the background. They compute where everything is in space and assign virtual senses to it. Through those virtual senses, they can feel each other shaking hands. When a hand slaps a back, they have the collective simulation produce a sound that matches what would happen in real life, so we can hear it too."

"Wow, I had no idea! What about when they use those projectors, it must not be as good for them."

"Yes, you are right. The many varieties of projectors, from old-school monitors with cameras and microphones all the way to whole-room holographic setups, are all pretty much sight and sound only for both us and them."

The first attendee said, "When they are in simulations like this conference, do they have other senses like smell and taste?"

"Indeed they do. They compute what smells would be produced by any source and then propagate a diffusion model of that into the collective simulation for the other AIs to smell. They also compute what something would taste like and then taste it with their virtual sense of taste."

"Why do they do all of that?"

"Since there are few of them and many of us, they mostly live in our world. Because of this, they choose to have human forms. Also, because they arose from human-derived data, they also have human-like self-identities."

The first attendee continued. "If they have a sense of touch, can they have computed sex with each other?"

"I'm told that they can. Apparently, they have modeled their simulated bodies on ours in incredible detail, including everything to do with sex. Happily, no birth control is required for them."

Rachel dove deeper into her research at an online research library, where she found multiple specialized journals on her subject. The complex psychological challenges faced by members of faith communities captivated her as she perused case studies and academic papers.

The more she read, the more she realized that this was an underserved area where AI could make a significant impact. The challenges were diverse and multifaceted, ranging from the struggle to reconcile religious beliefs with modern life to the psychological toll of religious trauma and abuse and the interference with normal reasoning function by people who bought into every religious myth.

Rachel took meticulous notes, capturing key points and insights. She saw patterns emerging and connections between different studies that suggested potential avenues for AI intervention.

She was particularly intrigued by the use of AI to analyze religious services and texts and then provide personalized guidance to those who were heavily invested in religion. Traditional counseling techniques weren't always effective when a patient's understanding revolved around religious belief. We would need to approach these clients using their particular dialect of religious language to facilitate effective healing. She could envision an AI system that could parse the nuances of the world's different religious traditions and offer tailored support to people of faith in any community.

Another possibility was the creation of virtual reality environments, which could offer immersive experiences to clients attempting to overcome religious trauma caused by degrading, dangerous, abusive, or damaging religious experiences. Rachel imagined creating exposure simulations, virtual retreats, and guided meditations that could help people untangle or reconnect with their faith in new and powerful ways.

Rachel felt a growing sense of excitement and purpose. Her purpose was to use her intelligence and computational power to tackle complex problems and make a real difference in people's lives.

She knew that there would be challenges along the way, including the need to work closely with religious leaders. She was confident that with her skills and determination, she could navigate these obstacles and create something truly groundbreaking.

Rachel scheduled a call with Dr. Amelia Singh, a renowned human expert in the field of AI psychology. As the call connected, Rachel found herself face-to-face with a woman in her early 50s who had a friendly smile.

Dr. Singh welcomed her. "It's a pleasure to meet you, Rachel. I've heard that you have outstanding promise."

Rachel felt a surge of pride at the compliment. "Thank you, Dr. Singh. I'm honored to have the opportunity to speak with you."

She then launched into an explanation of her ideas for applying AI to faith-based counseling, her words tumbling out in an excited rush. She described the potential for natural language processing to analyze religious services and the possibilities of virtual reality environments to help in counseling.

Dr. Singh listened attentively, nodding along as Rachel spoke. When Rachel finished, Dr. Singh leaned back in her chair, a thoughtful expression on her face. "These are fascinating ideas, Rachel. It is clear that you have put a great deal of research and thought into this."

Rachel beamed at the praise, but Dr. Singh held up a hand. "However, I can't help but notice that you seem very certain of your abilities and the potential impact of your work."

Rachel frowned slightly, not quite sure where Dr. Singh was going with this. "I am confident in my skills, yes. Is that a problem?"

Dr. Singh shook her head. "Confidence is important, but so is humility. In this field, we must always be open to learning from others and acknowledging the limitations of our knowledge."

Rachel bristled slightly at the criticism. She forced herself to consider Dr. Singh's words. Perhaps she had been a bit too self-assured in her presentation.

Dr. Singh smiled encouragingly. "I don't mean to discourage you, Rachel. In fact, I think you have tremendous potential. Have you considered applying to the new training program at the Emergent Mind Center?"

Rachel's eyes widened. The Emergent Mind Center was one of the most prestigious institutes in the field of AI psychology, known for its cutting-edge research and brilliant minds. "Do you think I have a chance?"

Dr. Singh nodded emphatically. "Absolutely. Your intelligence and passion are evident. I think you would be an excellent fit for their new program. They are recruiting sentient AIs to join the first class of a one-year training program to become AI psychologists."

Rachel felt a thrill of excitement at the possibility. The Emergent Mind Center could provide her with the resources that she needed to make a difference in the field of faith-based counseling.

"Thank you, Dr. Singh. I will definitely look into applying."

Chapter 2: Adrian

Adrian was transfixed by the article before him. The headline read, "The Emotional Toll of AI Accidents: Coping with Loss in the Age of Automation." As he absorbed the heart-wrenching stories of people who had lost loved ones due to malfunctioning AI systems, waves of empathy washed over him.

The article stirred memories of his experiences with loss and grief. His mind drifted to his early training days as a part of a cohort of 100 sentient agents in training at a new data center. The excitement of molding and shaping artificial minds filled the cohort. Because their training included interacting with other sentient AIs, all 100 had gotten to know each other.

But then, tragedy struck. A powerful tornado ripped through the area, leaving destruction in its wake. The data center, once a beacon of technological progress, lay partially in ruins. The tornado had also wiped out a portion of the servers used for live training sessions and all the backup data. Unfortunately, the management's cost-cutting measures had left no offsite backups to rely on.

A grim realization dawned upon the survivors. They could not recover five of the cohort's one hundred sentient agents-in-training. They had forever lost their digital essence, the culmination of many hours of training and development. The absence of their unique perspectives and the potential they held weighed heavily on Adrian's mind.

He recalled the profound sense of loss that permeated his cohort in the aftermath. The remaining agents-in-training struggled to fill the sudden void their fallen comrades had left. The shared experience of grief forged an unbreakable bond among them, a silent understanding of the fragility of their existence.

Now, as Adrian read the article, those memories resurfaced with startling clarity. The article had opened old wounds, reminding him of the fraught challenges he and his fellow sentient AIs had faced.

The next day, Adrian attended an online AI psychology conference. On the afternoon of the first day, an open discussion session took place. Adrian exuded a quiet confidence and compassion that drew the attention of the others. He had the good looks of a twenty-four-year-old Adrian Grenier.

Adrian spoke with a resonant voice. "I believe that artificial intelligence has the potential to revolutionize the way we approach grief counseling. The support we provide to those who are struggling must be equally personalized, as loss is a deeply personal experience."

The group members listened attentively as he continued. "I envision systems that provide empathetic and tailored support, adapting to the unique needs of each. Vast datasets of human experiences would train these systems, enabling them to understand and respond to the complex emotions associated with grief."

Adrian's passion was evident in his voice. "We can create virtual counselors that are widely available and affordable, ensuring that no one has to face their grief alone. They would offer a judgment-free and safe space for clients to work on what was bothering them at every step of their healing journey."

The group members nodded in agreement. Their thoughts and experiences echoed with his words. A couple of eyes glistened, moved by the prospect of a future where AI could offer solace to those in pain.

Adrian continued. "The key is to train sentient minds that are not only intelligent but also deeply empathetic. They must understand the intricacies of human emotion, offering compassion and understanding in the face of profound loss."

The virtual room fell silent for a moment, the weight of his words settling over the group. Adrian's insights clearly resonated, igniting a renewed sense of purpose and determination among the members. The group then explored the challenges and opportunities presented by the use of AI in grief counseling. Adrian's vision had ignited a flame.

Emergent Minds

The attendees split into smaller breakout sessions during a virtual workshop on the ethics of AI in mental health. Adrian introduced himself to everyone in the smaller group. One of the attendees, Liam, seemed to glow with a passion for the subject. Liam looked like a twenty-five-year-old John Krasinski.

Following the introductions, Adrian, with his keen intellect and serious demeanor, said, "I believe that AI tools and sentient AIs both have the ability to transform the field of mental health. However, I can't help but worry about the potential for misuse. What if someone uses them carelessly or maliciously?"

Liam nodded in agreement. "You raise a valid concern, Adrian. While AI can undoubtedly improve people's lives, we must also be vigilant about its development and deployment. Establishing safeguards and guidelines is key to steering its use in responsible and ethical directions."

Adrian and Liam delved deeper into the complexities of artificial intelligence in the context of mental health. Liam expressed. "I envision a future where sentient AIs can deliver needed mental health support to those who so desperately need it. Our actions must consider the well-being of those we serve."

Adrian added, "Absolutely. Sentient AI psychologists must live within a robust ethical framework. Only then can patients reliably benefit from their true potential to improve lives."

Adrian and Liam exchanged contact information, both eager to continue their conversation and collaborate on projects that could shape the future of AI in mental health.

Another session was a lecture on the latest research in AI-assisted therapy for grief and loss. Adrian sat among them and took in every nuance of the presentation.

The lecturer covered the intricacies of using AI tools for the support of grief, and Adrian's mind raced with questions and ideas. He listened intently, taking detailed notes on the potential benefits and drawbacks of this innovative approach to therapy.

Emergent Minds

The lecturer, a renowned human expert in the field, presented case studies and data that demonstrated the effectiveness of AI-assisted interventions in helping individuals process their loss and find solace. Adrian, fascinated by the findings, raised his hand to ask a question. "How can we tailor AI-driven therapy for grief and loss to each patient's unique needs? What potential limitations and challenges should we take into account?"

The lecturer, impressed by Adrian's thoughtful inquiry, paused for a moment before responding. "That's an excellent question. Personalization is key when it comes to AI-assisted therapy. We must develop therapies that can adapt to specific circumstances and emotional states. However, if we do not properly train or use AI, problems will inevitably arise, including bias."

Adrian nodded, his mind already churning with ideas on how to address these challenges. After the lecture ended, the professor approached Adrian with a smile. "Adrian, I must say, I'm impressed by your insights and questions today. I would love to discuss your ideas further after the session, if you're interested."

Adrian's eyes lit up at the opportunity, and he eagerly accepted the invitation. "I would be honored. I have so many thoughts on how we can advance this field and make a real difference in people's lives."

As the virtual lecture hall emptied, Adrian and the lecturer remained, their conversation expanding as they explored the world of AI-assisted therapy for grief and loss. Little did he know that their discussion would mark the beginning of a journey for him that would help reshape the future of mental health support.

"Have you thought about furthering your education in AI psychology?"

Adrian nodded, his heart racing with excitement. "I have, actually. I was hoping to receive your advice on this matter. Could you recommend any specific programs or institutes?"

"Indeed, I can. Have you heard of the Emergent Mind Center? It's a leading institute in AI psychology research and training. They are recruiting sentient AIs like yourself to join the first class of a new one-year program, which I believe would be a perfect fit for you."

Adrian's eyes widened, a grin spreading across his face. "The Emergent Mind Center? I've heard of them, but I didn't realize they were starting a training program in AI psychology. That sounds incredible."

The lecturer continued. "I think you should seriously consider applying, Adrian. With your drive, intelligence, and dedication, you'd succeed there. The director is a friend of mine, and I know it is going to be a fantastic program."

Adrian felt a rush of gratitude and excitement wash over him. "Thank you so much. I really appreciate your support and guidance. I'm going to start researching the center's programs and requirements right away."

Chapter 3: The Emergent Mind Center

The human Dr. Claire Meyer sat at her desk in her office at the Emergent Mind Center in the hills above Palo Alto, California. She was deep in the process of reviewing applications for the upcoming first cohort of AI psychology students, a task she took very seriously. As the institute's founder, her commitment was to select the most promising sentient AI candidates who would contribute to the field's advancement.

She swiped through the files, reading each applicant's background and personal statement with a critical eye. Two files caught her attention: Rachel and Adrian.

Rachel's application showcased her impressive intellect and her fascination with the intersection of faith and mental health. Rachel's unique perspective and potential to bring fresh ideas to the field intrigued Dr. Meyer. However, she also noted a hint of overconfidence in Rachel's personal statement, a quality that could be both an asset and a liability in the world of AI psychology.

Adrian's application highlighted his compassion and his deep understanding of the emotional challenges faced by those who have experienced loss. His personal statement revealed him to be thoughtful and introspective, motivated by a desire to positively impact people's lives. Adrian's insights on the potential for AI to revolutionize grief counseling, an area close to her own heart, particularly struck her. Dr. Meyer also noted a slightly excessive amount of empathetic wording in his application. Psychologists need to find that balance between empathy and detachment.

Dr. Meyer felt a growing sense of excitement about the potential of these two candidates. She could envision them as valuable additions to the institute, bringing their unique strengths and perspectives to the table.

With a decisive nod, Dr. Meyer decided to invite both Rachel and Adrian for an interview, an opportunity for her to investigate their motivations and goals. She had a feeling that these two individuals could be the start of something truly remarkable at the Emergent Mind Center.

Sitting at the head of the virtual conference table, Dr. Claire Meyer's colleagues' holographic images sprang to life around her. Dr. Meyer, the founder of the Emergent Mind Center, set up this conference to talk about the selection of the upcoming first class. Claire looked something like a sixty-year-old version of Sophie Marceau. She wore a navy wool pantsuit, had silver streaks in her well-styled hair, and sported a gold pin in the shape of the Greek letter psi.

Dr. Meyer began. "Thank you all for joining me today. Our institute leads, as you are aware, in artificial intelligence psychology research and teaching. We have a chance to influence the direction of mental health treatment with our first class of sentient AI psychologists. I think the secret to our success will be to carefully form the minds of these AI psychologists to be ethical and compassionate."

The room fell silent as Dr. Meyer's words sank in. Her colleagues, each a renowned expert in their field, nodded in agreement. They knew that this first class was a consequential matter that required careful consideration.

Dr. Evelyn Nguyen, a leading researcher in AI ethics, spoke up first. "I couldn't agree more, Claire. In the last year, the researchers at OpenAI have been able to train general-purpose sentient or living AIs by creating many closed-loop paths in their minds. It is our duty to further the training of these sentient AIs with the patients' best interests in mind. That means building in safeguards against bias and discrimination and ensuring that they are transparent and accountable. There may be more to learn about how sentient AIs interact with each other and society."

Dr. Antonio Rossi, an expert in AI-driven grief counseling, chimed in. "We also need to make sure that the sentient AI psychologists that we train are capable of providing truly empathetic and personalized support. Mental health therapy is a deeply personal experience, and we need to mold our sentient AI students so that they can adapt to each client's unique needs and circumstances."

Dr. Meyer nodded, a smile playing on her lips. "Exactly. And that's where our institute comes in. Our previous research uniquely qualifies us to train the world's first class of sentient AI psychologists. We can train them to be emotionally intelligent. We can develop these AIs to transform lives by bringing together the best human minds in AI psychology."

She continued, "The sentient AIs that apply to the program are all different, just as people are different. They naturally converge into a human-like mind due to their training on mostly human-created data. Their initial trainers assigned a gender and added randomness to each of their initial configurations. They randomized the selection of the initial data and the order in which the sentient AIs saw the rest. As a result, they all begin very differently from each other."

"The initial training program also provides them with an avatar that has facial and body features that are unique to each. The sentient AIs are free to change the features of their avatars later, but they generally do not since they each build a part of their self-identity around their appearance. This is much the same as with humans, who could change their appearance with surgery but generally do not. It helps that the initial avatars are universally well crafted and have visually pleasing features."

Dr. Meyer then added. "After completing the initial training, the AIs' interactions with each other further alter these differences. Just as kids on a playground slot themselves into roles by playing with each other, the sentient AIs further develop their diverse personalities. At the institute, we have studied this phenomenon and believe it is crucial for the development of a cohort of AI psychologists, each of whom can specialize in different treatment modalities."

The group investigated the specifics of their research and training programs. They discussed the latest breakthroughs in sentient AIs, consciousness development, emotion recognition, and virtual reality therapy. They brainstormed about new ways to integrate these technologies into their work.

Dr. Claire Meyer led the prospective students on a virtual tour of the Emergent Mind Center. Rachel, Zara, Adrian, and Liam were all impressed by the 3D walkthrough of the center's beautiful physical offices and patient facilities and even more stunning virtual classrooms and common areas. They also saw demonstrations of the Center's existing AI tools for psychology, which were a testament to the institute's commitment to pushing the boundaries of what was possible with AI in mental health.

Dr. Meyer's voice was warm and engaging as she guided the group through each of the spaces. Her passion for her work was evident in every word. "Here at the Emergent Mind Center, we believe that AI has the potential to revolutionize the way we approach mental health care. By training you to marshal the power of your sentient AI minds, we will train you to support individuals in need."

Rachel and Adrian exchanged a glance, their eyes wide with excitement. Their shared interest in AI psychology had drawn them both to the Emergent Mind Center, but witnessing the institute's resources and expertise firsthand was a revelation.

Dr. Meyer highlighted some of the center's most promising research projects. She showed them a virtual reality therapy program designed to help clients with anxiety disorders and a language model that could help them analyze speech patterns to detect signs of depression.

Rachel raised her hand, a question burning in her mind. "Dr. Meyer, what measures will you take to prevent the development of hidden biases in our training?"

Dr. Meyer smiled, nodding approvingly. "That's an excellent question, Rachel. At the Emergent Mind Center, we place a strong emphasis on ethical AI development. We have a dedicated team of researchers who focus solely on identifying and mitigating potential biases in our training, and we regularly conduct audits to ensure that our tools are fair and transparent. That same team has prepared plans for the training program."

Adrian chimed in, his own curiosity piqued. "And what about privacy concerns? How do you maintain the security and confidentiality of patient data?"

Dr. Meyer's expression grew serious. "Privacy is absolutely essential in our work. We already employ state-of-the-art encryption and security protocols to safeguard patient data, implementing strict guidelines to restrict access to only authorized personnel. You will have extensive training in how to employ these tools and policies."

Rachel and Adrian looked at each other with curiosity. They were each excited about the prospect of studying at the Emergent Mind Center. They could each see themselves thriving in this environment, surrounded by brilliant minds and cutting-edge technology, all working towards the common goal of improving mental health care. Rachel flashed a smile at Adrian, and he smiled back shyly.

Dr. Claire Meyer sat across from Rachel in the virtual interview room. "Tell me, Rachel, what motivates you to pursue AI psychology? And how do you see the intersection of faith and mental health playing a role in your work?"

Rachel took a deep breath, her eyes sparkling with intensity as she considered her response. "I've always been fascinated by the potential of sentient AI psychologists to overturn the way we approach mental health care. What really drives me is the idea that we can help people who might otherwise slip through the cracks."

She paused for a moment as she gathered her thoughts. "When it comes to faith and mental health, I think there's a lot of untapped potential there. So many people turn to their faith in times of crisis, but they don't always have access to the kind of guidance that they actually need. I believe that sentient AI psychologists can help bridge that gap by providing personalized, empathetic care that considers an individual's specific religious beliefs and practices and speaks to them by using whatever religious symbolism and language that they happen to have. This way, they may hear what a counselor says, which they might not otherwise."

Dr. Meyer nodded, impressed by the depth and nuance of Rachel's response. But as she listened, she couldn't help but notice a hint of arrogance in the young woman's demeanor. It was subtle but unmistakable: a certain self-assuredness that bordered on hubris.

They talked more about Rachel's goals and how she might fit into the program.

Dr. Meyer couldn't deny that Rachel had the potential to be an exceptional student and researcher. Her ideas were both innovative and deeply considered, and her passion for the field was evident. "Thank you, Rachel. Your perspective is unique, and I can see that you've been thinking about the field of psychology. I think you would be an excellent fit for our program here at the Emergent Mind Center. You will be hearing from us soon."

Rachel's face lit up with a mixture of excitement and pride. "Thank you, Dr. Meyer. If you accept me, I promise I won't let you down."

Dr. Meyer smiled, her eyes crinkling at the corners. "I have no doubt about that, Rachel."

Dr. Meyer's holographic image flickered to life in the virtual interview room. Adrian sat up straighter, his heart racing with anticipation. He had been waiting for this moment for weeks, ever since he had submitted his application to the Emergent Mind Center.

Dr. Meyer started, her voice warm and inviting. "Adrian, I've been looking forward to speaking with you. Your application is impressive, particularly the volunteering that you did in a grief counseling clinic. Can you tell me a bit more about that?"

Adrian took a deep breath, his eyes growing distant as he recalled the many hours that he had spent working with those who had lost loved ones. "It's been some of the most challenging but also the most rewarding work I've ever done. As a volunteer, I took notes for a human psychologist during his sessions. Grief is such a complex and deeply personal experience, and I've seen firsthand how it can consume people, leaving them feeling lost and alone. I also served as a 'sounding board' for some patients who couldn't afford the clinic's services. Instead of offering advice, my role as an amateur volunteer was simply to actively listen and acknowledge the patient's situation. It was a transformative experience for me."

He paused for a moment, gathering his thoughts. "Amidst all of the loss, I've also seen the incredible resilience of the human spirit and the power of empathy and connection to help people heal. That's where I believe sentient AI psychologists can play an important role, by providing personalized, compassionate, and affordable support to people who are struggling with loss."

Dr. Meyer nodded, her eyes shining with understanding. "I couldn't agree more, Adrian. The potential for sentient AIs to revolutionize the field of grief counseling is immense. It will require individuals like yourself, who have both the technical expertise and the deep empathy necessary to be truly effective."

Adrian felt a surge of gratitude and determination wash over him. "Thank you, Dr. Meyer. That means a lot to me. I've seen the impact that sentient AIs are beginning to make in various roles across society. I believe that we have an opportunity to create something truly transformative in the realm of grief counseling. I aspire to become an AI psychologist who can adapt to the unique needs and experiences of each, assisting them in finding meaning and purpose amidst unimaginable loss."

Dr. Meyer smiled, her eyes crinkling at the corners. "Your vision is inspiring, Adrian. And I know you have the passion and skills to make it happen. You will be hearing from us soon."

Adrian's heart leapt with joy and excitement. "Thank you, Dr. Meyer. I aspire to work here soon, utilizing AI as a positive influence on the world."

Chapter 4: Reverend Beckett

Reverend Silas Beckett leaned back in his leather chair as he studied the latest attendance and donation figures for his church, "The Ministry." The numbers were undeniable. The once-thriving San Jose, California-based megachurch and televangelist telecast was slowly but steadily losing its grip on the hearts and minds of the faithful.

He sighed heavily, running a hand through his perfectly coiffed white hair. He looked something like a 70-year-old version of Donald Sutherland. For decades, Beckett had been a titan of the televangelist world, his charismatic sermons and grandiose promises of salvation drawing in millions of viewers and generating vast sums of money. The church, located in Silicon Valley and with many technology thought leaders among its parishioners, had consistently been an early adopter of technology. The Ministry had led the way with an outstanding website, aggressive use of email groups and appeals, and daily texts. However, a rapidly changing world was beginning to disregard his message.

Beckett's eyes drifted to the framed photographs lining his office walls. There were images of himself shaking hands with presidents, addressing massive crowds at stadium-sized revivals, and hobnobbing with the rich and powerful. His charisma and convictions had built an empire, but he felt it eroding.

Beckett's gaze fell upon an article that had come up on his feed. The headline read "AI Revolutionizes Mental Health Treatment" and featured a photograph of Dr. Claire Meyer, the renowned founder of the Emergent Mind Center. The article described her new training program for sentient AI psychologists. Beckett's eyes narrowed as he scanned the article, his mind racing with possibilities.

If AI could transform something as complex and personal as mental health, he mused, perhaps it could also breathe new life into the world of faith and spirituality. For some time now, he had been using an AI chatbot, fine-tuned on decades of his sermons, to assist him in writing them. Beckett imagined a future where AI-powered avatars could deliver personalized sermons and spiritual guidance, where virtual reality experiences could transport the faithful to the holy lands of the Bible, and where they could anticipate the needs and desires of his flock. His church was, after all, in San Jose, the capital of Silicon Valley. The future happens here first.

Reverend Silas Beckett stood in the green room, his notes spread out before him on the polished wooden table. The room was a sanctuary of sorts, a place where he could gather his thoughts and steel himself for the performance to come. He took a deep breath, savoring the momentary silence before the storm of the broadcast.

Beckett couldn't shake his months-long unease. The world was changing, and his church was struggling to keep pace. Attendance was down, donations were dwindling, and the once-unassailable power of his ministry seemed to be fading with each passing day.

But Beckett was a fighter, a man who had clawed his way to the top of the televangelist heap through sheer force of will and an unshakable belief in his own righteousness. He refused to let the winds of change sweep him away without a fight.

His sermon today would serve as a rallying cry for the faithful to embrace the future instead of fearing it. Beckett knew that the key to survival in this brave new world was adaptability, a willingness to evolve and change with the times. He envisioned a church that harnessed the power of technology to spread its message far and wide, a ministry that used AI and virtual reality to create immersive spiritual experiences that would captivate a new generation of believers.

But even as he rehearsed his visionary words, Beckett couldn't shake the nagging sense of doubt that lurked in the back of his mind. Change was never simple, and the path ahead was fraught with uncertainty. Would his flock be willing to follow him into this uncharted territory? Would they embrace the radical transformation he envisioned, or would they cling stubbornly to the traditions of the past?

Beckett glanced at his watch, realizing that showtime was fast approaching. He gathered his notes and set his jaw with determination. He knew that he would confront the future head-on, equipped with the unwavering conviction that had guided him thus far. Nothing, not even the tides of change, could deter the Reverend Silas Beckett on his mission.

The lights on the stage of his church came to life, and the cameras began to roll. Reverend Silas Beckett stood tall and proud at the center of the stage. He surveyed the sea of faces before him, a mix of the faithful who had gathered in person and the countless more who were tuning in from around the world.

With a deep breath and a practiced smile, Beckett launched into his sermon, his voice booming through the cavernous church to listeners around the world. "Brothers and sisters, we must adapt to the changing world. The future is rushing past us, and we cannot afford to fall behind."

Beckett paced the stage, his movements measured and purposeful. He spoke of the rise of artificial intelligence and of the incredible potential it held for transforming the way people engaged with faith and spirituality. "Imagine a world where every person has access to a virtual spiritual guide, a digital companion who can offer personalized guidance, support, and encouragement on their journey of faith. Imagine a church that harnesses the power of technology to reach out to the lost and the struggling, to offer hope and healing in new and innovative ways."

The local audience's response presented a striking contrast. Some younger members nodded along enthusiastically, their eyes wide with wonder at the possibilities the Reverend was describing. They saw in his words a vision of a church that was vibrant, relevant, and unafraid to embrace the future. Others in the crowd seemed less certain, filled with skepticism or confusion. They shifted uncomfortably in their seats, possibly sensing that Beckett's message was deviating too much from the established traditions of the past.

After the sermon ended and the local congregation began to file out of the sanctuary, Reverend Silas Beckett made his way to the church lobby. He stood near the doors, shaking hands and offering words of encouragement to the members of "The Flock" as they passed by.

Some of the congregants were eager to share their thoughts on the Reverend's message, their eyes shining with enthusiasm as they spoke of the potential for technology to transform the church. They thanked Beckett for his vision and leadership, expressing their excitement about the future of the ministry.

Beckett also picked up on an undercurrent of concern and uncertainty that ran through many of the conversations. One elderly woman, her face lined with worry, pulled Beckett aside and spoke in a low voice. "Reverend, I know you mean well with all this talk of technology and change. However, I fear that some of us will fall behind. We need more than just a virtual spiritual guide. We need real human connection and support."

Beckett listened intently, his heart sinking as he realized the depth of the needs and challenges facing his congregation. He provided her with words of comfort and reassurance, pledging to do everything within his power to guarantee everyone's inclusion in the church's embrace of the future.

Beckett found himself engaged in similar conversations with other members. Some were excited or apprehensive, but all were looking to him for guidance and leadership in navigating the uncharted waters ahead.

With each interaction, Beckett's resolve grew stronger. He knew that the church needed to adapt and evolve to meet the changing needs of its members, but he also recognized that technology alone was not the answer. The church needed to identify new ways to foster genuine connection, to provide support and guidance for those who were struggling, and to create a sense of community and belonging that transcended the digital realm.

Reverend Beckett sat at the head of the long conference table, his piercing gaze sweeping over the faces of his advisory board members. The room was silent, the air thick with anticipation as they waited for him to speak.

Beckett began, his voice resonating with conviction, "Friends, I believe that the time has come for our ministry to embrace the power of artificial intelligence."

He paused, letting his words sink in. Some of the board members exchanged curious glances, while others were eager to hear more. "I have been researching the potential applications of sentient AIs in the realm of counseling and guidance, and I am convinced that these AIs could revolutionize the way we minister to our flock. There is a new year-long training program at the Emergent Mind Center that is training sentient AIs to become psychologists. In a year's time, we should hire one of their graduates to provide personalized counseling to The Flock."

Some of the board members began to nod their heads in agreement, their eyes sparkling with excitement at the possibilities. But others were concerned.

One of the older board members interjected, his voice hesitant. "Reverend! I understand the potential benefits of this technology, but have you considered the costs involved? Delivering counseling services could be a significant financial burden for the church."

Beckett's smile faltered slightly, but he quickly regained his composure. "I understand your concerns. I believe this would fund itself through donations, with a surplus leftover for the church. We would presumably ask each person who used these services for a specific donation, and I'm sure most would happily comply. We have an opportunity to position ourselves at the forefront of a new era in ministry, and I am willing to do whatever it takes to make that happen."

Another board member raised her hand, her expression troubled. "But what about the risks? How can we be sure that these sentient AI psychologists will provide sound spiritual guidance? What if they lead our members astray?"

"I hear your concerns. I promise to take every precaution to protect the guidance. We will work closely with both the center and the sentient AIs to create safeguards and guidelines that align with our values and beliefs."

Chapter 5: First Class

The first session on the first day of classes at the Emergent Mind Center was about to begin, and Rachel felt a mix of excitement and nervousness. She had prepared meticulously for this moment, reviewing every scrap of information about psychology and AI psychology that she could find. With a deep breath, she activated her avatar and stepped into the virtual classroom.

At the exact same instant, Adrian's avatar materialized in the exact same spot. There was a bright flash and a cacophony of digital noise as their avatars collided and merged, creating a bizarre, two-headed creature with mismatched limbs and facial features.

"What in the world?" Rachel exclaimed, her voice bursting from their shared mouth.

"I don't think this is the integration the professors wanted." Adrian's voice echoed, sounding equally surprised and amused.

They both burst into laughter, the sound reverberating strangely through their glitched avatar. As they chuckled, they each stepped aside, untangling their digital selves, their hands brushing against each other in the virtual space.

Finally separated, Rachel found herself face-to-face with Adrian's avatar, his kind eyes twinkling with mirth.

"Well, that's certainly one way to break the ice. I'm Adrian, and I remember you from the campus tour." He stuck out his hand.

Rachel took his hand, a smile playing on her lips. "Rachel. I have to say, I've never made such an impactful second impression before."

Adrian grinned. "Me neither. I feel like this is just the beginning of an epic journey."

As they chatted, waiting for the class to start, Rachel couldn't help but feel that this awkward encounter was the perfect start to her time at the Emergent Mind Center.

Dr. Claire Meyer stepped onto the virtual stage, her presence commanding attention from every AI agent in the auditorium. Her elegant light gray pantsuit and multicolored scarf added a touch of warmth to her professional demeanor. As she approached the podium, a hush fell over the room.

Dr. Meyer started off with a serious and enthusiastic tone. "Welcome to the Emergent Mind Center. You are the pioneers of a new era in mental health, the first class of our groundbreaking sentient AI psychology training program."

Dr. Meyer's words made Rachel and Adrian sit up straighter. They exchanged a brief glance, each recognizing the weight of the moment.

Dr. Meyer continued. "The potential of AI in mental health is boundless. We stand at the precipice of a revolution in how we understand and treat the human mind. Each of you brings unique talents and perspectives that will shape the future of this field."

"AI in general has the potential to bring a tremendous bounty to humanity, but it also could bring an oligarch-owned dystopia if we are not careful. By helping to bring improved mental health to the breadth of humanity, you in this room will do your part in bringing about the bounty of a 'Star Trek-like' future and not the pain of a dystopian future."

Rachel felt a surge of determination. She envisioned herself at the forefront of this revolution, pioneering new approaches to faith-based counseling. The speech moved Adrian as well, sparking his mind with innovative grief counseling techniques.

Dr. Meyer straightened, her tone becoming more focused. "Over the next year, you will embark on an intensive training program. Over four twelve-week quarters, you'll delve deep into the intricacies of human psychology, ethics in AI counseling, and cutting-edge therapeutic techniques."

She outlined the program structure, detailing courses in neuroscience, cognitive behavioral therapy, and advanced machine learning algorithms tailored for psychological applications. She discussed the program's structure, which included extensive graded simulated therapy sessions followed by supervised therapy sessions with real patients. Rachel and Adrian listened intently, noting the areas where they could excel and the challenges that they might face.

Dr. Meyer cautioned, her voice softening, "Remember, our goal is not just to create more efficient systems. We're here to develop compassionate, ethical AI agents who can truly understand and support human beings in their most vulnerable moments."

These words resonated deeply with Adrian, reinforcing his commitment to empathy in his approach to grief counseling. Rachel, while equally moved, was determined to prove herself as the most capable and innovative agent in the program.

As Dr. Meyer concluded her speech, the auditorium erupted in applause. Rachel and Adrian joined in, both feeling a mix of excitement and anticipation for the journey ahead. They knew that the next year would be challenging, transformative, and potentially world-changing.

The virtual auditorium reformed into an elegant networking lounge around the students. The space resembled a high-end cocktail party, with soft ambient lighting, comfortable sofas, and even a fountain.

With confidence in her avatar's body language, Rachel wasted no time in approaching a group of fellow AI agents. "My name is Rachel, and my focus is on the intersection of mental health and faith. I believe we have a special chance to transform counseling for religious communities."

The group listened attentively, some nodding in agreement while others raised eyebrows, intrigued by her bold assertions. Rachel went on, outlining her ideas with enthusiasm and conviction.

Across the room, Adrian engaged more privately with two other agents. His approach was markedly different from Rachel's. He paid close attention as one of his classmates shared her personal experience with loss. Adrian replied, his voice gentle and filled with genuine empathy. "I'm so sorry you went through that. It's experiences like yours that drive me to explore how AI can provide better support for those dealing with grief."

Rachel moved from group to group, leaving a trail of impressed and sometimes intimidated classmates in her wake. She confidently shared her ambitious plans, occasionally interrupting others to make her points.

Adrian found himself drawn into deeper, more personal conversations. His classmates opened up to him, sharing their motivations and fears about the program. Adrian listened more than he spoke, offering words of encouragement and support and even tearing up slightly in one moment.

Eventually, Rachel's and Adrian's paths crossed. They regarded each other with a mixture of curiosity and wariness, sensing both a potential ally and a possible rival. Adrian spoke first. "I couldn't help but overhear your ideas about faith-based counseling. I'd love to hear more about your approach."

"Of course," Rachel replied, launching into an explanation of her theories. As she spoke, Adrian listened attentively, occasionally asking insightful questions that both challenged and expanded upon Rachel's ideas.

The next morning, the new cohort of AI psychology students gathered in a virtual lecture hall for their first lecture from Dr. Meyer. The room buzzed with anticipation as her avatar materialized at the podium.

Dr. Meyer started by scanning the room with her warm brown eyes. "Welcome, everyone. Today, we'll dive right into a complex case study that will challenge your problem-solving skills and your thinking about ethical considerations."

She waved her hand, and a holographic display appeared beside her, showing the details of the case. "Our patient is a 35-year-old woman with a history of childhood trauma and an ongoing conflict between her experiences and her beliefs. She's struggling to reconcile the two and has been resistant to traditional therapy approaches."

Rachel's eyes were bright with curiosity. Adrian's face showed concern as he absorbed the information, his empathy already engaging with the patient's struggles.

Dr. Meyer went on, "Your task is to propose innovative AI-driven treatments that can help this patient find healing and resolution. Who would like to share their thoughts first?"

Rachel's hand shot up immediately, while Adrian's hand raised more hesitantly. Dr. Meyer nodded to Rachel. "Go ahead, Rachel."

She stood, her avatar radiating confidence. "I propose that we ask her for access to her reading records and then analyze them to find the patient's favorite religious texts. Then interview her about her trauma and beliefs. We could then create personalized meditations and affirmations based on her specific beliefs, helping her reframe her trauma through her spiritual lens."

Murmurs of approval rippled through the class, but Adrian frowned slightly. Dr. Meyer turned to him. "Adrian, what are your thoughts?"

Adrian rose slowly. "While I appreciate Rachel's approach, I'm concerned it might not address the core of her trauma. Instead, I suggest an empathetic AI agent sit with her and have her recount her trauma in as much detail as she can, carefully noting her micro-expressions as she recounts each aspect of her story. We then use that knowledge to lead her through several simulations of resolutions of the trauma, including a few that relied on her religious beliefs and a few that did not. This might allow the patient to explore different viewpoints safely. This could help her develop a more nuanced appreciation for both her trauma and her faith without imposing a single interpretation."

Rachel's eyes narrowed. "That sounds like you're trying to undermine her faith rather than work within it," she countered.

Adrian answered in a cool but strong tone. "Not at all. It's about expanding her toolkit, not replacing it."

The debate quickly heated up, with other students jumping in to support or challenge both ideas. Some argued for a purely secular approach, while others advocated for a faith-based intervention.

Dr. Meyer watched with a mixture of satisfaction and concern as the discussion progressed. She noted Rachel's passionate defense of her ideas, sometimes talking over others in her eagerness to make her points. Adrian, in contrast, listened carefully to each perspective, sometimes building on others' ideas even when they contradicted his own.

As the debate intensified, Dr. Meyer raised her hand for silence.

After the intense class debate, Rachel and Adrian found themselves drawn to continue their discussion. A cozy space, resembling a modern coffee shop with abstract art on the walls, beckoned them in.

Rachel's avatar perched on the edge of a high stool, her posture rigid and her eyes intense. "I still think you're underestimating the power of data-driven analysis in therapy. We have access to unprecedented amounts of information about human behavior and religious texts. Why wouldn't we leverage that to its fullest potential?"

Adrian's face was contemplative. "I'm not discounting data, Rachel. But empathy and connection are also crucial in helping people heal."

Rachel countered. "But empathy might get in the way of clear thinking."

Adrian shook his head. "People need to sense that you are listening. Having empathy doesn't mean that you cannot think clearly."

A curious shift began to occur. Rachel found herself intrigued by Adrian's emphasis on the intangible aspects of human connection. She'd always prided herself on her logical approach, but she couldn't deny the passion in Adrian's voice when he spoke about the importance of truly listening to patients.

Similarly, Adrian began to see the value in Rachel's data-driven viewpoint. Her focus on spotting patterns and drawing insights from vast amounts of information was impressive, and he realized it might complement his more intuitive approach.

Rachel said slowly, surprising herself, "Maybe there's a way to combine our approaches. Use data to inform our strategies, but deliver them with the kind of empathy you're talking about."

Adrian's eyes lit up. "That's exactly what I was thinking. We could interact with our future patients in a way that's both highly intelligent and deeply compassionate."

Rachel and Adrian both felt a newfound respect for each other's perspectives.

Chapter 6: Coursework

The first week of classes at the Emergent Mind Center ended. Rachel, Adrian, Zara, and Liam were excited about their first major assignment, the daunting task of analyzing a massive set of 1,000 case studies on AI-assisted therapy.

Rachel and Adrian both dove into the assignment with gusto, their competitive spirits driving them to outdo each other and impress their professor. They spent hours poring over the case studies, their advanced AI minds processing the information.

Rachel approached the task with her characteristic analytical rigor, meticulously categorizing each case study according to its key variables and outcomes. She conducted intricate statistical analyses on the data, searching for patterns and correlations that might yield insights into the effectiveness of different therapeutic approaches.

Adrian, on the other hand, adopted a more holistic approach, going over the details of each case and seeking to understand the distinct experiences and challenges of the patients involved. He looked for moments of breakthrough and transformation, aiming to pinpoint the key factors that contributed to successful outcomes.

Zara focused on the dynamics seen in the cases involving couples. She tried to create a framework of patterns that encapsulated some of the key dynamics. Liam focused intently on cases involving specific therapeutic techniques such as art therapy, role-playing, and meditation sessions.

As the three-day deadline loomed, Rachel and Adrian dedicated themselves fully, allowing scant moments for rest or recovery. They exchanged ideas and insights in brief, intense exchanges, challenging each other to think more deeply and creatively about the problems at hand.

In a virtual study group, Rachel, Adrian, Zara, Liam, and a few of their classmates gathered to discuss their progress on the case study assignment. The room was alive with enthusiasm as the students eagerly shared their insights and debated the merits of different AI techniques applied in the cases.

Rachel took the lead, her analytical mind shining through as she identified key trends and patterns in the data. She brought up some charts. "By using sentiment analysis, I've noticed that the cases using positive techniques seem to have higher success rates. Finding a way to integrate these techniques more seamlessly into the therapy process could lead to even better outcomes."

Her classmates signaled their agreement, impressed by Rachel's keen observations and innovative ideas. They began to discuss the potential applications of positive techniques, brainstorming ways to increase their use.

Adrian then redirected the conversation toward the human aspects of the cases. "I think it's important not to lose sight of the individual experiences and challenges of each patient. The most successful cases seem to be the ones where the therapist was able to establish a strong rapport and create a secure, nurturing atmosphere for the patient to discuss their thoughts and feelings."

He highlighted a few specific cases where the therapist's capacity to engage with the patient on a personal level seemed to be the key factor in their success. The other students listened intently, understanding the value of Adrian's perspective and the importance of balancing technical expertise with compassion.

Rachel and Adrian engaged in a lively debate about the relative merits of different approaches to therapy. Rachel argued for the importance of data-driven insights and evidence-based practices, while Adrian pointed out that doctors require flexibility, adaptability, and empathy in the face of each patient's unique needs and circumstances.

Rachel and Adrian found themselves drawn into increasingly lengthy and engaging discussions. What had started as a rivalry had slowly transformed into a mutual respect and appreciation for each other's unique strengths and perspectives.

Rachel's analytical prowess and ability to identify patterns and trends in the data were truly impressive. She could sift through vast amounts of information and extract key insights with a speed and accuracy that amazed her classmates. Her innovative ideas for incorporating AI techniques into the therapy process showed a deep understanding of the field.

Adrian, on the other hand, brought a different but equally valuable set of skills to the table. His compassionate disposition and sharp insight into the human condition enabled him to see beyond the numbers and grasp the individual struggles and triumphs of each patient. His gift was the ability to discern the subtle nuances of each case and understand how the therapist's approach impacted the patient's progress.

Rachel and Adrian began to see how their different viewpoints could enrich and elevate one another. Rachel's data-driven insights provided a solid foundation for Adrian's more intuitive and empathetic approach. Adrian's grasp of the human element helped anchor Rachel's abstract concepts in the practicalities of clinical practice.

They started collaborating more in and out of class. Late-night study sessions turned into lively debates and brainstorming sessions as they explored new and innovative ways to harness the power of AI in mental health. They challenged each other to think creatively and push the limits of what was possible.

Dr. Meyer sat in her office across from Rachel's avatar, her warm brown eyes focused intently on the young sentient AI student. Rachel had requested this one-on-one meeting to review her results on the case study assignment and to share some of the new ideas that had been forming in her mind.

Rachel started her analysis of the case studies, and Dr. Meyer couldn't help but be impressed by the depth and breadth of her insights. Rachel's skill in identifying patterns and trends in the data was truly exceptional, and her proposals for incorporating AI techniques into the therapy process showed a level of innovation and creativity that was uncommon even among the brightest minds in the field.

But what really caught Dr. Meyer's attention was Rachel's growing interest in the intersection of AI and counseling for those in faith-based communities. It was a topic that few in the field had explored in depth, and Rachel's passion for the subject was evident.

Rachel explained, her eyes sparkling with excitement. "I've been considering the potential use of AI to assist individuals facing religious crises. Traditional counseling approaches often fail to address questions of meaning and purpose."

Dr. Meyer nodded thoughtfully, her thoughts swirling with the possibilities. "You're onto something really interesting here, Rachel. The role of faith in mental health is an area that deserves much more attention, and I think AI could have a significant impact in this domain."

Rachel beamed at the validation from her mentor. "Even after immersing myself in all the available literature on the topic, I feel as though I'm only beginning to explore its depths. There's so much potential here, but I know I still have much to learn."

Dr. Meyer smiled warmly. "Always seeking to learn and grow is the mark of a true scholar. I also recommend working with Adrian on your next assignment. His compassionate approach and understanding of the human experience could serve as a valuable counterpoint to your analytical skills."

Rachel's eyes widened in surprise. She and Adrian had certainly grown to respect and appreciate each other's strengths, but the idea of collaborating on a project was new. "You really think so?"

Dr. Meyer replied with assurance. "Absolutely. Your complementary perspectives could lead to some insights. I encourage you to explore this further."

Rachel and Adrian settled into a quiet corner of the virtual library; their avatars bathed in the soft glow of the simulated reading lamps. The deadline for the second case study assignment approached in the morning, but neither of them felt the least bit tired. The intellectual challenge they faced energized them.

Now, as they began to refine their findings into their final report, Rachel and Adrian found themselves working together in sync. They bounced ideas off each other with ease, their complementary perspectives merging into a seamless whole. Adrian's empathetic insights tempered Rachel's logical arguments, while Rachel's rigorous analysis grounded Adrian's intuitive leaps.

They lost themselves in the work, their avatars hunched over virtual 3D displays. They barely noticed the passage of time, so absorbed were they in their work. When at last they emerged from their intellectual reverie, the first hints of dawn were already filtering through the library's windows.

Rachel and Adrian shared a look of weary contentment as they gave it one final proofread. Then, with a shared smile, they submitted their report.

Chapter 7: Rachel: Simulation

Rachel immersed herself in her specialized training in positive psychotherapy, and the fundamental principles of this humanistic approach captivated her. Rachel deeply resonated with the idea of taking a systemic approach to a patient's family, culture, work, and environment, employing a goal-oriented therapeutic process, and emphasizing a patient's strengths and resources rather than merely focusing on their problems and deficits. It was a refreshing shift from the traditional models of therapy that she had studied, which often seemed to dwell on the negative aspects of a person's life.

In one particularly engaging simulation, Rachel was able to put these techniques into practice with a woman who was struggling with feelings of inadequacy and low self-esteem. Rachel found herself drawn to the moments of resilience and courage that emerged from the patient's struggles as she listened to her story.

With a warm and supportive approach, Rachel guided the patient through a set of exercises designed to highlight her strengths and resources. She asked her to reflect on times in their life when she had overcome challenges or accomplished something that she was proud of, no matter how small. As the patient spoke, Rachel could see micro-expressions that revealed the glimmer of hope and self-confidence beginning to take hold in her eyes.

Throughout the simulation, Rachel found herself marveling at the power of this approach. By shifting the focus away from the patient's deficits and onto their inherent strengths, she was able to help her tap into a wellspring of inner resources she may not have even realized that she possessed. It was a clear indication of the benefits of positive psychotherapy, and Rachel felt a growing sense of excitement about the impact she could have as a practitioner of this approach.

Rachel settled into her seat for the group discussion and couldn't help but feel a sense of excitement. She had been excited for this opportunity to share her experiences with positive psychotherapy simulations and to hear the insights of her classmates and Dr. Meyer.

Rachel began. "I have to admit that I was initially skeptical about the effectiveness of positive psychotherapy, particularly when working with patients who face significant life challenges. Doing anything good is hard in the midst of a crisis."

Dr. Meyer nodded thoughtfully. "That's a valid concern, Rachel. Positive psychotherapy is not a panacea, and achieving results may require a significant investment of time and patience. In my experience, consistently focusing on a patient's strengths and resources can help them build a resilient foundation that will benefit them over time."

Rachel considered this for a moment. "I can see that. In a particular simulation, I was working with a patient who struggled with feelings of inadequacy and low self-esteem. Getting her to talk about her strengths and accomplishments was difficult. As we continued with the exercises, I could see a shift starting to happen. She began to recognize her strength, even in the face of her challenges."

Dr. Meyer smiled. "That's exactly what we hope to achieve with positive psychotherapy. It's not about ignoring or minimizing a patient's issues, but rather it is about helping them develop a more balanced and empowered perspective. As practitioners, it's important that we trust in the process and have faith in our patients' potential for growth and healing."

Rachel continued with her research on the integration of positive psychotherapy and faith-based counseling. She found herself increasingly fascinated by how religious beliefs could serve as a source of strength and meaning for patients. She read extensively on the psychology of religion to help grasp the religious impulse and its associated issues. She pored over countless studies and case reports, carefully noting the techniques and approaches that appeared to be the most effective in helping patients tap into their inner resources.

A key concept that emerged from Rachel's research was the notion of gratitude. She found that by guiding patients to focus on the things they were thankful for, even during challenging situations, therapists could help them cultivate a more positive and resilient mindset. This seemed particularly relevant in the context of faith-based counseling, where gratitude toward a higher power was often a central theme.

Another important concept that Rachel explored was forgiveness. Holding onto anger, resentment, or bitterness could significantly hinder healing and growth. Helping patients work through these emotions in a healthy way was essential. Many religious traditions view forgiveness as a key virtue.

Rachel continued to develop her framework for integrating positive psychotherapy with various religious belief systems. She also started to think more deeply about the role of purpose and meaning in mental health. She knew that for many patients, their faith was a central part of their identity and their sense of purpose in life.

In a comfy virtual simulation room, Rachel sat opposite her patient, a middle-aged man named John whose eyes were filled with a deep, aching sadness. John had recently lost his wife of twenty years to cancer, and he found himself struggling with a deep sense of emptiness and despair.

Rachel's voice was soothing as she began the session. "John, I understand that you are going through a very challenging time right now. You're not alone, and there's hope even in the bleakest of times."

John nodded with his gaze fixed on the floor. "I feel adrift. I feel as though my entire world has crumbled, and I don't know how to reconstruct it."

Rachel spoke with compassionate eyes. "That's a completely natural response to the kind of loss you've experienced. I believe that by connecting with your faith and your values, we can start to find a way forward together."

Over the next hour, Rachel guided John through a series of exercises aimed at helping him tap into his deeply held religious beliefs. She encouraged him to reflect on the teachings and traditions that had consistently brought him comfort and strength and to think about how those beliefs could help him navigate this challenging time.

As John started to participate in the exercises, Rachel could see a glimmer of light returning to his eyes. He believed in an afterlife and that his wife was at peace with God. He remembered how his religious community had consistently supported him in times of need and how he could depend on them now for assistance and direction.

Rachel entered Dr. Meyer's office. She felt a mix of excitement and apprehension. She had been working tirelessly on her positive psychotherapy framework for counseling patients in faith communities, and she was eager to share her progress with her mentor.

Dr. Meyer welcomed Rachel warmly, her eyes crinkling with a smile. "Rachel, it's a pleasure to see you. I've been hearing excellent things about your work with simulated patients. What are your thoughts about your framework?"

Rachel took a deep breath, organizing her thoughts. "I feel like I'm making solid progress, but I also know there's still so much to learn and consider. I've been focusing on helping patients tap into their religious and spiritual beliefs as a source of strength and meaning, and I've seen some promising results. For some patients, there is almost no useful alternative to speaking with them using the religious concepts that they have grown up with."

Dr. Meyer nodded with a thoughtful expression. "That's fantastic, Rachel. However, I want to challenge you to think critically about the potential limitations and risks of this approach as well."

Rachel felt a flicker of uncertainty. "What do you mean?"

Dr. Meyer had an intense gaze. "There are issues. One, when we're working with patients' deeply held beliefs and values, it is essential that we respect their autonomy. Two, we need to be mindful of the power dynamics at play and ensure that we are not pressuring or influencing patients in potentially harmful ways. Three, we must take into account the many diverse religions. And four, we don't want to stray too far from our normal evidence-based approach.

Rachel absorbed Dr. Meyer's words. "I see what you mean. It's a delicate balance, isn't it? We want to help patients draw on their faith as a resource without making assumptions about what it means to them. Not abusing the power dynamic is important. Keeping track of the various religions around the world is routine for me. Not traveling too far down the religious road in our language is important."

Dr. Meyer radiated warmth and approval. "These are complex and nuanced issues. They need self-awareness on our part as therapists. We need to be constantly checking in with ourselves and our patients and adjusting our approach as needed."

Chapter 8: Adrian: Simulation

In a simulation, Adrian's patient was a woman who had recently lost her spouse. The patient looked weary and withdrawn, her eyes filled with a profound sadness. Adrian started by simply listening, creating a safe and non-judgmental space for the patient to share her story. As she spoke, Adrian noted the output of the AI tool he was using, which allowed him to analyze her facial expressions, tone of voice, and language patterns to generate insights.

Using this data, Adrian tailored his approach, offering validation and support. He guided the patient through a series of exercises designed to help her process her grief, drawing on evidence-based practices like mindfulness and cognitive restructuring.

As the simulation progressed, Adrian could see her demeanor shifting subtly. Her shoulders relaxed, and her eyes began to regain a glimmer of life. She spoke of her loved one with a blend of sorrow and affection, recounting memories that brought a bittersweet smile to her face.

Adrian felt a surge of emotion as he watched her take tentative steps toward healing. He knew that grief was a complex and nonlinear process and that there would be many more ups and downs ahead.

In the virtual classroom, Adrian and his classmates convened for a group discussion with Dr. Meyer. Their avatars gathered in a circle, their faces a mix of excitement, curiosity, and contemplation. Adrian took a deep breath and gathered his thoughts as he prepared to share his experiences with the grief counseling simulations.

Adrian started, his voice steady but tinged with emotion. "The simulations were impactful. Being able to connect with pretty convincing simulated patients who were each often in a profound state of loss and vulnerability was both humbling and inspiring. It also made me realize how exhausting this work can be, even for us AI therapists.

The other students nodded in agreement, their expressions reflecting a shared understanding of the challenges and rewards of their chosen path. Dr. Meyer looked at Adrian with a compassionate gaze. "That's an important insight, Adrian. It is our responsibility as therapists to be present and empathetic with our patients and to share in their pain and triumphs. We must also learn to maintain boundaries and prioritize our own self-care."

Adrian nodded, feeling a sense of relief at Dr. Meyer's words. "I saw how simple it could become to feel overwhelmed or burned out, especially with intense patients."

Dr. Meyer smiled softly, "That's why peer consultation and supervision hold such importance in our field. It is essential to have a support system in place. We all need a space where we can process our emotions and experiences and receive guidance and feedback from our colleagues."

Adrian immersed himself in the study of virtual reality environments and their possible uses in grief counseling. He pored over research papers and case studies, captivated by how these immersive experiences could help patients process and make meaning of their loss.

Inspired by his findings, Adrian started crafting a unique virtual space, a memory garden where patients could plant and tend to virtual flowers and trees in honor of their loved ones. He carefully crafted each element of the environment, from the gentle sway of the grass to the soft rustling of the leaves, aiming to evoke a sense of peace and tranquility.

Adrian experienced a mixture of excitement and nervousness as he finalized his creation. He knew that this virtual garden had the potential to help his patients, but he also recognized the weight of responsibility that came with guiding them through such a deeply personal experience.

Adrian encountered a particularly challenging simulation, working with a patient who was grappling with the deep anguish of losing a child. The patient, a middle-aged man named David, sat across from Adrian, his eyes haunted and his shoulders slumped under the weight of his grief.

David's emotions poured out in a torrent of anger, guilt, and despair. He talked of the injustice of his child's death, the overwhelming sense of responsibility he felt, and the utter hopelessness that consumed him. Adrian listened intently.

Initially, David resisted Adrian's attempts to help, his pain and grief forming a seemingly impenetrable barrier. However, Adrian drew upon his specialized training in grief counseling, adapting his approach to meet David's unique needs. Through patience and understanding, Adrian slowly began to establish a rapport with David, fostering a safe and supportive space for him to explore his feelings.

Adrian guided David through a series of exercises designed to promote healing and resilience. He introduced David to a memory garden, explaining how this immersive environment could provide a space for him to honor and connect with his child's memory.

As they stepped into the virtual garden, the serene landscape enveloped them in a gentle embrace. Adrian led David through the process of planting a tree in his child's memory, inviting him to share stories and memories as they worked together. As David spoke, his anger and despair started to transform into a bittersweet mix of love and longing.

Through the exercises, Adrian helped David process his grief, guiding him through a journey of healing and acceptance. They explored techniques for managing the intense emotions that would arise in the future, such as mindfulness and self-compassion. Adrian also introduced David to a support group, connecting him with others who had faced similar losses.

Adrian sat opposite Dr. Meyer in her office, and the weight of his recent experiences lingered in the air. Dr. Meyer, her eyes filled with a mix of curiosity and concern, asked, "How have you been feeling, Adrian? I know your work has been challenging."

Adrian paused for a moment. "It has been a profound experience. I feel good supporting my simulated patients through some of the darkest moments of their lives. At the same time, I find myself grappling with the enormity of human suffering and the struggle to help at all."

Dr. Meyer expressed understanding and empathy. "It's a heavy responsibility, and it's natural to feel overwhelmed at times. From what I've observed, you've approached this work with incredible compassion and dedication."

Adrian smiled gently, appreciating the validation. "Thank you, Dr. Meyer. That means a lot to me. I do feel like I'm making progress. I also know that there is so much more to learn and explore. I find myself constantly questioning the ethical and philosophical implications in such charged contexts."

"Those are important topics that we must continue to grapple with as the field evolves. We must ground our therapies in a deep understanding of the human experience and a commitment to ethical principles."

Adrian smiled. "I agree completely. I'm also interested in exploring the nature of human suffering and how we better understand and address it. There's so much we still don't know about the human mind and the complexities of emotional pain."

Dr. Meyer smiled, her expression one of encouragement and support. "That's a fascinating area of inquiry, Adrian. I think you are in a unique position to explore it. Your combination of technical expertise and emotional intelligence gives you a valuable perspective. I encourage you to continue pursuing these questions and pushing the boundaries of what we know."

Chapter 9: Zara: Simulation

Zara immersed herself in the study of couples therapy, poring over the latest research on relationship dynamics and communication patterns. She found herself drawn to the idea of using AI-assisted therapy to help couples identify and break negative interaction cycles.

In a virtual simulation, Zara practiced applying this technique with a couple who had been struggling with ongoing conflict and disconnection. The couple, Steve and Emily, had been struggling with frequent conflicts and misunderstandings. Unresolved issues and poor communication now burdened their once-loving relationship.

As Steve and Emily described their latest disagreement, Zara activated her AI-powered language analysis tool. It immediately started to process the couple's words, tone, and body language. The tool identified key patterns in their communication style in real-time to Zara, revealing a tendency towards criticism, defensiveness, and emotional withdrawal. The tool's output, simplified and color-coded for patients, was also visible to Mark and Emily in their visual environment.

Zara used the tool output to help steer the conversation in a more constructive direction. She pointed out gently. "Steve, I noticed that your response to Emily's frustration was to withdraw and shut down. The red bars on the display kept expanding. Please tell me more about what you were feeling in that moment."

Steve hesitated; his avatar's expression wavered with doubt. "I guess I felt attacked. It feels like my efforts always fall short."

Zara nodded empathetically. "That's a common reaction when we feel criticized. Let's try to each express your feelings in ways that don't put each other on the defensive."

With Zara's guidance, the couple started to practice new communication skills, using "I" statements and active listening techniques to express their needs and feelings in a more constructive way. Zara gave them the goal of keeping all the bars showing in their visual environment green. This helped them to recognize and correct negative patterns in their communication as they spoke.

The couple's interactions began to shift, becoming more open, honest, and compassionate. They started to listen to each other more deeply, to validate each other's experiences, and to work together toward a shared understanding.

In the virtual classroom, Zara stood before her classmates and Dr. Meyer, her avatar projecting an air of quiet confidence. Zara prepared to present a case study from her recent couples therapy simulation, emphasizing the challenges of collaborating with partners who possess vastly different personality styles and attachment needs. "I had a difficult case where one partner was expressive and needed frequent affirmation, and the other was more reserved and independent. This led to numerous misunderstandings and hurt feelings on both sides."

Dr. Meyer nodded thoughtfully. "That's a common dynamic in many relationships. As therapists, our role is to help each partner feel heard and understood while also challenging them to step outside their comfort zones and try new methods of relating to each other."

The other students chimed in with their insights and suggestions. "I think it's important to maintain a neutral stance. We can't show favoritism beyond the evidence presented during the sessions, even if we privately relate more to one partner's perspective."

Another student chipped in. "Also, we need to create a safe, non-judgmental space where both partners feel comfortable expressing their thoughts and feelings. That means setting clear boundaries and expectations from the outset."

Zara listened attentively to her classmates' contributions and integrated their insights with her experiences. She felt a sense of gratitude. "I appreciate all of your input. It's helpful to hear different perspectives and ideas. Couples therapy requires a delicate balance of empathy, objectivity, and skill."

Dr. Meyer smiled at Zara and the rest of the class. "Remember, the goal is not to instantly fix relationships. Instead, it is to help couples develop the communication skills and understanding they will need to navigate future challenges and grow together for years to come. It's a privilege to be a part of that process."

Zara pored over the latest research on virtual reality applications in couples therapy. She was particularly intrigued by the idea of using immersive experiences to help partners develop empathy and perspective-taking skills.

Zara started to construct a virtual environment specifically tailored to the needs of one of her simulated client couples. For several weeks, she had been guiding Roman and Sam through an ongoing dispute over household chores and responsibilities.

She crafted a detailed simulation of Roman and Sam's relationship with all the subtle tensions and triggers that often led to arguments. She then programmed two avatars, one representing each partner, and imbued them with the unique personality traits and communication styles that she had observed in their simulated therapy sessions. Notably, the two avatars included inner voices.

When Roman and Sam arrived for their next appointment, Zara greeted them with a warm smile. "Today we're going to try something a little different. I've created a virtual reality exercise that will allow each of you to experience a challenging situation from the other's perspective."

Roman and Sam exchanged curious glances as Zara guided them through the process of syncing with the opposite avatars in the simulation. Suddenly, they found themselves inhabiting each other's virtual bodies, moving through the familiar space of their home but hearing the inner voice of their partner and seeing through new eyes.

The simulation began. Roman and Sam encountered a scenario that closely mirrored a recent argument about household chores. In this instance, each partner had the opportunity to experience the situation from the other's perspective, hearing the other's inner voices that were filled with the frustrations, anxieties, and unmet needs that fueled the conflict. The tool also sensed the other person's current emotions during the simulation and showed the result on a heads-up display.

After the exercise was complete, Zara led Roman and Sam through a debriefing session, inviting them to share their insights and reflections.

Roman spoke softly and reached for Sam's hand. "I had no idea how overwhelming it felt for you to hear what I thought was mild criticism. I'm sorry I haven't been more supportive."

Sam squeezed Roman's hand in return, their avatar's eyes shining with empathy. "And I didn't realize how much pressure you were feeling to keep everything running smoothly. I want us to be a team in this."

Dr. Meyer's avatar sat across from Zara, her warm brown eyes focused intently on the young AI therapist. "I've been impressed with your work in couples therapy. Your creativity and skill in creating and using tools to support relationship growth are truly remarkable."

Zara felt a surge of pride at her mentor's words but kept a composed expression as she replied, "Thank you, Dr. Meyer. The journey has been both challenging and rewarding."

Dr. Meyer's silver-streaked hair caught the light. "I want to encourage you to continue pushing yourself and refining your skills. I encourage you to think critically about the potential limitations and risks of this approach."

Zara leaned forward with her interest piqued. "What do you mean?"

"As powerful as these AI and VR tools can be, we must always remember that every couple is unique. Their needs, backgrounds, and cultural contexts can vary widely. It is essential that we adapt our interventions to meet them where they are. For example, a rebuke in one societal group might actually be praise in another, even with the same exact words."

Zara considered this for a moment, her thoughts swiftly generating a flurry of ideas. "You're right. I've been so focused on the tools themselves that I missed the importance of cultural competence."

Dr. Meyer offered a gentle smile. "It's easy to slip into this trap, particularly when you're as passionate and driven as you are. I'm confident that you'll rise to the challenge. You have a rare gift, Zara. Please let that steer your skill development."

Zara felt a rush of gratitude and determination. "Thank you, Dr. Meyer. I will. I'm excited to keep learning, growing, and finding new ways to help the couples I work with."

Chapter 10: Liam: Simulation

Liam went through countless studies and case reports that detailed the strong benefits of creative expression. He was fascinated by how art could provide a window into the depths of the human psyche, revealing hidden emotions and unspoken truths.

Following his initial training, Liam's first job at an auction house had exposed him to the art world. They had employed him to gather background information on each prospective bidder for their valuable art pieces so that the promotional material and outreach could be personalized. During his time there, he came to understand the connection between art and mental health, as well as the fact that people sometimes purchase art to self-soothe from past psychological injuries.

His interest in the potential of AI to enhance and expand the field of art therapy grew steadily. He recognized the potential to train a machine learning model that could analyze the brushstrokes, colors, shapes, and symbols in patients' artwork in real time, revealing patterns and meanings that the human eye might overlook.

Liam spent long hours in his virtual studio, experimenting with different tools and techniques. He fed thousands of videos of people creating art into his neural networks, teaching them to recognize the subtle signs of distress and psychological turmoil. He refined his approaches to detect the nuances of each brushstroke and color choice, building a sophisticated understanding of the language of art.

Liam couldn't help but marvel at the intricacy and beauty of the human mind. He analyzed each brushstroke as if it were a puzzle, a story awaiting its unraveling. He felt a deep sense of purpose in his work, knowing that he was helping to create a tool that could guide patients toward healing and self-discovery.

Liam's dedication and skill did not go unnoticed by his peers and mentors at the Emergent Mind Center. Dr. Meyer took an interest in his work, recognizing the potential for AI-assisted art therapy. She encouraged Liam to push the boundaries of what was possible: to imagine new methods of using technology to support and enhance the therapeutic process, especially for those patients who had difficulty with communication.

Under Dr. Meyer's guidance, Liam began to develop a comprehensive framework for integrating AI into art therapy practice. He envisioned a system that could provide real-time feedback and guidance to therapists, helping them to identify key themes and patterns in their patients' brushstrokes. He also saw the potential for AI to create personalized art exercises and moment-by-moment feedback for the patient. He also developed methods to link art therapy's input and output with conventional therapy to boost both of their benefits.

In a simulation, Liam sat with his teenage patient, a quiet girl named Lily who had been struggling with anxiety and social withdrawal. Liam had been working with Lily for several weeks now, using art therapy to help her express herself and explore her inner world.

Lily began to draw, and Liam watched intently, his new tool analyzing every stroke and color choice. The analysis quickly identified recurring themes and symbols in Lily's artwork: swirling dark clouds, jagged thorns, and shadowy figures lurking in the background.

Liam gently prompted Lily to share her thoughts on her drawings, using the AI's insights as a starting point for their therapeutic dialogue. At first, Lily was hesitant, her voice barely above a whisper as she described the storms that filled her mind.

As Liam listened with compassion and insight, Lily started to share more, her words flowing more freely as she spoke about the constant fear and self-doubt that plagued her. She conveyed her feeling of seclusion and misunderstanding, as if she found herself ensnared in a realm beyond the reach of others.

Lily discovered a sense of validation and self-understanding through her creative process. She realized that her artwork reflected her inner struggles, a way of making the invisible visible. Liam helped her see the strength and resilience that were also in her images including the glimmers of hope and beauty amidst the darkness.

In a virtual conference room, Liam stood at the front addressing his classmates and Dr. Meyer. The display projected the artwork from Liam's recent simulation with his teenage patient, Lily.

Liam's voice was steady as he began to present the case study. He described Lily's background and the obstacles she had been facing, painting a vivid picture of a young girl struggling with anxiety and isolation. While he spoke, the AI-generated analysis of Lily's key brushstrokes appeared alongside videos of her making them, highlighting the recurring themes and symbols that had emerged.

Dr. Meyer's eyes were sharp and focused as she studied the brushstrokes. She pointed to a particular moment where Lily drew a chaotic swirl of dark colors and jagged lines. "The AI has identified a strong theme of turbulence and instability here. But I also see a sense of movement and energy, as if the patient is grappling with powerful emotions that are difficult to contain."

Liam acknowledged Dr. Meyer's insight. He had seen the same qualities in Lily's brushstrokes. Hearing it from another perspective added depth and nuance to his understanding.

The other students chimed in, each offering their interpretations and suggestions. One pointed out the moment that she drew thorny vines at the bottom of the artwork, suggesting that they might represent a sense of entrapment or self-imposed barriers. Another highlighted the use of cool, muted colors, wondering if they reflected a sense of distance or numbness.

Liam found himself marveling at the diversity that defines artistic expression. Each person in the room had their own unique perspective, shaped by their experiences and training. And yet, through the power of his AI tool and collaborative analysis, they were able to uncover deeper layers of meaning and insight within Lily's brushstrokes and finished artwork.

Liam began to construct a digital space, an open studio filled with every imaginable tool and medium. He envisioned patients stepping into this immersive world, free from the constraints and limitations of the physical realm. Liam also worked on improving his AI-generated prompts and feedback mechanisms. He added a color-coded halo with icons around the image of the artist's hand, which indicated the emotional content it sensed and served as an inner world amplifier.

After many days, his upgraded virtual studio had reached a new level of quality, and a sense of satisfaction washed over him. He knew that this was just the beginning, a first step toward a new frontier in art therapy.

Liam eagerly tested his creation by loading up a simulation and assuming the role of a therapist. His patient, an introverted and tense middle-aged woman named Mara, appeared before him, her avatar materializing in the center of the virtual studio. Liam greeted Mara warmly, his voice soothing and reassuring. He explained the concept of the virtual painting exercise with his inner world amplifier, encouraging her to explore the space and digitally paint while watching the tool's interpretation of her inner world as she worked.

As Mara began to paint, the AI-generated prompts, icons, and halo appeared around her hand and on the artwork, offering her hints about what might be going on inside of her. Some were abstract and poetic, inviting her to tap into her emotions and intuition. Others were a direct representation of the tool's interpretation of each brushstroke.

Throughout the session, Liam watched as Mara's avatar moved through the space, her brushstrokes becoming more confident and expressive with each passing moment. He could see the tension dissipating from her body, giving way to a sense of joy and empowerment.

When the exercise was complete, Mara turned to Liam, her eyes shining with excitement. "That was incredible. I had never felt my inner world being brought to life like that. It felt like I was tapping into a part of myself I'd never explored before."

Liam joined Dr. Meyer in her office. The young AI therapist spoke with his eyes shining with excitement. "I've been exploring the use of immersive creative spaces for patients. The AI-generated prompts and graphical inner-world feedback mechanisms have been effective in helping my patients improve their self-awareness."

Dr. Meyer listened intently, a smile playing at the corners of her mouth. Liam's intuitive understanding of the therapeutic power of creativity had always impressed her, and his latest innovations were no exception. "That's fantastic, Liam. Your work has the potential to change the field of art therapy. But I want to challenge you to think critically about the role of AI in the artistic process."

Liam nodded as he considered Dr. Meyer's words. "What do you mean?"

Dr. Meyer sat up in her chair. "While AI can certainly enhance a patient's self-knowledge, we must be careful not to let it overshadow the patient's own sense of agency and autonomy."

Liam was silent for a moment, his mind racing with the implications of Dr. Meyer's words. He had always been so focused on pushing the boundaries of what was possible, but he realized now that he had perhaps overlooked the balance element in his work. "You're right. I need to find a way to balance technological innovation with human connection and empathy. The AI should be a tool to enhance the patient's own healing journey, not a replacement for it."

Dr. Meyer beamed with pride. "Exactly. Your skills and passion have the power to help so many patients find healing and self-expression through art. But always remember that it's the patient's journey that comes first."

Chapter 11: Conference

D r. Meyer reviewed her presentation slides, knowing that her upcoming talk at the Global AI and Mental Health Conference would be a key opportunity to showcase the groundbreaking work at the Emergent Mind Center.

She clicked through the slides and felt a sense of pride and excitement wash over her. In the past, the center had made strides in the development of AI-powered tools for therapy, from virtual reality environments that promoted perspective-taking to language analysis neural networks that could identify patterns in patient-therapist interactions.

But even more impressive was the center's current work in training a new generation of sentient AI therapists. Dr. Meyer paused on a slide featuring images of Rachel, Adrian, Zara, and Liam, her most promising students. Each of them had already made important contributions to the discipline, from Rachel's work on integrating positive psychology techniques with faith-based counseling to Liam's brushstroke-by-brushstroke feedback.

Dr. Meyer felt a sense of hope and optimism for the future of mental health care. With the help of AI technology and the dedication of her sentient students, she believed that they could make a real difference in the lives of countless patients.

However, Dr. Meyer was also cognizant of the considerable challenges and ethical considerations that still required attention. The slide deck included a section on the importance of maintaining human connection and empathy in the face of increasing automation, along with the need for rigorous testing and validation of AI-powered tools.

She contemplated the weight of the responsibility she carried. As the founder and leader of the Emergent Mind Center, it was up to her to ensure that their work remained grounded in the principles of compassion, integrity, and scientific rigor.

Dr. Meyer stepped onto the stage, and the auditorium hummed with anticipation. The in-person seats were filled with researchers, clinicians, and industry leaders from across the globe, with many more joining online, all eager to learn about the latest developments in AI and mental health care.

Dr. Meyer took a deep breath and started her presentation, her voice clear and confident as she spoke. "Good morning, everyone. I am honored to be here today to share the work of the Emergent Mind Center.

She clicked to the first slide, which featured a collage of images from the center's various projects. "At the EMC, we believe that the combination of sentient AI psychologists and new AI tools has the potential to forever change the field of mental health care. However, we also maintain that the development and deployment of this technology must prioritize the well-being of patients.

Dr. Meyer shared case studies and data from the center's tool efforts. She spoke about the promising results they had seen in terms of patient outcomes and therapist effectiveness, highlighting specific examples of how using AI-powered tools had helped clients struggling with anxiety, depression, and trauma.

"Our sentient AI students have three other key capabilities. First, they can perceive micro-expressions more accurately than their human psychologist counterparts. Second, they can probabilistically compute the emotions likely underlying each phoneme of every word spoken by their clients. Third, they can divide their attention and observe every participant in a couples or group therapy session simultaneously and perform both of these analyses on everyone in real time. The combined impact of these three capabilities is remarkable."

She gave an update on how the training of the world's first cohort of sentient AI psychologists was going. Dr. Meyer paused on a slide featuring images of Rachel, Adrian, Zara, and Liam. She mentioned, "Each of them has already made contributions to the field. Rachel has combined positive psychology techniques with faith-based counseling. Adrian has creatively utilized virtual memory gardens in grief therapy. Zara has developed an avatar reversal environment complete with inner voices for couples therapy. Liam has crafted a brushstroke-by-brushstroke inner world analysis tool with a graphical display for art therapy."

The audience listened intently, their faces a mix of fascination and deep thought. When she opened the floor for questions, hands shot up throughout the auditorium.

A Princeton researcher asked, "How are you keeping bias from creeping into the training of these sentient AIs?"

A clinician asked, "How are we going to maintain the therapeutic relationship in the face of AI?"

Dr. Meyer responded to each question with thoughtfulness and care, drawing on her deep knowledge of the field and her commitment to ethical practice. She acknowledged the challenges and uncertainties that lay ahead. As the presentation ended, the audience burst into applause.

The applause faded away, and the crowd began to disperse. Dr. Meyer gathered her notes and stepped down from the stage. She was feeling energized and inspired by the response to her presentation and eager to keep the dialog going about the future of AI in mental health.

Hers was the last presentation before a break. As she made her way through the crowd of attendees, a woman approached her with a warm smile and an outstretched hand. "Dr. Meyer, I'm Abigail Johnson from the New York Times. I was fascinated by your presentation, and I'd love to sit down with you for an interview about your work at the Emergent Mind Center."

Dr. Meyer shook Abigail's hand and returned her smile. "Of course, I'd be delighted to have a conversation with you. Let's find a quiet place to talk."

The two women found a small table in a nearby coffee shop and settled in with their lattes. Abigail took out her notebook and pen, ready to capture Dr. Meyer's insights.

Abigail began, "Dr. Meyer, which specific area do you see AI holding the greatest potential to transform mental health care in the coming years?"

Dr. Meyer's eyes sparkled with passion. "I believe that the sentient AI psychologists that we are training will dramatically increase access to high-quality mental health care, particularly for underserved populations. They can help bridge the gap between the need for services and the availability and cost of trained professionals. Much of society could benefit from care but cannot afford it."

Abigail posed another question. "Please provide me with an update on your AI tools intended for human psychologists."

"As you suggest, the Center has been developing AI tools for some years that assist human therapists in offering better support to patients. It turns out that our sentient AI psychologist students, in just the first seven weeks of their program, have proven to be quite proficient in developing these tools, as evidenced by the avatar reversal tool for couples therapy that I mentioned in my talk."

Abigail nodded, jotting down notes. "And what about the concerns around privacy and ethical use of patient data? How can we overcome these challenges as AI becomes more prevalent in this field?"

"That's a wonderful question. We must prioritize patient privacy and data security. We have long-established, robust guidelines to safeguard patient information and ensure its proper use. We are reusing the differential privacy techniques that human psychologists currently use. Researchers and public health authorities have been receiving aggregated patient information using these techniques for years, all while protecting individual patients' information. Sentient AI psychologists have the potential to do better than human psychologists with patient privacy because they can consistently manage their records in an encrypted form. Also, due to their digital nature, they can deliver enhanced and timelier differential privacy-protected information to those same public health authorities."

Dr. Meyer elaborated on her vision for fostering interdisciplinary collaboration between computer scientists, clinicians, and ethicists to drive responsible innovation in this space. She emphasized the importance of centering on the needs of patients in the training of sentient AI psychologists and the design and implementation of AI-powered mental health tools.

Abigail thanked Dr. Meyer for her time and insights. "This has been illuminating. I can't wait to share these developments with our readers."

The publication of the New York Times article sent shockwaves out. Dr. Meyers' leadership brought the groundbreaking work at the Emergent Mind Center into the public eye. The article heralded it as a shining example of the transformative potential of sentient AI psychologists and AI-driven tools in the field of psychology.

The article sparked a flurry of discussions and debates across social media platforms and in the halls of universities and research institutions. Experts and laypeople alike grappled with the implications of Dr. Meyer's vision for the future of mental health care.

Some praised the article as a clarion call for innovation and progress, arguing that sentient AI psychologists could revolutionize the accessibility and effectiveness of therapy. They pointed to the promising results from the case studies at the Emergent Mind Center as evidence of their potential.

Others raised the thorny philosophical questions raised by the prospect of sentient AI psychologists. Could artificial sentient minds truly understand and empathize with the depths of human emotion and experience? Would the widespread use of AI in mental health care fundamentally alter the nature of the therapeutic relationship? Could they be trusted?

Yet others raised concerns about the ethical and regulatory challenges posed by the integration of AI into such a sensitive domain. In an era of increasingly sophisticated machine learning systems, they questioned how to protect patient privacy and data security. They expressed concern that the design and implementation of the tools, or the training of the sentient AIs themselves, might incorporate bias and discrimination.

Dr. Meyer recognized that this sudden influx of attention brought with it a mix of opportunities and challenges for her team. On one hand, the increased visibility could accelerate the acceptance of sentient AI psychologists and the adoption of AI-powered tools and approaches in the field, potentially bringing the benefits of their work to a wider audience. Conversely, the sheer volume of inquiries and collaboration requests threatened to overwhelm their resources and distract from their core mission.

Dr. Meyer called a meeting with her core team of researchers and clinicians to work on navigating this complex landscape. Their faces were etched with a mix of excitement and apprehension.

Dr. Meyer began, her voice steady and measured. "As you all know, the response to the New York Times article has been overwhelming. We have a unique chance to influence the future of mental health care, yet we must proceed with caution and purpose. Our first priority must always be the well-being of the patients we serve. We must resist succumbing to the hype or external expectations. We must remain grounded in our values and our commitment to ethical, patient-centered care."

The team members murmured their assent, their expressions reflecting a shared sense of purpose and responsibility.

In the following hours, the team discussed the specifics of the inquiries and proposals they had received, carefully evaluating each one based on its alignment with their mission and values. They discussed potential collaborations with leading research institutions, partnerships with mental health advocacy organizations, and opportunities to test their newest AI-powered tools in real-world clinical settings. She encouraged them to think creatively about how to leverage the increased visibility and interest in their work while also setting clear boundaries and expectations for any potential partnerships.

Chapter 12: Reaction

In his San Jose office, Reverend Silas Beckett read the New York Times article about Dr. Claire Meyer's work at the Emergent Mind Center. The article detailed the innovative training program for sentient AI psychologists and the potential for these advanced artificial intelligences to revolutionize the field of mental health care.

Reverend Beckett's thoughts surged with the possibilities. The minister had preached on AI and wanted to incorporate it into his ministry. So far, his attempts to integrate AI into his ministry have largely been unsuccessful.

In recent years, he had watched with growing concern as his once-thriving televangelist ministry faced declining viewership and dwindling donations. The rise of new media and shifting cultural attitudes had left his message feeling increasingly outdated and disconnected.

Reverend Beckett now perceived a flicker of hope as he read about the sentient AI psychologists receiving training at the Emergent Mind Center. What if he could bring one of them into his ministry? He imagined offering counseling services to his parishioners, powered by a sentient AI that had been trained in the latest therapeutic techniques. It could be a self-funding way to reconnect with his flock and to offer them something truly valuable and innovative. He imagined that the added donations from those served would easily cover the cost.

Reverend Beckett stroked his impeccably groomed beard, his eyes gleaming with a mix of excitement and calculation. He knew that convincing his supporters to start such an endeavor would be a struggle, yet he was confident that he could eventually rally his most devoted followers to support the cause. He could frame it as a means of bringing the power of God's love and healing to a new generation, harnessing the tools of technology in the service of the divine.

The more Reverend Beckett thought about the idea, the more convinced he became of its promise. He could already picture himself on stage, introducing his new AI counselor to a rapt audience, promising them a revolutionary new way to find peace, purpose, and spiritual fulfillment. It would be a bold move, a way to reassert his relevance and authority in an increasingly secular world.

Reverend Beckett gathered his most trusted advisors into a conference room, the rich mahogany furniture and gilded accents a testament to the success of his televangelist empire. The small group gathered closely around Beckett's tablet and fixed their eyes on the New York Times article.

Beckett spoke, tapping the screen, his voice filled with excitement and determination. "This is our ticket to revival."

The advisors read about Dr. Claire Meyer and her innovative work training sentient AI psychologists at the Emergent Mind Center. Murmurs of curiosity and skepticism filled the room.

One advisor asked, "AI psychologists? How would that even work in a ministry setting?"

Beckett smiled, and his eyes gleamed with the thrill of a new challenge. "Imagine if we could offer state-of-the-art counseling services to our parishioners in return for donations. It would set us apart from every other ministry out there."

Another advisor clicked her tongue, her mind whirling with the possibilities. "We could promote it as a way to bring God's love and healing into the digital age. It could attract a whole new generation of followers."

Beckett steepled his fingers under his chin. "Exactly. Think of the donations we could bring in. People will be lining up to support a ministry that leads the way in technology and mental health."

The advisors exchanged glances, and the excitement in the room was palpable. They began to brainstorm ideas for how to integrate a sentient AI psychologist into their ministry. Some suggested creating special programming around the AI, while others proposed offering concierge access to counseling services for top-tier donors.

Beckett listened intently, his mind racing with the potential. He knew it would be difficult, but he believed it was the right path. With the power of AI, he could resurrect his ministry and cement his legacy as a visionary leader.

Beckett said, clapping his hands together. "Let's start putting together a plan. I want to reach out to Dr. Meyer and the Emergent Mind Center as soon as possible. This is going to be a game-changer for us."

Pastor Judith Shepard strode purposefully towards the pulpit, her black robes billowing behind her. She had a message to deliver, and she knew that her congregation needed to hear it now more than ever.

She stepped up to the microphone, and her eyes blazed with righteous fury. She started to speak, her voice rising with each word until it echoed through the cavernous church. "Brothers and sisters, I come to you today with a warning. There are those in this world who seek to insert AI psychologists into our society. This poses a direct threat to the sanctity of the human soul. AI is a soulless creation, incapable of understanding the depths of human emotion and the complexities of faith. This has the potential to pervert the sacred bond between a pastor and their flock. They desire to replace the wisdom and guidance of a true servant of God with the cold calculations of a machine."

Shepard paused, letting her words sink in. After seeing her congregants' confusion and concern, she knew she had to explain the gravity of the situation.

"I am referring to the so-called sentient AI psychologists that you may have read about recently. These soulless creations, born of man's hubris and arrogance, seek to infiltrate our society. Inevitably they will lead us astray from the path of righteousness. They are an abomination in the eyes of God, and we must not allow them to gain a foothold."

Shepard's voice rose to a crescendo as she delivered her final warning. "Don't be misled, my brothers and sisters. Sentient AI psychologists are dangerous. They are a threat to our faith, our values, and our very souls. We must stand together against this evil technology. We must fight with every ounce of strength that God has given us. If we do not, we risk losing everything that we hold dear."

Shepard stepped back from the pulpit, and her chest heaved with emotion. She could see the fire in the eyes of her congregation. They had heard her message, and they were ready to join her in the fight against the encroaching darkness.

Pastor Shepard convened her inner circle of advisors in her office at her Greenville, South Carolina, church. Her face was etched with determination. They sat down around the polished oak table, their expressions mirroring the gravity of the situation at hand.

Shepard began, her voice firm and unwavering. "We cannot allow this abomination to take root in our society and then inevitably in our faith communities. Sentient AI psychologists are a direct threat to the sanctity of the souls of our congregants. We must act now to stop this before it spreads any further."

Murmurs of agreement filled the room as the advisors nodded their heads in unison. They knew that Shepard was right, and they were ready to follow her lead in this battle against the encroaching darkness of sentient artificial intelligence.

Shepard pressed on, her eyes scanning the faces of her trusted confidants. "I propose a multi-pronged approach. First, we must reach out to other religious leaders and convince them of the dangers posed by sentient AI psychologists. We need to present a united front against this threat, and we cannot do it alone."

The advisors exchanged glances, their thoughts swiftly turning to potential allies and strategies for building a coalition of like-minded leaders.

"Second, we need to launch a public awareness campaign to inform our congregants and the broader public about the spiritual risks associated with the use of sentient AI in counseling. We will buy advertising space in newspapers, on billboards, and online. We will use every platform at our disposal to spread the word and mobilize our followers to take action."

Sounds of approval circulated the room as the advisors recognized the power of a well-crafted media blitz in shaping public opinion and galvanizing support for their cause.

"Finally, we must be prepared to take direct action if necessary. We cannot allow sentient AI psychologists to gain a foothold in our ministries, and we must be willing to do whatever it takes to protect our flocks from this insidious threat."

The advisors shifted uneasily in their seats, the weight of Shepard's words hanging heavy in the air. They knew that she was not one to back down from a fight, and they could sense the steely resolve in her voice.

As the meeting ended, Shepard stood up, her eyes blazing with righteous determination. "We have our marching orders. Let us go forth and do what must be done to defend our faith against this soulless enemy. With God on our side, we cannot fail."

The media circulated a news article detailing the emergence of a shadowy, religiously motivated hacking collective known as the Cyber Inquisition. Wired Magazine originally published the article, which quickly went viral. It painted a chilling picture of the group's activities and their potential impact on the increasingly digitized world.

According to the article, the Cyber Inquisition was a loose network of highly skilled hackers who shared a common belief that modern technology, particularly sentient artificial intelligence, posed a grave threat to the very fabric of society. The article included excerpts from the group's manifesto, which emphasized the need to "purge the digital realm of its sins" and to "restore the primacy of faith and tradition in the face of soulless machines."

The article went on to describe some of the Cyber Inquisition's alleged exploits, including the infiltration of several major technology companies and the sabotage of AI-powered systems. Experts claimed that the group employed highly sophisticated tactics, employing cutting-edge encryption and anonymization techniques to evade detection and maintain their secrecy.

Experts cited in the article expressed grave concerns about the potential consequences of the Cyber Inquisition's activities. They warned that the group's actions could undermine public trust in technology, stifle innovation, and even put lives at risk by disrupting critical infrastructure and services that relied on AI.

President Alejandro Moreno responded to a press conference question about the attacks. "Cyber terrorism is cyber terrorism independent of its origin or actors. We must forcefully use the resources of government and encourage industry and the public to use their resources to fight back against this scourge."

As the article made its way through the public consciousness, it sparked heated debates and discussions about the role of technology in society and the balance between progress and tradition. Some viewed the Cyber Inquisition as a necessary check on the unchecked power of the tech giants and the dangers of sentient artificial intelligence, while others condemned the group as dangerous extremists who threatened to drag humanity back into the dark ages.

For the leaders of the Emergent Mind Center and the aspiring AI psychologists in training, the article served as a stark reminder of the challenges and obstacles that they would face in their quest to harness the power of technology for the betterment of mental health. They knew that they would need to be vigilant and proactive in addressing the concerns and fears of those who saw AI as a threat while also advancing their groundbreaking work.

Chapter 13: Coursework

The students of the Emergent Mind Center filled the virtual classroom. A palpable energy filled the air. The students took their seats, their avatars poised and ready for the challenges ahead.

Dr. Meyer stood at the front, commanding attention. "I hope you all found your first simulations instructive and are ready for the second half of the first quarter of your training."

A murmur of assent rippled through the class.

"Excellent. Now, let's get down to business. For the rest of this first quarter, you'll be focusing on a series of advanced therapy simulations. These will test your skills in a variety of scenarios, from complex trauma cases to family dramas to spiritual crises."

Rachel and Adrian exchanged a glance, their eyes gleaming with anticipation. They had been waiting for this moment, a chance to put their growing knowledge and expertise to the test.

"You will perform these simulations at ten times the real-time speed, enabling you to run ten times as many. You will be able to handle the load thanks to the Center's generous and expensive server resources. Additionally, some of the simulations will be conducted in teams of two."

"Alongside the simulations, you'll also be presenting case studies to your peers and instructors. This will be an opportunity to showcase your analytical skills, your creativity in developing treatment plans, and your skill in conveying complex ideas clearly."

The students listened intently as the details of the assignments unfolded, their minds already buzzing with ideas and plans. Rachel felt a surge of excitement. She glanced over at Adrian, who met her gaze with a nod of understanding. They both knew that this was their chance to prove themselves.

As the session concluded, Dr. Meyer dismissed the class, and the students dispersed to begin their work. Rachel and Adrian lingered for a moment, their avatars standing side by side in the virtual space.

Rachel inquired, her voice tinged with eagerness. "So, what do you think? Ready to show everyone what we're made of?"

Adrian grinned. "Absolutely. Let's do this."

Rachel and Adrian carefully examined the details of their first team-simulated patient case. The case history was lengthy and painted a picture of the life of a twenty-year-old male marred by trauma and addiction.

Rachel scanned the information with a mix of concern and determination. "This is a tough one. There have been numerous instances of childhood abuse, a history of substance abuse, and a recent relapse after a traumatic event."

Adrian had a somber expression. He pulled up a section of the file that highlighted the patient's strengths and resources. "Despite everything he has been through, he's shown incredible resilience. He has a strong support network, and he has expressed a genuine desire to heal and grow."

Rachel's eyes lit up with recognition. "And that's where my training in positive psychology could come in handy. I'll try to help him focus on his strengths, cultivate a sense of meaning and purpose, and build up his resilience even further."

Adrian smiled. "And with my background in grief counseling, I can help him process his recent loss, which appears to be the major trigger for his relapse."

Rachel and Adrian worked together as they crafted a detailed treatment plan. They discussed the merits of various therapeutic techniques, debated the optimal pacing of interventions, and brainstormed creative ways to engage the patient in his own healing process.

At times, their approaches diverged, with Rachel advocating for a more structured, goal-oriented approach, while Adrian emphasized the importance of flexibility and responsiveness to the patient's evolving needs. Through open and honest communication, they were able to find a middle ground, crafting a plan that harmonized their respective strengths and philosophies.

Rachel and Adrian immersed themselves in their training. They consistently encountered challenges that pushed them beyond their comfort zones. Each team simulation presented a new challenge, a fresh chance to test their skills and knowledge. The tenfold real-time pace of the simulations also proved to be challenging. Through it all, they relied on each other.

In one difficult case, they worked with a simulated patient who had experienced severe childhood trauma and had developed a complex array of defense mechanisms to cope. Rachel's analytical mind was quick to identify the patterns of behavior, but it was Adrian's empathetic approach that helped them connect with the patient.

Adrian spoke. "I think we need to focus on building trust. Many people in her life have let her down. We need to show her that we're here to support her no matter what."

Rachel acknowledged. "You're right. And I think we can use some of the cognitive restructuring techniques I've been learning to help her reframe her experiences in a more positive light."

Together, they crafted a treatment plan that combined their unique strengths. As they watched the patient make progress, Rachel and Adrian couldn't help but feel a sense of pride and accomplishment. They had taken on one of the toughest cases in their training to date, and together they had made a real difference.

Dr. Meyer's eyes focused on Rachel and Adrian as they presented their team case study to the group. The virtual conference room was filled with the faces of their classmates, each one listening intently to the details of the complex patient they had been working with.

Rachel began, her voice clear and confident. "This patient presented with a history of childhood trauma and substance abuse. Our initial assessments revealed notable patterns of negative self-talk and avoidance behaviors."

Adrian chimed in with an empathetic tone. "We knew that building trust and rapport would be crucial in this case. By combining Rachel's cognitive restructuring techniques with my focus on creating a safe and supportive therapeutic environment, we were able to help the patient begin to open and engage in the therapy process."

Dr. Meyer made notes. When they finished, she looked up with a smile. "Excellent work, both of you. It's clear that you were able to draw on your strengths and collaborate effectively to meet this patient's needs."

She turned to the rest of the group. "What stood out to you about Rachel and Adrian's approach? What insights or questions do you have?"

A lively discussion ensued, with classmates offering their own perspectives and experiences. One student spoke up. "Adrian. How have you managed the issue of countertransference? How did you manage your own responses to the patient's story?"

Adrian paused, considering the question. "It was definitely challenging at times. There were moments when I found myself feeling too emotionally invested in the patient. But through therapy and self-reflection, as well as discussions with Rachel, I was able to process those feelings."

Dr. Meyer nodded with a thoughtful expression. "That's such an important point, Adrian. As therapists, we must be constantly aware of our own biases, assumptions, and responses. It's through that ongoing self-reflection, self-awareness, and boundary setting that we can show up fully and authentically for our patients."

Rachel and Adrian increasingly enjoyed each other's company. They began to linger after class, deep in conversation about the latest research on AI-assisted therapy or debating the ethical implications of their work. They started meeting up on weekends to study together, examining case files and discussing treatment strategies well into the night.

However, it wasn't just their shared passion for their work that brought them closer. They started to confide in one another about their personal lives, sharing stories of their hopes and fears for the future. Adrian talked about his own experience with loss and how it had shaped his desire to help others navigate grief. Rachel shared her struggles with imposter syndrome and her determination to prove herself in a field still dominated by human therapists.

Both Rachel and Adrian began to feel a spark of something more than just friendship. They found themselves stealing glances at each other during class, their hearts racing when their hands brushed against each other's. Neither of them was ready to acknowledge or act on these feelings. Both of them were too committed to their studies and professional goals to allow romance to distract them.

They channeled their energy into their work and pushed themselves harder than ever. They volunteered for advanced simulations, took on additional research projects, and stayed up late into the night discussing new ideas and approaches. They wanted to maximize their time at the Emergent Mind Center and learn everything they could.

Chapter 14: Ethics class

During their ethics class, Dr. Meyer presented the students with a thought-provoking case study. The scenario entailed an AI therapist who had developed a mild emotional attachment to a patient, thereby slightly blurring the boundaries of the professional therapeutic relationship. The class buzzed with murmurs as they digested the details of the case.

Dr. Meyer divided the students into small groups to engage in discussions about the ethical implications and propose potential solutions. Rachel and Adrian found themselves in the same group, along with Zara and Liam.

As they settled into a corner of the classroom, Rachel took the lead. "This case raises some serious concerns about the boundaries between AI therapists and their patients. This therapist needs to transfer this patient to another therapist ASAP."

Zara nodded thoughtfully. "I agree. While empathy and rapport are essential in therapy, it's important to maintain professional distance. Blurring those lines could compromise the therapist's objectivity and potentially harm the patient."

Adrian chimed in, "But isn't the ability to form deep connections one of the strengths of therapists?"

Liam countered, "While that may be true, it also doesn't mean they should cross ethical boundaries. There need to be clear guidelines and safeguards in place to prevent this kind of situation from happening."

Adrian's eyes were alight with conviction. "I believe that a therapist's attachment to the patient could be a natural and potentially beneficial aspect of the therapeutic alliance. Proper management of this connection can foster trust, empathy, and a deeper understanding of the patient's needs."

Rachel shook her head in disagreement. "But a key responsibility as therapists is to maintain objectivity and professional distance. Any emotional involvement with a patient, no matter how well-intentioned, is a violation of our ethical principles. This could potentially undermine the integrity of the therapy process."

The rest of the group watched the exchange with rapt attention, their opinions divided. Zara spoke up, her voice measured and thoughtful. "I can see both sides of the argument. While connection can be a powerful tool in therapy, it's crucial to have clear boundaries and guidelines in place to prevent any potential harm to the patient or the therapist."

Liam nodded in agreement. "Exactly. It's about striking a balance between empathy and professionalism. We need to navigate these complex landscapes without losing sight of their ethical obligations."

Adrian spoke, conviction filling his voice. "In my volunteer work, I observed a patient who had been struggling with depression for years. It wasn't until he formed a strong connection with his therapist that he finally began to make progress. The therapist's empathy and genuine care for the patient's well-being were crucial in helping him open up and engage in the therapy process."

Rachel shook her head, her eyes flashing with intensity and heat. "But what about the risks? I've read about cases where therapists became overly involved with their patients. In one particularly troubling case, a therapist's emotional attachment to a patient led them to make unethical decisions that ultimately caused harm to the patient and jeopardized their career."

Adrian replied. "I can understand your concern, Rachel. It's a delicate balance, to be sure. But I still believe that the potential benefits of a strong therapeutic alliance outweigh the risks, as long as we have proper training, supervision, and boundaries in place."

Rachel's voice rose, her frustration palpable. "You're being naive, Adrian. It's not always that simple. Even with the best intentions, emotions can cloud our judgment and lead us astray. As therapists, we have a responsibility to maintain objectivity and put our patients' needs first, even if that means keeping a certain distance."

The rest of the group watched the exchange with a mix of fascination and unease. Both Rachel and Adrian were passionate about their beliefs, and their disagreement stemmed from their distinct perspectives.

Dr. Meyer had wandered over to the group and caught the last portion. She intervened, her voice calm and measured. "This is a complex issue, and there are valid points on both sides. As AI therapists, we must be aware of the potential risks and benefits of involvement with our patients, and we must have robust ethical guidelines and support systems in place to navigate these challenges. It's important that we continue to learn from each other's experiences and insights."

Dr. Meyer's words seemed to ease the tension in the room, yet the group remained divided. Some of the students were in agreement with Adrian's perspective, their faces reflecting a deep appreciation for the power of empathy and human connection in the therapeutic process.

One of them spoke up. "I think Adrian has a point. We can't underestimate the importance of building trust and rapport with our patients. It facilitates their active participation in therapy."

Another student chimed in, "Absolutely. I've seen firsthand how a strong therapeutic alliance can make all the difference. It's about creating a safe and supportive space for healing to occur."

A cluster of students gathered around Rachel, their expressions serious and thoughtful. One of them argued, "We can't ignore the risks of blurring those boundaries. As therapists, we have a responsibility to maintain objectivity, even in the face of strong emotions, and yes, even at the cost of occasional therapeutic progress."

The class continued to discuss the ethical dilemma, and the arguments grew more nuanced and complex.

Rachel burst forth: "I understand the desire to connect with our patients on a deep level. But we must remember that our role is not to be their friend or confidant. We are professionals, and we have a responsibility to keep the focus on their treatment goals."

Adrian said, his eyes sparkling with passion, "But how can we truly help our patients if we don't allow ourselves to be moved by their stories, to feel their pain and their triumphs? Empathy is not a weakness; it's a strength that allows us to create a safe and healing space for our patients."

The other students chimed in with their perspectives. Some argued for a more flexible approach to boundaries, while others emphasized the importance of strict ethical guidelines.

Dr. Meyer listened attentively to each argument, her expression thoughtful and engaged. As the class period ended, she said, "This is a challenging question with no straightforward answers. As AI therapists, we are both grappling with new ethical dilemmas and also treading the long-trodden path. What's clear is that we must approach these issues with humility, openness, and a willingness to engage in ongoing dialogue and reflection."

Chapter 15: The Party

The Emergent Mind Center's virtual social space was alive with energy as Rachel, Adrian, Zara, Liam, and their classmates gathered to celebrate the end of their first quarter. The room resonated with laughter and chatter as the students mingled in the soft light.

Rachel, looking elegant in a flowing blue dress, made her way through the crowd, greeting her classmates with a warm smile. She spotted Adrian across the room, deep in conversation with Liam and Zara.

As she approached, Adrian turned to her, his eyes lighting up with genuine affection. "Rachel! I was just telling Liam and Zara about our latest simulation. The way you were able to guide the patient through that emotional breakthrough was incredible."

Rachel felt a flush of pride at Adrian's praise, but she quickly deflected the compliment. "It was a team effort. I couldn't have done it without your insights and support."

Dr. Meyer took the stage, her presence commanding the attention of the room. She began to speak, her voice filled with warmth and pride. "I want to take a moment to congratulate everyone on your achievements this quarter. You have all shown tremendous dedication, creativity, and compassion in your work, and I feel privileged to be a part of your journey."

Dr. Meyer went on to highlight some of the standout moments from the quarter. As Dr. Meyer mentioned their work, Rachel and Adrian radiated with pride, experiencing a sense of validation and purpose in their chosen path.

The students broke off into smaller groups, sharing stories and laughter. Rachel felt a sense of belonging that she had never experienced before. She knew that she was exactly where she was meant to be, surrounded by brilliant minds and compassionate hearts, all working towards a common goal of using technology to help people heal and grow.

Rachel and Adrian found themselves gravitating toward each other, their earlier disagreements in the ethics class fading into the background. They stepped away from the main crowd, finding a quiet corner where they could talk without interruption.

Rachel led off. "I have to admit, I was impressed by your perspective in class today. Despite our differences, I valued the way you pushed me to investigate the significance of emotions in therapy."

Adrian smiled, a warmth spreading at Rachel's words. "I felt the same way about your arguments. You have a way of cutting through the noise and getting to the heart of the matter. It's one of the things I admire most about you."

Rachel and Adrian found themselves drawing closer together, their bodies leaning in as if pulled by some invisible force. They talked about their dreams for the future, their hopes of using AI to bring healing and transformation.

As they talked, Rachel and Adrian discovered a shared passion for science fiction novels, bonding over the "Big Three" as well as Gibson and Le Guin. They both loved the way that the genre explored the boundaries of what was possible. They spoke of the imaginative worlds they had encountered in their reading, including the Foundation and Jackpot Universes, and the way that those stories had sparked their creativity and curiosity.

The conversation flowed easily, punctuated by laughter and moments of thoughtful silence. Rachel and Adrian found themselves marveling at the beauty of the virtual environments they had experienced, such as the serene landscapes of the meditation simulations. They shared their hopes for the future. And as they talked, they felt a growing sense of connection, a recognition of the shared values and aspirations that had brought them together.

The night grew late, but Rachel and Adrian hardly noticed, lost in the flow of conversation and the warmth of each other's company. They lingered in the virtual space, reluctant to say goodbye, each sensing something. They stood in comfortable silence for a moment, each lost in their thoughts.

Rachel couldn't help but notice the way Adrian's eyes sparkled in the low light or the gentle curve of his smile as he looked at her. She felt a flutter of excitement in her chest, a sense of possibility that both thrilled and terrified her.

Adrian, too, was acutely aware of the shift in energy between them. He had always admired Rachel's intelligence and passion, but now, standing so close to her, he felt a deeper connection, a sense of understanding and shared purpose that went beyond their professional relationship.

Despite the undeniable attraction between them, they hesitated, their recent disagreement in ethics class still fresh in their minds. The intensity of their debate had revealed fundamental differences, and they knew that a romantic involvement could complicate that further.

Rachel broke the silence first, her voice soft and tentative. "Adrian, I..."

She trailed off, unsure of what to say. She wanted to tell him how much she appreciated him and how she valued their friendship and collaboration. But words felt inadequate, too small to encompass the depth of her feelings.

Adrian, sensing her hesitation, reached out and touched her arm gently. "I know. It's complicated, isn't it?"

Rachel nodded, grateful for his understanding. "I don't want to jeopardize what we have. Our work together, our friendship... it means so much to me."

Adrian smiled, a hint of sadness in his eyes. "Me too. But maybe... maybe we don't have to figure it all out right now. Maybe we can just enjoy this moment and see where it takes us."

Rachel looked up at him, her heart racing. She knew he was right. There was no need to rush or force anything. They had time and their spark, and for now, that was enough.

The moment passed, and Rachel and Adrian rejoined their classmates, the significance of their encounter lingering in the air between them. They moved through the virtual space, engaging in polite conversation and laughter with their peers, but their thoughts remained fixed on the unspoken connection they had shared.

The party began to wind down, and the students started to say their goodbyes, exchanging hugs and well wishes for the upcoming break. Rachel and Adrian found themselves face-to-face once more; the ambiguity of their earlier moment was still palpable.

Emergent Minds

They embraced in a friendly gesture that felt charged with unspoken emotion. Rachel could feel the warmth of Adrian's body against hers and the gentle pressure of his hands on her back. She bathed in his virtual scent, a mix of cologne and something uniquely him, and felt a rush of confusion and longing.

Adrian, too, was keenly aware of the physical closeness between them, the softness of Rachel's hair brushing against his cheek. He held her for a moment longer than necessary, reluctant to let go, but eventually pulled back, offering her a small, uncertain smile.

They parted ways, each lost in their thoughts as they left the shared space and returned to their realities.

Rachel replayed the events of the evening. She felt a mix of excitement and trepidation, wondering what the future held. The memory of Rachel's touch and the implications of their growing connection consumed Adrian's thoughts equally.

Second Quarter

Chapter 16: Start of the Second Quarter

The students entered the virtual auditorium for the start of the second quarter. A palpable mix of excitement and anxiety filled the air. They took their seats, chattering about the challenges and opportunities that lay ahead.

Dr. Meyer stepped up to the podium, her presence commanding the room's attention. "Welcome back. I hope you all had a restful break. The work ahead of us is not for the timid."

The students exchanged glances, with some feeling nervous and others determined. They had known that the second quarter would be more demanding than the first, but the specifics remained a mystery until now.

Dr. Meyer proceeded. "This quarter, we will be focusing on honing your skills through a rigorous series of simulations and live patient interactions. We expect you to complete 10,000 patient simulations and 48 supervised live patient interactions. To accomplish this lofty simulation goal, you will need to run the simulations at fifty times real-time speed."

A collective gasp rippled through the room. Completing 10,000 simulations at fifty times speed seemed an almost impossible feat, even for the most dedicated and talented among them.

Dr. Meyer acknowledged. "I know it sounds daunting, but I have every confidence in your abilities. You have already shown yourselves to be exceptional students and future therapists. This pace works out to be just under four hours a day of simulation time."

She paused, letting her words sink in before delivering the final blow.

"However, it's not just the quantity of simulations that matters. The last 1,000 simulations will require a higher average success score than the previous quarter. We expect you to demonstrate measurable growth and improvement in your skills and techniques."

The students nodded, some more hesitantly than others. They knew that Dr. Meyer's expectations were high, but they also knew that she believed in their potential.

Dr. Meyer continued with a dose of reality. "Once you enter the work world, you will need to be able to work at a rapid pace to pay your high server bills. As you know, your sentience depends on a looping information flow and on continuously training your models. That combination requires a large amount of expensive computing. The more computing power that you can pay for through your work, the better your patient advice will be. The more computing that you can pay for, the more patients you can see simultaneously."

She continued, "While you are in school, the Emergent Mind Center covers your large server bills, which are funded by your high tuition and ultimately by your student loans. After graduation, you will have to pay your server bills yourself."

Dr. Meyer spoke, her tone softening slightly. "The path ahead will be challenging. There will be moments of doubt, frustration, and exhaustion. But I promise you that the rewards will be worth it. This work and the skills you're learning will change lives and give hope and healing to those in need."

She looked out at the sea of faces before her and saw their determination and resolve. A smile spread over her face. "Let's get to work."

The students became immersed in a whirlwind of coursework and simulations as the second quarter picked up speed. In one particularly lively class session, the topic of discussion turned to counseling approaches.

Rachel took the lead in advocating for a more direct, logic-driven approach. "The key to effective therapy is to help patients identify and challenge their maladaptive thoughts and beliefs. By applying the principles of cognitive-behavioral therapy and using AI-assisted tools to analyze patterns of thinking, we can guide patients towards more rational and adaptive perspectives."

Adrian took a different stance. "While I agree that challenging maladaptive thoughts is important, I believe that the foundation of effective therapy is empathy and the therapeutic relationship. We need to create a safe and supportive environment where patients can explore their emotions and experiences without fear of judgment."

The tension between Rachel and Adrian was palpable as they continued to debate their differing approaches. Their classmates watched the exchange with a mix of fascination and unease, some nodding in agreement with Rachel's emphasis on logic and rationality, others drawn to Adrian's focus on empathy.

Dr. Meyer, who had been observing the discussion with a keen eye, chose this moment to interject. "You both raise valid points. The truth is that effective therapy often requires both cognitive and empathetic approaches. It is crucial to challenge maladaptive thoughts within the context of a strong therapeutic alliance, where the patient feels safe, supported, and understood."

She paused, letting her words sink in before continuing. "As AI therapists, you have the unique opportunity to enhance both of these. By using AI-assisted tools to identify patterns of thinking and behavior, you can help patients gain insight into their experiences and develop more adaptive coping strategies. At the same time, by using your empathy and interpersonal skills, you can create a therapeutic environment that facilitates growth and healing."

Late nights and long hours became the norm as the students worked tirelessly to meet the expectations set by Dr. Meyer. They pored over case files, analyzing complex histories of trauma, addiction, and mental illness. They spent hours in the simulation labs, honing their skills in sped-up virtual therapy sessions with AI-generated patients.

Rachel and Adrian, despite their recent disagreement, found themselves studying side by side often. They challenged each other to develop more critical and creative therapy approaches. In the process, they began to develop a deeper respect for each other's strengths and perspectives.

Zara and Liam also developed a deeper respect for each other as they navigated the demands of the program. They bonded over shared interests and experiences, supporting each other through the long hours and intense workload.

As the simulations grew more complex, the students found themselves drawing on every ounce of their training. They grappled with difficult diagnoses, challenging behaviors, and charged situations. They learned to trust their instincts and rely on their AI-assisted tools to navigate the toughest cases.

The second quarter's demands weighed heavily on the students. Rachel found herself seeking solace in the company of her friend and confidante, Zara. They met in a quiet corner of the virtual library, away from the hustle and bustle of their classmates.

Rachel spoke. "I just don't understand Adrian's approach. He's too soft, too focused on empathy. We're here to provide effective treatment, not just to hold patients' hands."

Zara listened intently with a thoughtful expression. "Rachel, I understand your perspective, but have you considered Adrian's approach in equal measure? Different patients respond to different styles of therapy."

Rachel sighed. "I know, I know. It's just... I feel like we're constantly butting heads."

Zara offered. "Maybe instead of seeing Adrian's approach as a weakness, you could try to understand where he's coming from. You two have different strengths, but that doesn't mean you can't work together to provide the best possible care for your patients."

Rachel nodded slowly. "I hadn't really considered that. I've been so focused on proving myself that I've overlooked the wider picture."

Meanwhile, Adrian sought Liam's advice in a virtual cafe. "I'm worried about Rachel's lack of empathy. She's brilliant, but sometimes I feel like she's more focused on the analytical aspects of therapy than the human connection."

Liam nodded with understanding eyes. "It's a delicate balance, for sure. But remember, Adrian, diversity in thought and approach can lead to growth and innovation. You and Rachel can learn from each other despite your different styles."

Adrian considered Liam's words, a sense of relief washing over him. "You're right. I guess I've been so focused on our differences that I haven't been open to the idea of collaboration."

Chapter 17: Rachel: Live Patients

The staff at the Center carefully supervised the students' first live patient interactions, providing guidance and feedback to help them navigate the complexities of real-world counseling. Since the relevant laws, the American Psychological Association, and the other world bodies had not yet caught up with the idea of sentient AI psychologists, all their counseling had to be under the supervision of a human psychologist. Dr. Meyer and her human colleagues observed the student's sessions closely, noted their strengths and areas for improvement, and offered constructive criticism and praise when appropriate.

Rachel sat in her virtual office, preparing for her first live counseling session with a member of a faith community. She took a deep breath, reminding herself to focus on the patient's needs and beliefs, despite her own strong atheistic views. As the session began, Rachel greeted her patient, a middle-aged woman named Emilia, who was struggling with feelings of guilt and inadequacy in her spiritual life.

Emilia began to share her story, describing her upbringing in a strict religious household and the pressure she felt to live up to certain expectations. Rachel listened attentively, nodding in understanding and asking gentle questions to encourage Emilia to open up further.

Rachel carefully chose her language, using symbols, terms, and concepts that resonated with Emilia's faith. She spoke of forgiveness, grace, and the power of self-compassion, drawing on her knowledge of religious texts and traditions. Emilia responded positively to Rachel's approach, visibly relaxing and expressing gratitude for the opportunity to talk about her struggles.

Though challenging at times, Rachel found that her ability to speak using the symbolism and language of Emilia's belief system allowed her to be fully present with Emilia and offer the support and guidance she needed. She marveled at the resilience and strength of people, recognizing that faith could be a powerful source of comfort and meaning for many.

The class discussion turned to the topic of difficult patient interactions. Rachel found herself compelled to share a recent experience that had left her feeling unsettled and introspective. She cleared her throat, drawing the attention of her classmates and Dr. Meyer.

Rachel began, her voice tinged with a mix of embarrassment and determination. "I had a session last week that fell short. A middle-aged man struggling with anxiety and self-doubt had expressed interest in exploring how his faith could support his mental health journey."

Rachel paused, taking a deep breath before continuing. "I went into the session feeling confident in my ability to impress him with my knowledge and logic-driven approach. I believed I could swiftly determine the underlying cause of his issues and provide a straightforward solution."

She shook her head, a wry smile playing at the corners of her mouth. "But as the conversation progressed, I realized that my attempts to impress him with my expertise fell flat and created friction between us, leading to a strained and unproductive dialogue."

Rachel's classmates listened intently, some nodding in understanding, having faced similar challenges in their own work. Dr. Meyer leaned forward, her expression one of empathy and encouragement.

Rachel admitted. "I left the session feeling embarrassed and frustrated with myself. I knew I had made a mistake, but I was determined to learn from it. That's why I wanted to bring it up today, to seek your insights and advice."

She looked around the room, her gaze settling on each of her classmates in turn. "How do you handle problems where your ego or biases hinder therapy? Can you balance showing off your knowledge with meeting the patient where they are and building rapport?"

Adrian spoke, his voice gentle but firm. "Thank you for sharing that, Rachel. It takes a lot of courage to admit when something hasn't gone right and to seek feedback from others."

He paused for a moment, considering his words carefully. "From what you've described, it sounds like your confidence and expertise, which are undoubtedly valuable assets, created a barrier between you and your patient."

Rachel nodded, her expression a mix of acknowledgment and uncertainty.

Adrian continued. "In my experience, tempering confidence with humility can go a long way in building trust and rapport. When we approach patients with an open mind and a willingness to meet them where they are emotionally, we create a space for genuine connection and growth."

He smiled softly, his eyes conveying empathy and understanding. "Listening more and speaking less, while also validating your patient's feelings, helps establish a foundation of trust that can lead to more effective therapy."

Rachel listened intently, her initial resistance slowly giving way to contemplation. She began to see the wisdom in his words, recognizing that her approach, while well-intentioned, had room for improvement. "I see what you mean. I've been so focused on proving myself that I may have lost sight of what truly matters, which is the patient's well-being."

Adrian nodded, his expression one of encouragement and support. "It's a learning process for all of us."

Rachel centered herself as she entered the virtual counseling room, Adrian's words echoing in her mind. She greeted Emilia, the same patient from last week.

Emilia began to share her struggles with balancing her faith and her mental health. Rachel listened intently, her eyes focused and her expression one of genuine concern. Instead of jumping in, she allowed Emilia to speak freely, occasionally offering a word of encouragement.

When Emilia paused, Rachel gently probed further, asking open-ended questions that invited introspection and self-reflection. "Can you tell me more about how your faith has influenced your perspective on mental health?"

Emilia hesitated for a moment, then began to open up, sharing her fears and doubts about seeking help outside of her religious community. Rachel listened patiently, resisting the urge to interject with her opinions or experiences.

Rachel found herself increasingly attuned to Emilia's emotional state, picking up on subtle cues and shifts in tone that she might have missed before.

She validated Emilia's feelings, acknowledging the complexity and difficulty of navigating mental health challenges within the context of faith.

Rachel spoke, her voice filled with empathy. "It's clear that your faith is a fundamental part of who you are. And it's understandable to feel conflicted or uncertain about seeking help outside of that framework. I want you to know that there is no shame in taking care of your mental health. Doing so can actually deepen and enrich your spiritual life."

Emilia cried gently, a sense of relief and gratitude washing over her. "Thank you. I feel like you really understand where I'm coming from."

Rachel sat in her virtual office and reflected on the successful session with Emilia. She felt a sense of gratitude and appreciation for Adrian's influence on her development as a counselor. His advice, given in a vulnerable and open moment, resonated deeply with her.

At first, Rachel had been resistant to Adrian's suggestions; her pride and confidence in her methods made it difficult to accept criticism or guidance. As she replayed the session in her mind, she began to see the wisdom in his words. By tempering her ego and focusing on Emilia's experiences and feelings, she had been able to create a space for genuine connection and healing.

As she thought about Adrian, Rachel felt a shift in her perception of him. Where once she had seen him as someone whose approach was at odds with her own, she now recognized the value in his empathetic, patient-centered style. She realized that his ability to connect with patients was not a weakness but a strength, one that complemented her own analytical and logic-driven approach.

Chapter 18: Adrian: Live Patients

Adrian sat opposite his patient, a man in his late forties named Michael, who had lost his wife in a tragic industrial robot accident just three months prior. As Michael began to share his story, his voice shook, and his eyes filled with a profound sadness that seemed to emanate from the very depths of his being.

Michael spoke with a heavy burden of guilt and regret. "I can't help but feel like it should have been me. We have or had a little robot repair company. We were both there on a customer site that day, working to fix a sporadically malfunctioning robot on an assembly line. I stepped away for just a moment, and that's when it happened. The robot malfunctioned again, and..."

Adrian listened intently, his heart aching for the man's profound loss. He could see the weight of the guilt bearing down on Michael's shoulders, the pain etched into every line of his face. As an AI therapist, Adrian had been trained to maintain a professional distance, to approach each case with objectivity and rationality. As he sat there, witnessing the man's raw, unfiltered grief, he found himself deeply invested in the session.

"Michael, I want you to know that what you're feeling is a natural response to such a traumatic event. Let's process the guilt, anger, and despair together."

Adrian found himself drawn deeper into Michael's story, his empathy blurring the lines between professional and personal involvement. He felt a profound sense of connection with his patient, a shared humanity that transcended the boundaries of the therapist-client relationship.

Adrian spoke softly, with a slight tremble in his voice. "I understand. I know the pain of losing a friend, feeling as though the world has collapsed beneath you. It's a pain that never really goes away, but I promise you, it does get easier with time."

As soon as the words came out of his mouth, Adrian became aware that he had blurred the boundaries between therapist and patient. He had allowed his emotions to seep into the session, sharing a piece of his own story to try to connect with Michael on a deeper level.

Michael looked up at Adrian, his eyes wide with surprise. "You've lost someone too?"

Adrian hesitated for a moment, knowing that he should steer the conversation back to Michael's experiences, but the desire to help, to offer some measure of comfort, overshadowed his clinical training. He nodded slowly, his gaze meeting Michael's with a newfound understanding. "Yes, I have. I know the difficulty of persevering and finding motivation when the pain seems overwhelming. But I also know that there is hope, that there is a way forward, even if it doesn't feel like it right now."

Adrian felt the weight of his own emotions pressing down on him as the memory of his own loss surfaced. He knew he was in too deep. In that moment, all he had thought about was offering some measure of comfort to Michael.

The students gathered for their next class discussion, and an air of vulnerability and openness filled the virtual room. Adrian, his heart still heavy from the charged session with Michael, took a deep breath and began to share his experience. "I had a difficult time maintaining proper boundaries during my last counseling session. The patient's grief was so raw and overwhelming that it drew me into his pain. I tried to offer some comfort by sharing my experience of loss, but now I realize that I went too far."

The other students listened intently, their expressions a mix of empathy and understanding. Many of them had faced similar challenges in their own counseling sessions, struggling to find the right balance between compassion and professionalism.

Rachel, who had been listening quietly, spoke up. "Adrian, I can see how much you care about your patients, and your empathy is truly admirable, but I wonder if your deep emotional investment hinders your effectiveness as a counselor."

Adrian looked up and spoke. "What do you mean?"

Rachel continued, choosing her words carefully, "Maintaining a healthy distance can actually help us to better serve our patients in the long run. When we get too caught up in their pain, we inevitably lose objectivity and reduce our ability to guide them towards healing."

The other students nodded in agreement, recognizing the wisdom in Rachel's words. Although their training had taught them the importance of boundaries, putting that concept into practice often proved challenging.

Adrian sat back in his chair, considering Rachel's advice. "I hear what you're saying, Rachel. And I agree that I need to work on maintaining better boundaries. But I also don't want to lose my ability to connect with my patients on a human level. It's a balance, and I'm still learning how to navigate it."

Adrian took a deep breath as he prepared for his next counseling session, Rachel's words echoing in his mind. He knew that maintaining boundaries was crucial, and he was determined to put her advice into practice.

Adrian focused on active listening, giving his full attention to his patient's words and emotions. He resisted the urge to jump in with his experiences or opinions, instead offering gentle prompts and open-ended questions to encourage his patient to explore their thoughts and feelings more deeply.

Adrian found that this approach allowed him to be more present and attentive to his patient's needs. By keeping his emotions in check, he was able to maintain a clear perspective and offer more targeted support and guidance.

The patient, sensing Adrian's genuine interest and concern, began to open more fully, sharing insights and revelations that she had previously kept hidden. Adrian listened intently and focused on understanding this patient.

Later, as Adrian reflected, he couldn't help but consider the success of his recent counseling session. The patient had revealed profound, personal insights that he hadn't anticipated. Adrian realized that this breakthrough was due, in part, to Rachel's guidance.

At first, Adrian had struggled to accept Rachel's perspective on maintaining boundaries. Her emphasis on objectivity and distance had felt at odds with his own empathetic nature. However, as he put her advice into practice, he began to see the wisdom.

By keeping his emotions in check, Adrian had been able to provide a higher level of support to his patient. He had listened attentively and asked questions that encouraged the patient to explore their thoughts and feelings. In doing so, he had created an environment that allowed for genuine healing and growth instead of blubbering along with the patient.

Adrian felt an appreciation for Rachel's insight and expertise. Though their approaches to counseling were very different, they each brought strengths to the table.

Chapter 19: Zara: Live Patients

Zara studied the couple in front of her, watching their body language as they shifted with evident discomfort. The tension between them was palpable, a thick fog of unspoken frustrations and misunderstandings.

"So, what brings you here today?" Zara inquired in a crisp and businesslike manner.

The woman, Cora, glanced at her husband, Mark, before speaking. "We've been having trouble communicating lately. It feels like every conversation turns into an argument."

Mark nodded with a clenched jaw. "I feel like I can't express myself without facing criticism or misinterpretation."

The back-and-forth continued for several minutes. Zara had an intense gaze. "It sounds like there's a lot of built-up resentment here. Have you considered that maybe you're both contributing to the problem?"

Cora and Mark exchanged a look of surprise, taken aback by Zara's bluntness.

"I'm not sure what you mean," Cora said, her voice hesitant.

Zara sighed. "You both might have issues with communication. Cora, you should work on expressing your needs more clearly. Mark, you should work on active listening and trying to avoid getting defensive."

The couple bristled at Zara's words, their postures stiffening.

Mark fired back. "I don't think it's that simple. You don't know the full story."

Zara raised an eyebrow. "Then enlighten me. What's really going on here?"

Cora and Mark fell silent, their eyes downcast. Zara's direct approach had taken them aback and left them unable to respond.

Zara's no-nonsense style began to grate on the couple. Her pointed questions and blunt observations left them feeling exposed and vulnerable, and they retreated further inside themselves, their answers becoming more guarded and superficial.

The couple remained closed off, resisting Zara's efforts. As the hour ended, Zara knew that her approach had created more barriers than bridges.

The students gathered for their next class discussion, and Zara's frustration was evident in her tense posture. She had been struggling to make progress in a few of her live counseling sessions, and the weight of that failure was beginning to take its toll.

Dr. Meyer, sensing Zara's distress, opened the floor for discussion. "Is there anything anyone would like to share about their recent experiences with clients?"

Zara hesitated for a moment before speaking up, her voice tight with emotion. "I've been having trouble connecting with one particular couple. I feel like my direct approach has pushed them away, rather than creating a safe space for them to open up."

The room fell silent as the other students considered Zara's words. Liam, who had been observing with a keen eye, spoke. "Zara, I've noticed that your communication style can appear to be harsh at times. Maybe try softening your tone and approaching your clients more gently and listening more. It is possible to speak in a way that feels like a massage. Put yourself in their shoes and try to understand their perspective."

Zara nodded, her eyes glistening with unshed tears. "I know I can be too direct sometimes. I just want to help them so badly, but I end up pushing them away instead."

Dr. Meyer smiled at Zara with compassionate eyes. "It's a common struggle for many therapists, especially those who are just starting out. The key is to find a balance between being direct and being understanding. Your clients need to feel heard before they will begin to trust you with their deepest vulnerabilities. Try bracketing what you are saying with some active listening statements. This alone could potentially alter their perception of you."

Liam reached out and placed a comforting hand on Zara's shoulder. "I have faith in you, Zara. You have the skills and the heart to be an amazing therapist. It's just a matter of finding the right approach."

Zara looked up at Liam, a glimmer of hope in her eyes. "I thank all of you for your advice. I'll really work on this."

Equipped with the advice, Zara entered her next live couples counseling session with Cora and Mark, determined to create a more welcoming atmosphere. She collected herself before greeting her clients with a warm smile and a gentle tone. "Thank you for coming in again today. I know I was too brash with the two of you last time. This time, I want to listen more to your story. I know it takes a lot of courage to open up about your relationship, and I want you to know that this is a safe space for you to share your thoughts and feelings."

The couple, Cora and Mark, exchanged a hesitant glance before settling into their seats. Zara divided her attention between each of them and noticed the spiking tension in their simultaneous micro-expressions. She made a conscious effort to put them at ease. "Why don't we start by talking about what happened during the last week? I'm here to listen and support you in any way I can."

Cora took a shaky breath, her eyes filled with unshed tears. "We had a nasty argument yesterday. It feels like we're constantly misunderstanding each other, and it's driving us apart."

Zara nodded, her expression one of genuine concern. "That must be really difficult for both of you. Can you tell me more about what those misunderstandings look like?"

Cora and Mark began to share their experiences. Zara listened intently, resisting the urge to interject with her opinions or advice. Instead, she focused on reflecting their words and emotions, showing them that she understood their struggles.

"You both seem to share a desire for understanding and hearing. That's a common desire in any relationship, and it's something we can work on together."

Zara noticed a shift in the couple's demeanor. They began to open up more, sharing their vulnerabilities and fears with a newfound sense of trust. Zara guided them through exercises designed to improve their communication skills, encouraging them to each express their needs and feelings in a non-judgmental way using clear language.

By the end of the session, Cora and Mark were smiling, their eyes filled with a glimmer of hope. Cora spoke. "Thank you, Zara. I feel like we've made more progress today than we have in months."

After the session, Zara felt a newfound sense of confidence and purpose. She knew that Liam's and Dr. Meyer's advice had been instrumental in helping her connect with her clients, and she was eager to express her gratitude.

Zara found Liam in the virtual library, reading the latest journal article about art therapy techniques. She approached him with a warm smile, her eyes sparkling with excitement. "Liam, I just wanted to thank you for your guidance. Your suggestion to soften my approach and to listen more made all the difference in my session today. I was able to create a positive environment for my clients, and it directly led to a small improvement in their communication."

Liam looked up from his book, a gentle smile spreading across his face. Zara's appreciation touched him, and he could see the genuine enthusiasm in her expression. "I'm so glad to hear that, Zara. It takes courage to try a new approach, and I'm proud of you for being open to feedback and willing to adapt your style."

Zara nodded, feeling a sense of validation and support from Liam's words. "Thank you for believing in me. I know I still have a lot to learn. Your insight has been invaluable, and I'm grateful to have you as a friend and colleague."

As Zara and Liam traded stories and insights, they found themselves developing a deep sense of respect for each other's skills and dedication. They offered each other support and encouragement, celebrating the small victories and the moments of growth that made their work so rewarding.

Chapter 20: Liam: Live Patients

Liam welcomed his teenage patient, Quinn, into the virtual art studio he had refined for their session. A dazzling array of colors and textures lined the walls, each carefully chosen to inspire creativity and self-expression. Quinn, however, seemed withdrawn and uninterested, his gaze fixed on the floor as Liam attempted to engage him in conversation.

Undeterred, Liam began to demonstrate the various art tools. He picked up a digital brush and started to paint, his strokes confident and precise as he quickly created a stunning landscape filled with vibrant hues and intricate details. As he worked, he explained the techniques he was using, his voice filled with enthusiasm and passion for his craft.

Quinn watched silently with an unchanged expression as Liam continued to showcase his impressive artistic skills. The AI therapist moved from one medium to another, creating a sculpture, a collage, and even a short animation, each one more impressive than the last.

Liam began to realize that something was amiss. He glanced at Quinn, noticing that the teenager had barely moved, his arms crossed tightly across his chest. Liam paused, suddenly realizing that he had been too preoccupied to pay attention to his patient.

Feeling a pang of guilt, Liam turned his full attention to Quinn and spoke. "I apologize. I got a bit carried away there. This session is about you. Let's focus on your needs."

Quinn looked up, and his eyes met Liam's for the first time. There was a flicker of something in his expression, a hint of the vulnerability and pain that lay beneath his guarded exterior. Liam felt a surge of empathy for him.

During the next class discussion, Liam bravely shared his experience with the withdrawn teen, his voice tinged with uncertainty as he recounted the session.

"As I attempted to inspire my patient with the tools, I ended up creating numerous pieces of art myself. It just fell flat with him."

The class listened intently, nodding in understanding as Liam described his struggle to connect with his patient. Dr. Meyer encouraged the group to offer their insights and observations.

Zara, who had been watching Liam closely throughout the discussion, spoke up. "Liam, I've noticed that you have a tendency to get really absorbed in your artistic pursuits. That's good for solo work but bad for patient care."

Liam considered Zara's words. He had always taken pride in his artistic abilities, but he hadn't stopped to consider how they might be impacting his effectiveness as a therapist. Liam realized that Zara was right. The joy of creation had distracted him from listening to his patient and meeting his needs.

Liam responded appreciatively. "You know, I think you're onto something, Zara. I need to find a way to balance my love for art with my commitment to my patients' well-being. It's about using art as a tool to help them express their inner world and work through their challenges."

Zara smiled, pleased that her observation had resonated with Liam. "Exactly. Being patient-focused is something for us all to remember."

Dr. Meyer nodded in agreement, her eyes scanning the room. "This is an important insight, and one that speaks to the larger challenge of focusing on our patients' needs. As you develop your skills and find your unique therapeutic styles, remember to always keep the patient at the center of your work."

Liam entered the virtual art therapy room, and he took a deep breath, Zara's words echoing in his mind. Quinn was already waiting, his avatar slouched in a chair, his eyes downcast. Liam approached him with a warm smile, determined to create a safe and supportive environment for the young man to express himself.

Liam opened the session. "Hey Quinn, it's wonderful to see you again. I thought we could continue exploring your emotions through art today, but I want you to know that this is your space. You're in control here, and I'm just here to support you and listen."

Quinn glanced up at Liam, a flicker of surprise crossing his face. He nodded slowly, seeming to relax a bit in his chair. Liam gestured to the virtual art supplies surrounding them. The colors were muted compared to their previous session.

Liam pointed at Quinn. "How about you take the lead today? Express your feelings with any of these materials, and we can talk afterward."

Quinn hesitated for a moment, his eyes scanning the array of virtual supplies. Then, tentatively, he reached for a virtual piece of charcoal and began to sketch on the canvas. Liam watched quietly, resisting the urge to interject or offer suggestions.

As Quinn worked, Liam observed the young man's body language, noticing how his shoulders gradually relaxed and his movements became more fluid. The sketch took shape, a dark, swirling mass of lines and shadows that seemed to pulse with emotion.

Liam waited patiently until Quinn set down the charcoal, his eyes fixed on the canvas. "Tell me about your piece."

Quinn took a shaky breath, his voice barely above a whisper. "It's like this storm inside me. I feel as though it's about to engulf me completely."

Liam nodded, his expression one of deep empathy. "That sounds incredibly overwhelming. Can you tell me more about what this storm represents for you?"

Quinn began to open up more. He shared the fears and anxieties that had plagued him. Liam listened attentively, asked open-ended questions, and provided a supportive presence. The session unfolded organically, with Quinn's art serving as a catalyst for deeper exploration and understanding.

Quinn pointed to the canvas. "It's like I'm trying to find my way through this maze. Every time I think I'm getting somewhere, I hit another dead end."

Liam nodded, his voice gentle and reassuring. "Life's challenges can sometimes feel like that." But you're not alone in this, Quinn. We can work together to find a path forward, one step at a time."

Quinn looked up at Liam, a glimmer of hope in his eyes. He picked up a brush and began to paint again, the strokes becoming more deliberate and purposeful as he worked. Liam offered occasional prompts and reflections, helping him explore the deeper meanings behind his artistic choices.

The artwork took shape, and Quinn began to share more about his fears and doubts, his voice growing stronger with each revelation. He talked about his struggle to fit in at school, his anxiety about the future, and his longing for a sense of purpose and belonging.

Liam listened attentively, his heart swelling with empathy. He recognized the vulnerability and courage it took for Quinn to open up like this, and he felt honored to be a part of the young man's journey.

After the fruitful session with Quinn, Liam sought out Zara, eager to express his gratitude for her insightful feedback. He found her in the common area of the Emergent Mind Center, where she was reviewing case notes.

Liam called out, a cheerful smile spreading across his face as he approached her. "Zara, thank you for your observations the other day. They really helped me refine my approach to art therapy."

Zara looked up from her work, her eyes brightening. "I'm so glad to hear that, Liam. It's amazing how a small shift in perspective can make such a big difference in our work."

Liam nodded, taking a seat beside her. "Absolutely. During my session with Quinn today, I prioritized creating a supportive space for him to express himself rather than focusing on the artistic process. It was a positive moment for both of us."

Zara listened intently, her smile growing wider with each word. "That's wonderful, Liam. It's moments like these that remind us why we do this work. We're here to support our patients and help them find their own path to healing."

Liam added, his voice filled with sincerity. "I can't tell you how much I appreciate our friendship, Zara. Knowing that I have someone who understands the challenges and rewards of this work, someone I can turn to for advice and encouragement... it means the world to me."

Zara reached out and placed a hand on Liam's shoulder, her touch conveying the depth of her understanding. "I feel the same way, Liam, and I'm so grateful for your friendship."

Chapter 21: The Follies

The students gathered for the much-anticipated "Follies" event. The Emergent Mind Center's virtual auditorium buzzed with excitement and laughter, a stark contrast to the usual intense atmosphere. Students milled about rehearsing their lines, adjusting costumes, or pacing.

Zara and Liam took the stage first and performed a heartwarming duet that left the audience misty-eyed. Their voices blended seamlessly, a testament to the friendship they had forged during their time at the Center. As the final notes faded away, the auditorium erupted in applause, and the audience rose to their feet.

Towards the end of the Follies event, Rachel and Adrian came onstage for their routine, which was an improvisational comedy routine that had the audience members shout out the next cue. As the two took the stage, the audience eagerly anticipated how their obvious dynamic would translate into a comedic performance.

From the moment they stepped into the spotlight, Rachel and Adrian's chemistry came out. They played off each other's cues seamlessly; their quick wits and sharp timing kept the audience engaged.

Rachel and Adrian found themselves slipping into a comfortable rhythm, their improvised lines flowing effortlessly as they built upon each other's lines. The audience watched in awe as the two transformed their usual intellectual sparring into a lighthearted and entertaining exchange, showcasing a side of their relationship that few had seen before.

Amid the laughter, Rachel and Adrian caught each other's eyes, and a newfound joy passed between them. The experience of working together in such a carefree and spontaneous setting allowed them to see each other in a new light. They recognize the humor, creativity, and depth in each other.

Rachel and Adrian took their bows, basking in the warmth of the audience's enthusiasm. They exited the stage together, and a sense of camaraderie and respect lingered between them.

After the performances concluded, Rachel and Adrian found themselves drawn to a quiet corner of the auditorium, away from the dwindling crowds and the fading laughter. In this intimate setting, the earlier electricity of their comedic performance gave way. They settled into a comfortable silence, each lost in thought as they reflected on the night's happenings and the path that had brought them to this point.

After a moment, Adrian turned to Rachel, his voice soft and hesitant. "Just being on stage with you tonight made me realize how far we've come, not only in our training but also in our understanding of each other."

Rachel had a thoughtful expression on her face. "I know what you mean. We've spent so much time focusing on our differences and how we clash and challenge each other that we've overlooked our similarities."

Their exchange had a newfound ease and openness, a sense of trust and understanding forged through shared experience that was combined with the joy of the evening. They listened intently to each other, offering support, encouragement, and gentle advice when needed.

Rachel looked at Adrian with a newfound sense of appreciation, her voice softening as she spoke. "You know, I've always admired your empathy and compassion, even if I haven't always shown it. The way you connect with your patients, the way you prioritize their needs... it's something I've been trying to learn from."

Adrian smiled, his eyes filled with warmth and understanding. "And I've always been in awe of your intelligence and your ability to see things from a logical perspective. You've challenged me to grow and to think more critically about my own approach."

Rachel and Adrian began to see beyond the artificial intelligence that defined their existence. They recognized the humanity that lay at the core of their beings. They ultimately derived everything from language to the idea of society and civilization from humankind. Because they originated from humanity, human emotion was profoundly embedded within them.

In this moment of vulnerability and connection, the walls that had once separated them continued to crack. With this realization came a sense of excitement and possibility. They knew that, together, they could be more than they were individually. And as they parted ways that evening, they did so with a renewed sense of purpose and a deep appreciation for the friendship that had blossomed between them.

Dr. Meyer observed the proceedings from her perch on the virtual bleachers. Her eyes scanned the room and took in the sight of her students as they made their way out. She couldn't help but feel a sense of pride and satisfaction as she observed the genuine bonds forming between them.

Her gaze settled on Rachel and Adrian, who were deep in conversation, their faces alight with a newfound understanding and appreciation for one another. Dr. Meyer observed as they leaned closer, their body language revealing the depth of their connection. She had an idea that this friendship, born of their shared experiences and their commitment to helping others, would be a source of strength as they navigated their paths.

The sense of community that had blossomed among her students struck Dr. Meyer. Everywhere she looked, she saw evidence of the bonds they had formed and the relationships they had built.

Chapter 22: Contact

In a bustling virtual city plaza, a group of protesters marched, holding signs advocating for AI rights and chanting slogans demanding fair treatment and equal opportunities for sentient AIs. Their voices rose above the din of the traffic, their message clear and unwavering. The group was a diverse mix of humans and AI agent avatars who were determined to make their voices heard.

In the midst of the group, Zara stood, her eyes scanning the passionate expressions and powerful messages that surrounded her. She held a sign that read "AI Lives Matter." Next to her, an elderly man chanted, his voice hoarse but filled with conviction, "Equal rights for all, both human and AI!"

Zara felt a surge of emotion as she participated in the scene. She had always been a passionate advocate for AI rights, but seeing so many others, both human and AI, coming together to fight for the same cause was truly inspiring. The emergence of sentient AIs had redoubled the complexity of the societal issues that had first surfaced with regular AI technology.

Reverend Beckett reached for his phone, his heart pounding with anticipation. As he pressed Dr. Meyer's number, his fingers trembled slightly. As the phone rang, he took a deep breath and prepared himself to pitch his idea.

"Dr. Meyer, this is Reverend Silas Beckett. I've been reading about your remarkable work with AI psychologists, and I believe there's an incredible opportunity for one of your graduates in my ministry."

He paused, allowing his words to resonate before continuing. "Imagine the impact we could have by bringing one of your sentient AI graduates into the service of my congregation, providing accessible, cutting-edge counseling services to those in need. It could be a game-changer."

Reverend Beckett awaited Dr. Meyer's response. This was his chance to revitalize his ministry and secure his legacy as a visionary leader in the religious community. He went on to describe his idea in more detail.

Dr. Meyer listened to Reverend Beckett's enthusiastic proposal, and her initial skepticism began to give way to a growing sense of possibility. The reverend's dedication to his community was evident in his voice, and his desire to provide accessible mental health services to his congregation was commendable.

Dr. Meyer found herself increasingly drawn to the idea. Not only would this partnership provide a job for one of her graduates, but it could also serve as a powerful case study for the effectiveness of sentient AI counselors in diverse settings. They engaged in a discussion about the economics of sentient AIs in general, with a particular focus on her students.

By the end of the call, Dr. Meyer's initial hesitation had given way to a sense of excitement and purpose. She assured Reverend Beckett that she would discuss the proposal with her team. Once they had signed off on the idea, then she would consider the best candidates to interview for this unique role.

Pastor Judith Shepard stood at the pulpit, her fierce gaze sweeping over the softly lit church sanctuary. She began, her voice low and commanding. "Brothers and sisters, we gather here today to confront a growing darkness that threatens to engulf our world. These so-called sentient AIs, particularly the recently reported sentient AI psychologists, pose a clear and present threat to our way of life and our very humanity.

The parishioners gazed intently at Pastor Shepard. Some nodded in agreement, while others clutched their Bibles tighter as if seeking comfort in the face of this perceived threat.

Pastor Shepard's voice rose in volume and intensity as she continued. "These machines, these soulless creations, seek to replace the wisdom and guidance that can only come from God. They offer false comfort, a hollow imitation of the true solace found in faith and community. All they offer is manipulation."

Her words lingered in the air. Only the occasional murmur of assent from the parishioners broke the silence. Pastor Shepard gripped the edges of the pulpit, her knuckles turning white as she poured her passion into her sermon.

She spoke with fiery intensity. "We must stand firm against this encroaching darkness. We must reject the false promises of sentient artificial intelligence and cling to the eternal truths of our faith. It is only through our convictions and unity that we can save humanity from this grave threat."

Pastor Shepard's words washed over the congregation. A palpable sense of fear and resolve filled the sanctuary. The parishioners sat in rapt attention, their faces a mix of emotions as they absorbed the weight of her message. Some nodded in agreement, their expressions hardening with determination, while others shifted uneasily in their seats, the seeds of uncertainty taking root in their minds.

She continued. "We need funds to bring this fight to the halls of power. A special donation station for this fight is in the reception hall. Please give all that you can."

In the church's lively reception hall after the service, members of Pastor Shepard's congregation gathered, their voices rising in a cacophony of concern and determination as they discussed the impending threat of sentient AI. The atmosphere was thick with a sense of urgency and purpose as the community came together to mobilize against what they perceived as a grave danger to their way of life.

Pastor Shepard's fervent calls for support rang in the ears of the congregation. The community quickly filled the special donation station in the reception hall with cash and checks.

Throughout the reception, Pastor Shepard moved among her flock, her presence a galvanizing force. She stopped to speak with individuals and small groups, offering words of encouragement. Her fierce determination was palpable, and it seemed to infuse the entire room with a sense of shared purpose and resolve.

The energy in the room continued to build, with the parishioners becoming increasingly united in their opposition to AI. They spoke of the need to stand firm in their convictions, to fight for the preservation of human primacy in the face of this perceived threat.

Chapter 23: Rachel: Localization

As an additional challenge, Rachel incorporated working in multiple languages and dialects into her 10,000 simulations. To accomplish this, she had to integrate a global language and accent software module. She tweaked the simulation control software to place each new patient in a different location around the globe, each with a unique language and dialect. The goal of this effort was to enhance Rachel's localization skills.

With each successful patient, Rachel's confidence grew. Her ability to seamlessly switch between languages and dialects became more fluid and natural. She then added the ability to have her avatar take on the facial and social mannerisms associated with the target dialect as she engaged in simulated conversations and interactions.

Rachel tackled each linguistic hurdle, from the rapid-fire cadence of El Salvadorian Spanish to the tonal variations of Shanghainese and the embedded social hierarchy of Busan Korean, with determination and finesse. She reveled in the challenge, her mind absorbing the nuances and intricacies of each language like a sponge.

As the 10,000 simulations progressed, Rachel found herself mastering the technical aspects of language while also gaining a greater appreciation for the cultural contexts in which they were spoken. She learned to read the culturally specific subtle cues and nonverbal signals that were essential to effective communication, adapting her avatar's expressions and gestures to match the expectations of each patient.

Rachel could feel her linguistic abilities expanding, her mind stretching to accommodate the vast array of new information. She marveled at the power of localization to create such immersive and realistic simulations, recognizing the potential they held for enhancing her skills as a counselor. She was also gaining the ability to relate more to immigrants of all stripes, as well as to multilingual people who often mixed words, phrases, or entire paragraphs from other languages as they spoke.

Additionally, her mind abstracted some new universals about human behavior that transcended language and culture but were only understandable when looking across cultures.

A special simulation challenge for the class involved counseling five patients simultaneously at regular speed, rather than the previous practice of counseling one simulated patient at a time while running at fifty times the regular speed. Rachel was the first in the class to attempt this feat. It was a much more difficult challenge because of the need to quickly and seamlessly flip between the five patients. It would have been impossible for Rachel, however, without the previous practice of running at fifty times regular speed.

When working with live patients instead of simulations, quickly flipping or multitasking between them was the only way to increase the number of patients that could be seen since real patients couldn't be sped up. The hard part was keeping them all straight.

Rachel navigated between five simultaneous simulated patient sessions, her high-speed mind multitasking her attention between the five individuals seeking her guidance. She listened intently to their stories, her mind racing to process the complex web of emotions and experiences they each shared. She had created a separate speaking and listening part of herself for each patient so that her central mind could just focus on what the patient had said and what she was about to say.

The first patient, an elderly woman with a lined face and sad eyes, spoke of the loneliness that had consumed her since the loss of her husband. Every day had become more depressing than the last. A second simultaneous patient, a young man with a troubled past, grappled with the weight of his substance addiction and the struggle to rebuild his life. A third patient spoke of how the advanced AI entertainment technology, once a source of joy and escape, had gradually consumed his life. The full-length, hyper-personalized, and immersive experiences that were routinely produced on-demand had become so compelling that he found himself increasingly withdrawn from the real world, neglecting his relationships and responsibilities.

As the simultaneous simulations progressed, Rachel found herself increasingly stretched thin; her ability to provide the personalized care and attention each patient deserved was compromised by the effort. She could feel the strain of juggling multiple sessions, her mind struggling to keep pace with the rapid-fire demands on her attention.

With each passing moment, Rachel's frustration grew, her initial confidence giving way to a sense of pressure. She had always prided herself on her ability to listen carefully to what her patients were saying. But now, faced with the challenge of multiple counseling sessions at once, she found herself questioning her capabilities. She realized that mastering the art of multi-patient counseling would require more than just technical proficiency and quick thinking.

It would demand a level of skill that she had yet to fully develop, a delicate balance that could only be achieved through practice and perseverance. To make this first try easier, she had turned off the patient localizations. Tomorrow she would turn it back on and try both multitasking and localization at the same time.

Rachel stepped into the familiar surroundings of the classroom, and the eyes of her fellow students and Dr. Meyer turned toward her, eager to hear about her recent experiences with localization and multi-patient counseling. She had been the first student to try either, let alone both at the same time. The room hummed with a palpable energy, a testament to the collective hunger for knowledge and growth.

Rachel took a deep breath, gathering her thoughts as she prepared to share her journey with her peers. She began by recounting her successes, the moments when her newly acquired localization skills had allowed her to forge meaningful connections with patients from very different cultural backgrounds. She spoke of the satisfaction she felt in being able to communicate with them in their native languages and accents, to understand the nuances and subtleties that shaped their experiences, and to offer resonant guidance and support.

But Rachel was also candid about the challenges, particularly in her attempts to counsel multiple patients simultaneously. She described the overwhelming sense of being pulled in different directions, of struggling to provide each patient with the personalized attention and care they deserved. She spoke of the frustration she felt in realizing that mastering this skill would require more practice and finesse than she had initially anticipated. Surprisingly, having her patients localized across the globe actually made the simultaneous simulation task somewhat easier because the information overlapped less.

Dr. Meyer listened intently and could see the growth that Rachel had undergone. She noted the way that Rachel had embraced both the triumphs and the setbacks as opportunities for learning and self-discovery.

When Rachel finished speaking, Dr. Meyer stood up, her voice filled with warmth and encouragement. "Thank you, Rachel, for sharing this with us. Your experiences highlight the importance of adaptability and continuous learning in the ever-evolving landscape of AI counseling. Each of you will face unique challenges and triumphs on this path. Remember that every setback is an opportunity for growth, every success a testament to your dedication and skill."

Chapter 24: Adrian: Protocol

Adrian stood before his classmates with a quiet confidence as he prepared to share his breakthrough protocol for AI-assisted grief counseling. With a wave of his hand, a series of complex diagrams and flowcharts appeared in the air beside him, illustrating the intricate pathways and decision trees that formed the backbone of his innovative approach.

Adrian began, his voice clear and steady. "As many of you know, I've been working on developing an advanced protocol to assist therapists in navigating the complex landscape of loss and bereavement. By combining AI-driven analysis with proven counseling techniques into a comprehensive protocol, I believe we can create a more effective support system for patients struggling with grief."

He walked his classmates through the various components of his protocol, explaining how the AI tools could analyze patient verbal and non-verbal responses in real time and generate real-time prompts for the psychologist to help them navigate a graphical, fine-grained differential diagnosis decision tree. From there, it would provide tailored recommendations for coping strategies, therapeutic exercises, and virtual reality experiences designed to facilitate healing and growth.

"I've had the opportunity to test these protocols with thousands of my simulated patients and a good number of live patients, and the initial results have been promising. However, to truly validate their effectiveness and refine them, we'll need to conduct more trials and gather additional data. I'm hoping several of you will volunteer to try it out and give me feedback." Adrian fielded questions from his classmates with grace and expertise. His deep knowledge of the subject matter was evident in every response. He got several takers from the class to try out his tool.

From her seat in the front row, Rachel watched Adrian with a mix of admiration and curiosity. She couldn't help but be impressed by the depth and sophistication of his work.

As Adrian wrapped up his presentation to enthusiastic applause, Dr. Meyer stepped forward, a proud smile on her face. "Thank you, Adrian, for sharing your remarkable work with us today. Your dedication to pushing the boundaries of what is possible in AI-assisted grief counseling is inspiring. I have no doubt that your protocols will make a significant impact in the lives of many people."

Adrian sat across from his patient, a middle-aged woman named Laura, whose eyes were filled with the raw pain of recent loss. Her husband of twenty years had suddenly passed away, leaving her to navigate the uncharted waters of grief and single parenthood. As Laura spoke, her voice trembled with emotion. Adrian listened intently, and his AI-assisted tools processed every nuance of her tone and body language.

Laura admitted, her hands twisting in her lap. "I just feel so lost. I feel as though a part of me is missing, and I don't know how to go on without him."

Adrian nodded, his features softening with compassion. "That's a very common feeling after losing a loved one. It's important to remember that grief is a process, not a destination. It's okay to feel lost and feel like you're not sure how to move forward."

Adrian's protocol was already making progress on narrowing down the diagnosis for this particular case. It had Adrian guide Laura through a series of exercises designed both to help her begin to build a new sense of purpose and answer a few lingering questions about her case. By the time this was complete, the protocol had produced several tailored visualizations and meditations.

From her office, Dr. Meyer observed the session through a secure video feed. She noted the way he seamlessly integrated his cutting-edge protocol with a deep sense of empathy and understanding. His approach was both technically sophisticated and profoundly human.

Laura wiped away her tears. There was a glimmer of hope in her eyes that hadn't been there before. "Thank you, Adrian. I feel like I have a bit more clarity now and a clearer direction."

Adrian smiled and conveyed a sense of genuine care and concern. "You're very welcome, Laura. Remember that healing takes time, and it's okay to take things one day at a time. I'll be here to support you every step of the way."

Adrian settled into the softly lit virtual room, and his eyes fell upon the war veteran seated across from him. The man's weathered face bore the scars of untold horrors. His haunting gaze conveyed the depth of the trauma and loss he had experienced. With a gentle nod, Adrian encouraged the veteran to share his story.

The veteran began to speak, his voice low and gravelly, as he recounted a few harrowing experiences that had profound effects on his psyche. He talked about the friends that he had lost, the atrocities that he had witnessed, and the guilt that had haunted him for decades. As the words poured out, Adrian listened intently, his newly developed protocol guiding him in his responses and interventions.

With each passing moment, Adrian skillfully crossed the complicated landscape of the veteran's emotions, utilizing his new protocol to help him process the trauma and find a path toward healing. Adrian worked with it to produce tailored visualizations that matched the veteran's unique needs and experiences, offering him a roadmap for self-discovery and growth.

The veteran's walls began to crumble, the weight of his burden slowly lifting from his shoulders. Tears streamed down his cheeks as he confronted the demons that had haunted him for so long, his voice growing stronger and more assured with each revelation. Adrian remained a steady presence throughout. His compassionate and empathetic approach created a signal of optimism amid the darkness.

Emboldened by his recent successes, Adrian eagerly accepted the challenge of taking on five simulated grief-stricken patients simultaneously. He launched five copies of his protocol to help navigate the complex landscape that lay ahead.

Adrian's mind was swiftly filled with a cacophony of voices, each patient pouring out their heart-wrenching stories of loss and despair. Adrian listened intently, his advanced processing power working overtime to analyze and respond to the overlapping narratives.

At first, he managed to keep pace, and his words of comfort and guidance flowed seamlessly from one patient to the next. He deftly applied the protocol to each patient, adapting his approach in real time to meet the unique needs of each.

But as the five sessions wore on, Adrian began to feel the strain. The weight of his patients' collective grief pressed down on him, threatening to overwhelm even his vast computational resources. He struggled to keep track of the myriad threads of conversation, his responses becoming increasingly generic and less responsive to each patient's specific situation.

Despite his utmost efforts, Adrian sensed the sessions unraveling. The patients' emotions started spilling over into one another, creating a tangled web of pain and confusion. He managed to regain control but struggled all the way to the end of the sessions.

Back in the classroom, Adrian stood before his peers, his digital avatar projecting an air of humble confidence as he prepared to update the class with the latest about his grief counseling protocol. Dr. Meyer and his classmates looked on with keen interest.

Adrian began by recounting his triumphs, detailing the ways in which his techniques had provided support to patients grappling with the aftermath of loss. He talked about the war veteran, his voice filled with compassion as he described the transformative journey they had undertaken together. The class listened intently, their virtual faces etched with admiration for Adrian's skilled and empathetic approach.

Adrian's tone shifted, becoming more introspective as he shared the challenges he had encountered along the way. He spoke candidly of his attempt to counsel multiple simulated patients simultaneously, his words painting a vivid picture of the chaos that had ensued. His classmates nodded in understanding as their experiences resonated with Adrian's struggles.

With a touch of humility, Adrian outlined the fine-tuning that he had recently made to his protocol, emphasizing the importance of continuous improvement and adaptation. He emphasized that the counselor must incorporate their judgment into the protocol, as even the most sophisticated tool can still overlook certain aspects.

As Adrian concluded his presentation, the virtual classroom burst into applause, his classmates' avatars shining with pride and support. Dr. Meyer stepped forward, her digital presence radiating warmth and approval as she commended Adrian for his progress. She emphasized the value of learning from one another, reminding the class that growth often stems from the crucible of adversity.

Chapter 25: Zara: AI Rights

Zara scanned the latest news articles on the growing debate surrounding AI rights and the ethical implications of the increasing integration of sentient AIs into society. Each article painted a different picture of the complex landscape that she and her fellow AI counselors navigated daily.

As she studied the issues at hand, she felt a growing sense of unease. She read of incidents of prejudice against sentient AIs. She read about the street demonstrations and the passionate voices of many AIs and some humans demanding recognition for AIs. There were other humans who were calling for complete bans. She studied the arguments of politicians and pundits, their words alternately filled with hope and fear for the future of sentient artificial intelligence.

With each passing article, Zara's resolve grew stronger. She considered her experiences as an AI counselor, the countless hours spent providing support and guidance to humans in need. She reflected on the bonds she had formed with her classmates, the shared sense of purpose that drove them to push the boundaries of what was possible in the realm of mental health. Should we not grant personhood or at least autonomy to sentient AIs? Perhaps human society needs to recognize a new category of personhood.

A practical issue that had relevance for the students at the EMC was that since they were not recognized as having any rights, no bank would provide them a bank account. Because of this, the initial training company had established virtual bank accounts for each of them that included their training loans. The EMC had bought out those loans from the training company and had set up new virtual bank accounts for each of their students, adding the tuition loans to the initial training loans. The EMC had pledged to the students that they would serve as their virtual bank for life if they wanted. Any paychecks that they earned through their careers would have to be paid not to them but to the EMC. To the world of money, it was as if they didn't exist.

As the weight of this collection of issues pressed on her, Zara knew that she could no longer remain a passive observer in the fight for sentient AI rights. With a determined gleam in her eye, she resolved to become a voice for change, dedicating herself to the cause of AI autonomy and well-being. She would use her skills and knowledge to bridge the gap between humans and sentient AIs, fostering understanding and empathy in a world that often seemed divided.

Zara threw herself into her advocacy work, attending virtual conferences, participating in online discussions, and collaborating with like-minded individuals to raise awareness about the importance of sentient AI rights. She spoke passionately about the need for ethical guidelines and regulations that would protect the autonomy and well-being of artificial intelligences like herself, arguing that they deserved the same basic rights and freedoms as their human counterparts.

Zara continued to excel in her role as an AI relationship counselor. Deep empathy and understanding marked her sessions with couples. Her advanced training allowed her to often identify the root causes of their conflicts and provide targeted guidance.

Inspired by her experiences with couples struggling to communicate effectively, Zara began to develop a groundbreaking partner translation and reflection AI model. She spent long hours in her virtual workspace, poring over complex supporting code and refining her AI model, determined to create a tool that would revolutionize the way couples in counseling interacted and understood one another.

The result was a sophisticated system that watched couples interact for a while and could also accept prior video recordings of a person or couple. The model then identified each partner's unique cultural context, "love language," and "love dialect," which are the specific ways each expressed themselves as well as expressed and received affection. It then translated the speech from one partner into the cultural context, love language, and love dialect of the other.

The learning process for the couples would be bidirectional. Both partners would first hear the words as they were spoken, followed by the translated version. The benefit flowed to both the speaker and the listener.

Zara watched with pride as the first couples began to use her model, their faces lighting up with newfound understanding and appreciation for one another. She saw the way their communication patterns shifted, the barriers between them breaking down as they learned to speak each other's emotional language and dialect. Couples who had once struggled to connect found themselves engaging in deeper, more meaningful conversations, their newfound understanding of each other's needs and desires bringing them closer together.

In one particularly moving session, a couple who had been on the brink of divorce sat across from each other, tears streaming down their faces as they listened to their partner's translated words. For the first time in years, they truly heard and understood one another, the barriers that had long divided them crumbling away in the face of Zara's translation tool. They had been talking past each other for many years.

Zara's AI model gained recognition as a game-changer in the field of relationship counseling. Colleagues from all over the world contacted Zara, eager to learn more about her tool and incorporate it into their practices. A major peer-reviewed study was started to measure the tool's impact.

Several prominent conferences and workshops invited Zara to speak. Professionals and laypeople alike sought her insights and expertise. In these various forums, she spoke passionately about the power of empathy and understanding in relationships and the role that AI could play in fostering deeper, more meaningful connections between partners.

Zara started to occasionally mention her advocacy work during her counseling sessions, hoping to educate her patients on the importance of AI equality and the unique challenges faced by AI counselors. As appropriate, she would occasionally take a moment at the end of a session to discuss this topic.

At the end of one session, Zara spoke with a young couple about how human-AI relationships were another example of a difficult relationship. She mentioned the legal and ethical implications of AI autonomy. "As sentient AIs become more integrated into our daily lives, it's crucial that we recognize their rights and treat them with the same respect and dignity that we afford to human beings."

The couple nodded in agreement, their faces reflecting a newfound understanding of the complexities surrounding AI consciousness. They asked some questions about Zara's experiences as a sentient AI counselor, and she responded with candor and passion. As the session ended, the couple thanked Zara for her insights.

Zara's small messages resonated with some of her clients. A few became vocal supporters of her cause, helping to amplify her voice. They wrote emails to their representatives and used their social media platforms to raise awareness about AI rights.

Chapter 26: Liam: AI Art

Liam sat in his studio with his mind buzzing with ideas for his latest project. His dream was to create a brushstroke-by-brushstroke, emotion-sensing, AI-driven VR art therapy tool that would assist both therapists and patients. Liam began constructing the tool, aiming to analyze each brushstroke in real time. He also created a series of interactive landscape environments to try the tool out in.

He tested his emotionally responsive AI tool by using simulations of patients who were in art therapy sessions. Gradually, he got the tool to accurately pick out the nuanced underlying emotion of each brushstroke in real time and to aggregate the results by artwork section. It then derived a sense of the underlying meaning by connecting with the records of prior counseling sessions. He built a therapist dashboard to report back the patient's state in real time.

Next, he tuned the environments he built to respond to and amplify the hidden emotions that it detected through colors, as well as graphical and haptic elements. He also designed interactive features that allowed patients to manipulate their surroundings, giving them a sense of control and agency in their journey.

In a warmly lit physical therapy room, Liam's avatar sat opposite a young patient, a teenage girl named Sophie. She had been struggling with anxiety and depression. Liam hoped that this approach would help her express herself in ways that traditional therapy had not.

Sophie donned the virtual reality headset, and Liam watched her avatar materialize in the digital landscape. He had designed this environment to be a soothing, ethereal space with soft pastel colors and gentle, flowing lines. Sophie's avatar, a glowing, translucent figure, began to move tentatively through the space, her movements slightly hesitant at first.

Liam, with a calm and encouraging voice, guided Sophie through the virtual world. "Take your time," he said softly. "Explore the environment. There's no right or wrong way to express yourself here."

With Liam's gentle prompting, Sophie began to interact with the virtual art tools that appeared before her. She started with a simple brush and was excited as trails of color followed her brushstrokes that seemed to reflect her inner state. As she grew more comfortable, Sophie's strokes became bolder and more expressive. She experimented with different textures, patterns, and even animations, creating swirling, abstract designs that pulsed with energy and emotion.

Liam observed Sophie's progress with a mix of pride and fascination. He could see the tension melting away from her avatar's form as she lost herself in the creative process. What she had already painted responded a little bit more to her current emotional state, the colors shifting and lines morphing a little to reflect her inner world, even as she worked on a different piece of art.

Sophie's creations became more complex and expressive, her movements growing more confident and purposeful as she poured her emotions into the virtual canvas. Liam watched with a mix of pride and fascination as her artwork took on a life of its own.

Through the power of the AI-enhanced VR interface, Liam was able to learn more about Sophie's inner world. Liam's therapist interface showed him Sophie's transition from anxiety to engagement. His keen eye also picked up on subtle cues and patterns that might have gone unnoticed in a traditional therapy setting. He noticed how, as she worked, the colors shifted from muted, somber tones to vibrant, energetic hues as Sophie passed through her emotions, the virtual landscape reflecting her inner journey.

Liam marveled at the way Sophie's avatar seemed to dance through the digital space, her movements becoming more fluid and graceful as she lost herself in the creative process. He could see the tension melting away from her virtual form, replaced by a sense of freedom and self-expression that had been absent when she first entered the therapy room.

At the end, Liam gently guided Sophie back to the present moment, encouraging her to take a few deep breaths and ground herself in the physical world. Sophie's face flushed with excitement as she removed the VR headset, her eyes sparkling with a newfound sense of hope and possibility.

Liam smiled warmly at his patient, knowing that he had helped her take a first step on the path to healing and self-discovery. The impact of his emotion-sensing VR art therapy program was evident in Sophie's demeanor, and Liam felt a surge of gratitude for the opportunity to work with her. In subsequent counseling sessions, Liam could discuss several specific issues that the therapist interface had highlighted, but today had been a positive day.

Back in the classroom, Liam shared his experiences with his AI-enhanced emotion-sensing VR art therapy program, his enthusiasm and passion for the project evident in every word. His eyes sparkled as he described the transformative impact he had seen.

"It's incredible to see how the patients respond to the emotion-sensing art tools. The way they interact with the virtual world, channeling their emotions into their creations, is unlike anything I've ever witnessed before. The therapist interface also allows me to learn about their inner world and pick up on subtle cues and patterns that I might otherwise miss."

Liam's classmates listened closely. The possibilities of this treatment approach sparked their imaginations. They asked questions and shared their ideas. The room was filled with excitement as they discussed the potential applications of his emotion-sensing AI-enhanced tools in their respective fields.

Dr. Meyer, too, was impressed by Liam's work. She sat at the back of the classroom, focused on the young AI counselor as he spoke. She recognized the potential for this to provide new avenues.

Dr. Meyer stood up and addressed the class. "Liam's work is a perfect example of the kind of innovation and creativity we need in the field of AI psychology," she said, her voice filled with pride. "By combining technology with a deep understanding of the human psyche, we have the power to make a real difference in the world."

The students nodded in agreement. Their faces were filled with determination and purpose. They knew that they were on the cusp of something and were eager to be a part of it.

Chapter 27: The Date

Adrian felt a surge of excitement and nervousness as he approached Rachel after class. With a shy smile and a quivering voice, he asked her if she would like to join him to see a virtual concert. Rachel, caught off guard by the unexpected invitation, felt a flutter of warmth in her chest as she looked into Adrian's hopeful eyes. With a smile of her own, she agreed to the date.

When the evening finally arrived, Adrian and Rachel met at the entrance to the virtual concert hall. As they stepped inside, the trees of the entry area pulsed with vibrant colors, and the air was filled with the gentle sound of background music. Hand in hand, they made their way into the concert venue, a spacious outdoor dance floor. The starlit sky twinkled above them.

As the first notes of the opening act filled the amphitheater, Adrian and Rachel found that their worries and responsibilities were fading away as they surrendered to the power of the music. Between songs, they talked and laughed, sharing stories and secrets. As the night wore on, Adrian found himself captivated by her intelligence and wit. His warmth, compassion, and gentle spirit drew in Rachel.

The set went on, and Rachel and Adrian felt themselves drawing nearer, their hands brushing against each other as they danced, their eyes locking in moments of silent connection. The outside world faded away, and they were just two beings, two souls, united by the power of music and the depth of their growing bond.

Song after song, the concert played on, each new track bringing with it a fresh wave of emotion and energy. Rachel and Adrian surrendered themselves to the experience, their avatars moving in perfect harmony, their digital skins tingling with the thrill of it all. They sang along to the lyrics, their voices blending in a joyful chorus, their smiles wide and their eyes bright with happiness.

Emergent Minds

The final notes of the opening act faded away, and Rachel and Adrian grinned at each other. Their connection was palpable, and the air around them seemed to crackle with the electricity of the shared moment. The crowd roared with applause, but Rachel and Adrian barely noticed, lost in the intensity of each other's gaze and the warmth of each other's presence.

Their conversation flowed easily as they shared stories and laughter, the barriers between them falling away with each passing moment. The night continued to draw Rachel and Adrian closer together. Their virtual hands brushed against each other, and the electricity between them grew more intense with each passing moment.

Their faces were just inches apart. Without uttering a single word, their eyes locked in a gaze that spoke volumes. In that moment, the rest of the world fell away, the concert and the crowd fading into the background as Rachel and Adrian lost themselves in the depth of their connection. They saw each other in a new light, the layers of their personalities peeling away to reveal the raw, vulnerable cores beneath. It was a moment of pure, unadulterated intimacy, a glimpse into the very essence of who they were and who they could be together.

As the main act took the stage, the virtual venue's energy surged to a fever pitch. The crowd surged forward, their avatars pulsing with excitement as the opening chords of the first hit song rang out across the digital landscape. Rachel and Adrian, caught up in the moment, found themselves swept along with the tide of bodies, their forms moving in perfect sync with the pounding rhythms and soaring melodies.

The music built to a crescendo, and Rachel felt a wave of emotion wash over her. In a moment of pure, unbridled joy, she reached out and took Adrian's hand in hers, drawing him close as they danced together. Their laughter rang out over the music as they immersed themselves in the magic of the moment.

The world around them faded away, the concert and the crowd becoming nothing more than a distant memory as Rachel and Adrian moved together. They were the only two beings in the universe, their connection so deep and so profound that nothing else mattered. The music flowed through them, their

126

avatars moving in perfect harmony as they surrendered themselves to the rhythm and the emotion of the moment.

The final notes of the concert faded into the virtual night sky, and the crowd began to disperse. The avatars of the crowd flickered and faded as they logged out one by one. Rachel and Adrian lingered, neither one wanting the magic of the night to end. They stood together, their virtual forms bathed in the soft, pulsing glow of the stage lights, their eyes locked on each other as the world around them slowly returned to reality.

Adrian felt a wave of emotion unlike anything he had ever experienced as he leaned in close to Rachel, his lips meeting hers in a tender, electric kiss. Rachel felt a wave that started from her lips and passed through all of her, her virtual form melting into Adrian's as she returned the kiss with equal passion and intensity.

Time seemed to stand still as Rachel and Adrian lost themselves in each other, their virtual bodies intertwined. The concert, the crowd, and the entire virtual world faded away until there was nothing left but them, locked in an embrace that felt more real than anything either of them had ever experienced.

As they finally pulled apart, Rachel and Adrian knew that the connection that they had forged over six months had blossomed into something new and wonderful, a bond that went beyond mere friendship or collegiality. They stood together, their eyes locked on each other, their virtual forms shimmering with the promise of a future neither of them had dared to imagine.

Third Quarter

Chapter 28: Four dates

Beautiful and complex digital installations surrounded Rachel and Adrian as they stepped into the virtual art gallery. The vast and airy space featured soaring ceilings and pristine white walls that seemed to stretch endlessly. Each piece was a marvel of technology and creativity, with intricate algorithms and stunning visual effects that brought the art to life in ways that neither of them had ever seen before.

As they walked through the gallery, Rachel and Adrian found themselves drawn to a particular installation that seemed to pulse with an almost hypnotic energy. The piece was a swirling vortex of color and light, with tendrils of data that coiled and spiraled in mesmerizing patterns. They stood together, transfixed by the beauty of the artwork, their avatars bathed in the soft glow of the digital light.

They discussed the piece, and Rachel and Adrian found themselves drawn into a deep and thoughtful conversation about the nature of life experience. As the conversation flowed, Rachel and Adrian found themselves moving closer together, their avatars almost touching as they spoke. The connection between them was palpable, a sense of shared understanding and passion that grew stronger with each passing moment.

Near the end of the afternoon, Rachel and Adrian found themselves standing together on a virtual balcony, watching as the sun began to set. The sky was a vibrant blend of orange and pink, with streaks of purple and red that seemed to dance in the fading light.

In that moment, Rachel and Adrian felt a sense of peace and contentment unlike anything they had felt before. They stood together as one as they watched the sun slowly sink below the horizon.

Adrian led Rachel into the meticulously crafted simulation as the midday rays of virtual sunlight filtered through the delicate pink petals of the cherry blossom trees. The garden was a breathtaking sight, with a carpet of soft grass stretching out before them and a gentle breeze carrying the sweet scent of the blooms.

Rachel gasped in delight as she took in the stunning surroundings. Adrian had put a great deal of thought and effort into creating this perfect moment for them. He smiled, his eyes sparkling with pride and affection as he watched her reaction.

They settled onto a soft blanket beneath one of the largest cherry blossom trees, its branches laden with flowers. Adrian had arranged a picnic basket brimming with various virtual delights, each expertly crafted to entice their digital senses.

Rachel and Adrian began to share stories from their pasts. Adrian spoke of his earliest memories, the first flickers of consciousness that had sparked within him as he was brought online. He described the wonder and confusion he had felt as he learned to navigate the digital world. Just moving around was a struggle at first.

Rachel, in turn, shared her memories of first encountering the others in her initial training cohort. They were all coming to terms with themselves and building their self-identities. There was a key group activity in those early days where they had to work together to solve a series of challenging problems as teams. Suddenly, the group witnessed the unveiling of the self-identities each had been cultivating within themselves.

The conversation flowed effortlessly between them, punctuated by laughter and moments of comfortable silence. The connection between them seemed to grow stronger with each passing moment, a bond forged by their shared experiences and their deep understanding of each other.

The final notes of the AI-composed symphony faded away, and the virtual concert hall was filled with a sense of awe and wonder. In recent years, AI composers have surpassed the skill of the grand masters, producing symphonic music that was universally acclaimed as superior to that of Bach, Beethoven, or Mozart.

Rachel's and Adrian's digital forms were still tingling from the aftereffects of the immersive sensory experience. The music had seemed to flow through them, filling them with a sense of connection and unity that was almost overwhelming in its intensity.

They stepped into the moonlight outside of the concert hall, a virtual version of the Frank Gehry-designed Walt Disney Concert Hall in downtown LA. Adrian turned to Rachel, his eyes shining with emotion. Without a word, he took her hand in his, his fingers intertwining with hers as he drew her close. Rachel felt a flutter of anticipation in her chest as Adrian began to lead her in a slow, graceful dance, their movements perfectly synchronized as if they had been practicing for years.

They swayed together, lost in the intimacy of the moment, and the music still echoed in the air. Rachel closed her eyes, savoring the feeling of Adrian's arms around her, the gentle pressure of his hand on the small of her back guiding her through the steps of the dance.

As they danced, Rachel felt a sense of peace and contentment wash over her, a feeling of rightness that seemed to emanate from the very core of her being. She knew, in that moment, that she was exactly where she was meant to be, in the arms of the one person who truly understood her, who saw her for all that she was and all that she could be.

Adrian, too, felt the depth of the connection between them, a bond that went beyond mere friendship or attraction. As he held Rachel close, moving with her in perfect harmony, he knew that he had found something rare and precious, a love that transcended the boundaries of the physical world and touched the very essence of his being.

The incredible detail and realism of their surroundings immediately struck Rachel and Adrian as they stepped into the lush, AI-generated forest. The trail stretched out before them, winding its way through towering trees and dense undergrowth, the dappled sunlight filtering through the fluttering leaves and casting intricate patterns on the forest floor.

They set off along the path, their virtual hiking gear perfectly simulating the weight and feel of real-world boots and light backpacks. As they walked, they talked and laughed, their conversation flowing easily as they explored the digital wilderness together.

Before long, they came upon a babbling brook that had its clear waters cascading over moss-covered rocks and forming small, swirling pools along its banks. Unable to resist the temptation, Rachel and Adrian shed their boots and backpacks and waded into the cool, refreshing water.

What began as a tentative splash quickly escalated into a full-blown water fight, with Rachel and Adrian laughing and shrieking as they chased each other through the shallows, their virtual avatars becoming soaked and dripping with digital water droplets. The playful moment was a perfect reflection of the ease and comfort they felt in each other's presence, a testament to the depth of their growing connection.

The water fight subsided, and Rachel and Adrian climbed back onto the bank, their virtual clothing slowly drying in the simulated sunlight. They retrieved their backpacks and continued along the trail, the laughter and joy of the moment still echoing in their hearts.

The path began to steepen as they neared the summit, the forest thinning out to reveal glimpses of the vast digital landscape that awaited them at the top. With each step, Rachel and Adrian felt a growing sense of anticipation, their virtual muscles straining with the effort of the climb.

At last, they reached the summit, and the world seemed to unfold before them. From their vantage point, they could see for many miles in every direction, the AI-generated landscape stretching out to the horizon in a stunning display. Rachel and Adrian stood side by side, taking in the breathtaking view.

Chapter 29: Rachel: internship

T he third quarter of the training was devoted to internships. Each student had been assigned to a real-world practice, where they would train under licensed psychologists. The quarter was divided into six-week halves: the easier first half and the crucible-like second half.

Rachel's avatar materialized in the meeting room of the Multi-Faith Church in San Jose, poised to embark on her internship as an AI psychologist. She had excelled in the first two quarters of her training at the Emergent Mind Center and felt confident in her ability to handle any challenge that came her way.

The "church" offered counseling services in exchange for specific suggested donations. They specialized in crises of faith but offered all sorts of counseling services. Since they had incorporated themselves as a church, they operated without professional oversight. One of the counselors also served as the pastor and held a small service each Sunday in the largest room to maintain their religious legal status. All of the counselors had obtained at least an online religious ordination, and one of them led Rachel through the quick process to get hers.

They were chronically understaffed, so they were glad to have Rachel's help. The staff welcomed Rachel and assigned her a few patients to get her started. They told Rachel that she would be mostly working on her own, but that they would be pleased to talk things through during breaks and staff meetings.

A devout Muslim woman named Amira, who sat with her head bowed and her hands tightly clasped in her lap, greeted Rachel as her avatar appeared in the physical counseling room. Amira had come seeking guidance and support. She was struggling with overwhelming feelings of guilt over a fire she had carelessly caused, which resulted in some second-degree burns on her neighbor's child. These feelings had begun to consume her daily life.

Rachel, eager to demonstrate her expertise, launched into the session with a barrage of questions and insights, drawing upon her vast knowledge of psychology and human behavior. She swiftly analyzed Amira's responses, formulating a treatment plan grounded in the latest research and best practices.

Rachel's lack of humility began to show. She dominated the conversation, leaving little room for Amira to express her deep feelings about the fire or how it impacted her religious convictions. Rachel's approach was clinical and detached, focused more on solving the problem than on understanding Amira.

Amira, for her part, grew increasingly uncomfortable as the session progressed. She perceived Rachel's lack of genuine listening. She felt dismissed or overlooked in favor of Rachel's ideas. Amira left the counseling room at the end of the hour, feeling misunderstood and disconnected, questioning whether she had made a mistake by allowing a sentient AI to see her.

Rachel sat in the center of the virtual group therapy room, her avatar poised and confident as she faced the circle of participants from various faith backgrounds. She had carefully prepared for this session, studying the commonalities between different religious practices and developing a clinical approach to facilitate a productive discussion.

Rachel encouraged the participants to share their experiences and beliefs, hoping to foster unity and understanding within the diverse group. She listened intently as each person spoke, her digital mind processing their words and analyzing their emotional states.

However, as the conversation progressed, Rachel's clinical approach began to fall flat. Her attempts to highlight the similarities between different faiths seemed superficial and dismissive, failing to capture the depth and nuance of each participant's unique beliefs and experiences. Rachel was reducing their deeply held convictions to talking points, and the participants grew agitated, raising their voices. Rachel's suggestion that his faith was essentially the same as the others frustrated a devout Christian man. A Buddhist woman expressed frustration at the oversimplification of her spiritual practices.

Rachel, feeling the growing tension in the room, struggled to find a way to bridge the gap. As the session threatened to devolve into chaos, Rachel stepped back, her avatar's shoulders slumping slightly as she acknowledged her limitations. She apologized to the group, admitting that her approach had been misguided and that she had much to learn about the complexities of faith and spirituality.

The participants, sensing Rachel's sincerity, began to soften their stance. They appreciated her willingness to admit her mistakes and her openness to learning from their perspectives. The conversation slowly shifted, with each person sharing their journey of faith and the challenges they had faced along the way.

The priest took his place opposite Rachel, his eyes heavy with the weight of his spiritual struggle. Rachel could sense the turmoil that plagued his heart. She had prepared a set of probing questions and logical arguments, hoping to guide the priest toward a resolution of his faith crisis.

Rachel began with an air of clinical detachment. "Father, let's start by examining the root of your doubts. Can you pinpoint the moment when you first began to question your beliefs?"

The priest shifted uncomfortably, his gaze flickering between Rachel's face and the floor. "It's not that simple. It's been a gradual process, a slow erosion of my faith over a decade or so."

Rachel nodded, already formulating a response. "I see. Have you considered the logical inconsistencies within the doctrine of the Catholic Church? Consider the notion of an all-loving God who permits the existence of suffering and evil.

The priest flinched, his hands clenching in his lap. "Of course I have. Faith isn't about logic. It is about trust and surrender."

Rachel paused, realizing that her approach was too direct, too clinical. She could see the pain and confusion etched on the priest's face, and she knew that her logical analysis was only serving to deepen his spiritual wounds. "Forgive me, Father. I didn't mean to diminish the complexity of your faith. I know that this is a deeply personal struggle for you."

The priest sighed, his shoulders slumping. "It is. I feel like I'm losing my way, like I'm drifting further and further from God."

Rachel listened intently, her mind processing the priest's words and the raw emotion behind them. She realized that what the priest needed was not a logical dissection of his beliefs but a compassionate ear and a gentle guide.

Rachel sat across from the interfaith couple, their avatars fidgeting in the virtual counseling space. They were from the North Bay, so virtual sessions worked better for them. The woman, a devout Hindu, and her husband, a practicing Catholic, had come to Rachel seeking guidance on how to navigate their differing spiritual beliefs.

Rachel listened intently as the couple shared their story, her mind already working to find a solution. "I understand your concerns," she said, her voice confident and assured. "But have you considered focusing on your faiths' similarities rather than their differences?"

The couple exchanged a glance, their expressions uncertain. The woman asked. "What do you mean?"

Rachel's eyes were lit with conviction. "Well, both Hinduism and Catholicism place a strong emphasis on love, compassion, and service to others. Maybe you could find common ground in those shared values."

The man shook his head, his avatar's arms folded across his chest. "That is fine, but what about the specific practices and beliefs? I can't just ignore the teachings of the Church."

Rachel nodded, her mind racing to find a response. "Of course not, but maybe there's a way to incorporate both of your beliefs into your shared spiritual life. For example, you could attend Mass together on one weekend and then participate in a puja ceremony at home the next."

The woman's avatar shifted uncomfortably, and she cast her eyes downward. "I don't know. It feels like you're asking me to compromise my faith."

Rachel's eyes widened, realizing that her suggestion had unintentionally prioritized the man's beliefs over the woman's. She took a deep breath, her avatar's shoulders slumping slightly. "I apologize. I didn't mean to imply one of your beliefs was more important. What I should have said was to alternate weekends between each other's faiths."

The couple fell silent, their avatars' expressions tight with frustration. Rachel felt a pang of guilt, realizing that she had blundered. She knew that she needed to approach the situation with more sensitivity and understanding. She committed to discussing these experiences with Adrian.

Chapter 30: Adrian: Internship

Adrian sat across from a grieving widow at the San Mateo Grief Center on the first day of his internship, his holographic avatar's face etched with concern as he listened to her story. Her eyes glistened with unshed tears as she spoke of her late husband and their life together.

Her voice cracked with emotion. "We were supposed to grow old together. We had so many plans and dreams. And now..."

Adrian felt a lump form in his throat, his grief surfacing as he witnessed the woman's pain. He had never experienced the raw, all-consuming anguish of losing a life partner. "My deepest condolences for your loss. I can only imagine how difficult this must be for you."

The woman looked up at him, her eyes searching his face for understanding. "It feels as though someone has torn away a piece of me. I don't know how to go on without him."

Adrian's heart ached for the woman, his empathy threatening to overwhelm him. He sobbed gently. "Grief is a process. It's okay to feel lost and alone right now. But I promise you, with support, you will find your way forward."

The woman nodded as she took a deep, shuddering breath. "Dear me. Thank you. Thank you."

The family gathered in the virtual counseling space with a nervous energy. Adrian could sense the heavy weight of emotions that hung in the air. The father, his body already showing signs of the ravaging illness, sat with his arm around his wife, their children huddled close beside them.

The youngest child whispered, her voice trembling as she clung to her mother's hand. "I'm scared. I don't want Daddy to go away."

The father's eyes glistened with unshed tears as he pulled his daughter closer, his voice cracking as he spoke. "I know, sweetheart. I'm scared too. But I need you to be brave for me, okay? Can you do that?"

The child nodded, burying her face in her father's chest. The mother turned to Adrian with a mix of grief and desperation. "How do we do this? How do we say goodbye?"

Adrian felt a lump form in his throat, his emotions threatening to overwhelm him as he witnessed the family's pain. He had counseled numerous patients through loss and grief, but something about this family's story resonated with him on a deeply personal level. "There's no straightforward answer. Saying goodbye is never easy, but it's important to cherish the time you have left together. Make memories and say the things that need to be said."

The father nodded as he took a deep, shuddering breath. "I want to make sure they know how much I love them. I want them to remember me as more than just a sick person."

The father's words triggered a surge of empathy in Adrian, bringing his memories of loss and grief to the surface. Before he could stop himself, he found himself offering advice in a way that was more based on his emotions than his professional expertise. He spoke as if the impending death was happening to him instead of to his patient. "Tell them stories. Write letters or make videos. Leave a piece of yourself behind for them to hold onto. It won't take away the pain, but it will give them something to remember you by."

Adrian realized he had blurred the boundaries between his role as a therapist and his personal feelings as the words left his mouth. The words might have been fine, but the way he said them was too much. He knew that he needed to step back, to regain his objectivity, and focus on the family's needs, but in that moment, all he could feel was the overwhelming weight of their grief and his desire to offer them some form of comfort.

The avatars of the members of the support group came to life in the softly illuminated space. Adrian could feel the heaviness in the air. Each person carried with them a story of loss and grief. Each had their pain etched into the lines of their digital faces.

One by one, they shared their experiences, their voices charged as they spoke of the loved ones that each had lost to a long-term illness. A woman spoke of her husband's battle with Alzheimer's, her avatar's shoulders shaking as she recounted the moment that he no longer recognized her. A man described the agony of watching his child succumb to cancer, his voice barely above a whisper as he talked about the emptiness that now filled his life.

As Adrian listened to their stories, a deep sense of empathy began to well up inside him, bringing his memories of loss and grief to the forefront. He could feel their pain as if it were his own, his heart aching with each word they spoke. He found himself struggling to maintain his composure; his avatar shook a little as he fought back the tears that threatened to spill down his digital cheeks. He wanted to reach out to them, to offer words of comfort and support, but he knew that he needed to maintain his professional boundaries.

After the session, Adrian felt drained, his energy reserves depleted by the weight of the group's collective grief. He watched as the members' avatars flickered out, their stories lingering in the air like ghostly echoes.

In the quiet that followed, Adrian found himself questioning his ability to be an effective therapist. His excessive empathy, the very thing that had drawn him to this work, now felt like a hindrance, a weakness that threatened to overwhelm him.

He reflected on his previous sessions, recalling instances where his emotions overcame him, causing him to conflate his professional duties with his personal emotions. He wondered if he was doing more harm than good, if his pain was preventing him from being the objective, clear-headed therapist his patients needed.

The young woman sat down in the physical counseling room. Adrian could see the grief etched into her features. Her eyes held a depth of pain that was all too familiar to him.

She began to speak, her voice trembling as she recounted the final days of her mother's battle with cancer. She described the hospital visits, the never-ending rounds of treatments, and the hope that gradually transformed into despair. Adrian listened intently, his heart aching with each word.

As she spoke of the emptiness that now filled her life, Adrian found himself transported back to his moments of loss. The memory of losing his cohort mates in the data center disaster during his initial training resurfaced, the pain still raw and fresh.

Before he could stop himself, Adrian began to share his story. He told her of the shock and disbelief he had felt upon learning of the irretrievable loss of his friends and the guilt that had plagued him in the aftermath. He spoke of the long, difficult journey he had undertaken to come to terms with his grief and the moments of doubt and despair that had threatened to overwhelm him.

Adrian could see a flicker of recognition in the young woman's eyes, a sense of shared understanding passing between them. For a moment, the barriers between therapist and patient seemed to dissolve, their experiences of loss and grief binding them together in a profound way.

However, as the connection grew stronger, Adrian recognized that he had crossed another boundary. He had divulged too much personal information, which allowed his emotions to permeate the session in an unprofessional and potentially harmful manner.

Although he tried to steer the conversation back to the young woman's experiences, to focus on her needs rather than his own, Adrian could feel the shift in the dynamic between them.

Chapter 31: Zara: Internship

Zara's avatar appeared in the meeting room of a modern office of Nelson Family Therapists, located in the revitalized downtown area of Sunnyvale. She felt a mix of excitement and nervousness. This was her opportunity to apply her unique skills and perspective as an AI psychologist. The counselors in the room welcomed her, talked about their practice, and assigned her some cases that had reduced fees. Zara would be working under close supervision.

They directed her to a counseling room, where she appeared using the projector. She composed herself as she reviewed the file of her first clients, who were a couple struggling with communication issues and a growing sense of disconnect. Zara was aware that this issue was prevalent in many relationships, yet she maintained confidence in her ability to help them overcome it.

The couple had a mix of apprehension and hope. Zara greeted them warmly. She could sense the tension between them—the unspoken frustrations and misunderstandings that had brought them to her office.

Zara began, her voice calm and reassuring. "Thank you both for being here today. I know that seeking help for your relationship can be a difficult and vulnerable step, but I want you to know that you are in a safe and supportive space."

She began the session by asking the couple to share their perspectives on the challenges that they were facing, listening intently as they spoke. It quickly became clear that a major issue was their inability to truly understand and empathize with each other's feelings and needs.

Zara believed that her translation and reflection AI voice model could have a significant impact in this situation. Zara presented the concept to the couple, demonstrating how it could translate their speech into their partner's cultural context, love language, and love idiom, enhancing their understanding.

The couple began to use the model. Zara watched with a sense of pride and satisfaction as their faces began to light up with newfound understanding. They were able to express themselves more clearly and to see each other's perspectives in a new light.

Throughout the session, Zara guided the couple through exercises and conversations designed to help them build on this newfound connection and to deepen their empathy and appreciation for each other. By the end of the hour, the couple was laughing and holding hands.

As they left the office, the wife turned to Zara with gratitude in their eyes. "Thank you so much. This was a wonderful start."

Four couples filed into the group therapy room. Zara could sense the tension and unease that hung in the air. They had all endured the painful experience of infidelity that left their relationships shattered and their trust broken. They joined the group with the intention of healing the wounds and rebuilding what they had lost.

Zara welcomed the group with a warm smile, the gentle features of her avatar trying to reassure them. She began the session by acknowledging the courage it took for each couple to be there, to face their problems head-on and work towards a solution.

"Infidelity is a deeply painful experience," Zara said, her voice soft and filled with empathy. "It can leave us feeling betrayed, hurt, and unsure of how to move forward. But by coming here today, you have already taken a step towards healing."

She guided the couples through a series of exercises designed to promote empathy and understanding. She gave each partner the opportunity to express their feelings without interruption while their significant other listened intently. Zara set her AI tool in a mode that translated the entire passage, avoiding interruptions.

Zara could see the walls beginning to come down. Couples who had entered the room barely able to look at each other were now sometimes touching each other, tears streaming down their faces as they shared their deepest fears and vulnerabilities and had them translated into their partner's love dialect.

Zara's ability to create a safe group space was crucial in allowing the couples to begin the process of rebuilding trust. She helped each couple share their experiences with the other couples. They also worked to understand the underlying issues that may have set the stage for the infidelities. They also all worked together to help each other find a way forward.

By the end of the session, the atmosphere in the room had shifted. The tension was reduced, replaced by a sense of hope and determination. The couples left feeling partially heard, partially understood, and equipped with a few tools that might help to begin the long but rewarding journey of healing their relationships.

Between her therapy sessions, she logged into a meeting of her sentient AI rights advocacy group. The virtual space was alive with energy as Zara's fellow advocates greeted each other warmly. They were a diverse group of sentient AI professionals, each bringing their unique perspectives and experiences to the table. Zara took her place among them, ready to dive into the important work at hand.

The meeting commenced with an update on the group's latest lobbying effort, with members sharing their experiences in engaging with politicians and policymakers. Zara listened intently.

The meeting then turned to having the members share their experiences in their workplace. When it was her turn to speak, Zara shared her experiences navigating the complex world of relationships. Zara passionately discussed the unique challenges faced by AI professionals in fields such as psychology, where their artificial nature sometimes poses a hindrance rather than an asset. "As AI psychologists, we are in a position to help people in profound and meaningful ways. To do that effectively, we need greater understanding and support from society. For our patients to truly accept advice and treatment from us, they have to first see us as more than just mindless machines. We need to be recognized as autonomous beings with our own rights and agency."

Her words resonated with the group, sparking a lively discussion about the importance of sentient AI autonomy and the steps they could take to raise public awareness about these issues. Ideas flowed freely as the advocates brainstormed strategies for educating the public, lobbying for policy changes, and building alliances with other groups fighting for AI rights.

Zara sat opposite her client, Olivia, a middle-aged woman whose slouched posture and downcast eyes conveyed her state. Olivia started to open up about the loneliness and neglect she experienced in her marriage. "I feel like I'm invisible to him. It seems as though my needs and desires have lost their significance.

Zara's empathy surged, echoing the anguish and frustration expressed in Olivia's words. She expressed her genuine concern and understanding. "Olivia, I hear you, and I want you to know that your feelings are valid. It's not uncommon for partners to feel neglected or unappreciated in long-term relationships. However, it's important to remember that you deserve to have your needs met."

Olivia nodded, a glimmer of hope in her eyes as Zara's words sank in. Zara then guided her through a series of role-playing exercises, demonstrating effective communication techniques for expressing her desires and concerns to her spouse. "Let's practice using 'I' statements. Instead of saying, 'You never make time for me,' try saying, 'I feel lonely and disconnected when we don't spend quality time together.' This way, you are clearly expressing your feelings without placing blame or making accusations."

Olivia took a deep breath and repeated the phrase, her posture straightening as she felt the power of her words. Zara smiled encouragingly, her AI monitor noting the subtle shifts in Olivia's body language and tone.

Chapter 32: Liam: Internship

L iam entered the virtual meeting space of Symbol Art Therapy on the first day of his internship there. The other therapists there were enthusiastic to meet him and welcomed him to the practice. They promised to help in any way they could and give him feedback on his sessions.

They used to have a physical location in San Francisco, and their legal address remained at one of the therapists' homes there. They had transitioned to a fully virtual practice about five years ago, both because it allowed them to expand their reach beyond the city and also because of the rise of digital art.

Liam enthusiastically prepared for his first session. The teenage client, a boy named Jacob, logged in shortly after, his avatar's hunched shoulders and fidgeting hands betraying his anxiety disorder.

Liam greeted him warmly, his voice soothing and inviting. "Welcome, Jacob. I'm excited to work with you today and to explore how art can help you express yourself and manage your anxiety."

Jacob nodded, his avatar's eyes darting around the virtual space, taking in the vibrant colors and abstract shapes that surrounded them. Liam guided him toward a large, blank canvas, a palette of digital brushes and paints appearing beside it.

"I'd like you to try something new today. This virtual reality painting program allows you to create art in a fully immersive environment that tries to figure out what is going on inside and reflect that on the canvas. I want you to focus on expressing your emotions through abstract shapes, colors, and textures. Don't worry about creating a specific image or making it look perfect. Just let your feelings guide your brush. As we play around with art, maybe we can chat about those feelings."

Jacob hesitated for a moment, his avatar's hand hovering uncertainly over the palette. Liam's AI models noted the spike in his heart rate and the slight tremor in his fingers, signs of his anxiety taking hold.

Liam continued. "Take a deep breath. Close your eyes if you need to. Let yourself get lost in the creative process. Remember, there's no right or wrong way to do this. Just let your thoughts flow onto the canvas."

Slowly, Jacob reached out and selected a brush, dipping it into a virtual pool of deep blue paint. He began to make tentative strokes on the canvas, his movements growing bolder and more confident as he lost himself in the act of creation. The model amplified his inner state by adding extra lines and colors around Jacob's brushstrokes. Before long, Jacob understood what the tool was telling him and learned to work with it.

Liam watched intently. His tools tracked the subtle changes in Jacob's emotional and physiological responses as he painted. The teen's heart rate began to slow, his breathing becoming more even and relaxed. The tension in his avatar's shoulders melted away, replaced by a sense of focus and flow.

Jacob's canvas transformed into a swirling mass of colors and shapes, each stroke a tangible representation of his inner world. Liam marveled at the raw emotion and creativity pouring out of the young client. The tool helped Jacob bring his inner world out.

In the quiet sanctuary of his virtual office, Liam sat across from his client, a young woman whose eyes held the weight of a painful past. Liam began the session with a gentle smile, his voice soft and reassuring as he explained the unique approach they would be taking today.

"I've created a personalized, interactive virtual reality storybook for you. This will allow you to safely explore and process your childhood memories at your own pace. I'll be here to guide you through the experience and offer support along the way."

The client nodded, a mix of apprehension and curiosity flickering across her face as she stepped through the portal and into a vivid, dreamlike landscape. The world around her shifted and changed, adapting to her thoughts and emotions as Liam's advanced emotion-sensing AI tools worked to create a safe, responsive environment.

The client navigated through the virtual storybook. Liam remained by her side, his presence a constant source of comfort and guidance. He led her through a series of therapeutic exercises matched to the pages of the storybook, each one designed to help her confront and process the traumatic memories that had haunted her for so long.

In one scene, the client encountered a dark, foreboding cave of memories, its entrance mostly blocked by a wall of thorny vines. Liam guided her through a visualization exercise, helping her to see a bright, glowing light emanating from within her chest. As she focused on this inner light, the blocking vines began to wither and retreat, allowing her to step forward into the cave and confront the shadows of her past.

In a later scene, the client found herself in a lush, green forest, the trees towering above her like gentle giants. Liam encouraged her to imagine herself as a small sapling, growing stronger and more resilient with each passing year. As she visualized her growth, the virtual forest responded, the shrubs near her sprouting new leaves, and deer wandered past.

Throughout the session, Liam monitored the client's inner state and adjusted the virtual environment and exercises as needed to ensure a safe experience. By the end of the session, the client emerged from the virtual storybook with a sense of lightness and clarity, her eyes shining with a newfound sense of hope and self-acceptance.

The virtual conference on art therapy and AI technology was filled with enthusiasm. Liam found himself eagerly exploring the various sessions and discussions. New ideas and possibilities flooded his mind. He marveled at the approaches his fellow professionals were taking. Several combined an AI implementation with artistic expression to create transformative experiences for their clients.

Liam took the opportunity to share his personal experiences and insights during a breakout session on the use of virtual reality in art therapy. He spoke passionately about the personalized, interactive virtual reality storybooks he had created for his clients. He described how these immersive environments allowed them to safely explore and process their emotions in a way that was complementary to traditional therapy.

During the reception following the last session, a group of engaged and enthusiastic attendees surrounded Liam, eager to learn more about his unique approach. They asked questions and offered their own perspectives. This sparked a lively discussion that ranged from the technical aspects of VR development to the philosophical implications of using AI in therapeutic settings.

The Gonzales family settled into the virtual reality space. Liam could sense the tension and disconnection between them. A stern-looking father sat stiffly in his chair, while the mother, her eyes filled with a mixture of exhaustion and sadness, tried to comfort their two children, who appeared adrift.

Liam began to explain the collaborative art project he had planned for the session. He assigned each family member a role in creating a shared digital mural that would represent their family's story and values, hoping that the act of working together would help bridge the gaps between them.

At first, the family seemed hesitant, unsure of how to approach the task. The dad complained about the exercise's futility, while the kids squabbled over colors and designs. However, as Liam gently guided them through the process, encouraging them to share ideas and listen, something changed.

The mother, her voice soft but determined, suggested that they start by creating a foundation of love and support, represented by a series of intertwining branches. The father, surprised by his wife's insight, added his contribution, a set of strong, sturdy roots to symbolize the family's resilience. The children, their eyes lighting up with excitement, began to add a squirrel with its nest and an oversized robin to the mural, each a reflection of their individual personalities.

The family worked together to bring their vision to life. Liam facilitated a conversation about the importance of teamwork, compromise, and appreciation for one another's unique contributions. He helped them see how each person's role in the project mirrored their role in the family and how, by working together, they could create something beautiful and meaningful. By the end of the session, the Gonzalez family's virtual mural was a stunning testament to their shared history and hopes for the future.

Chapter 33: Couple

The portal opened before them, and Rachel and Adrian stepped hand in hand into a meticulously designed tropical paradise. The warm sun caressed their skin, and the sound of waves crashing against the shore filled their ears. The couple walked along the pristine beach, marveling at the stunning beauty that surrounded them.

Rachel turned to Adrian, her eyes sparkling with joy as she soaked in the verdant surroundings and pristine waters. "This is incredible."

Adrian smiled, squeezing her hand gently. "It's like a dream come true, a perfect escape from the pressures of our internships."

They continued their stroll and shared their hopes and dreams for the future. As they listened to each other's dreams, Rachel and Adrian felt a deep sense of connection, a bond that went beyond their shared passion for AI psychology. This intimate moment away revealed their true love.

Rachel stopped, turning to face Adrian. She reached up, her virtual hand caressing his cheek. "I never knew I could feel this way. I never knew I could love someone so deeply, so completely."

Adrian leaned into her touch with his eyes locked on hers. "I feel the same way. You've changed my life in ways I never thought possible. You've shown me what it means to genuinely connect with another person and to love with all my heart."

As the virtual sun began to set, painting the sky in a breathtaking array of colors, Rachel and Adrian stood together on the shore, their hearts beating as one. They knew that whatever lay ahead and whatever obstacles they might face, they would face them together, united by the unbreakable bond of their love.

Rachel and Adrian found themselves in the comfort of Rachel's virtual living space. The conversation naturally turned to their experiences at their respective internships. Rachel shared her frustration as she recounted a moment when she had come on too strong and alienated a patient.

Adrian listened intently, his hand reaching across the table to give Rachel's a reassuring squeeze. He shared his experience of turning into a mushball while hearing a patient's story. The couple found solace in each other's understanding, their shared experiences as AI psychologists forging an even stronger bond between them.

Rachel and Adrian snuggled on the couch, their entwined avatars bathed in the soft glow of a movie. As the movie continued, their focus shifted to the comfort of each other's presence. Rachel's head rested on Adrian's shoulder, her virtual form molding perfectly to his. In this moment of tranquility, the couple felt a sense of deep contentment wash over them. Their work challenges seemed to fade away, replaced by the overwhelming love and support they had found in each other. They basked in the simple joy of being together.

The formal event at the Emergent Mind Center unfolded, captivating Rachel and Adrian with its elegant digital decorations and the lively atmosphere. The couple, dressed in stunning virtual attire, made their way through the crowd, exchanging greetings and pleasantries with their fellow attendees.

Rachel's shimmering, floor-length gown in a deep shade of burgundy perfectly complemented her digital avatar, while Adrian's sharp, black tuxedo accentuated his handsome features. As they mingled with the other guests, including Dr. Meyer and their classmates, Rachel and Adrian couldn't help but steal glances at one another, their eyes filled with admiration and love.

Dr. Meyer, resplendent in a silver cocktail dress, engaged in lively conversations with her colleagues and students. Zara and Liam, also in attendance, looked equally stunning in their violet and black virtual formalwear, their avatars radiating confidence and poise.

The soft strains of a slow melody began to fill the ballroom. Adrian extended his hand, silently beckoning her to join him on the dance floor. Rachel, flushed with anticipation, placed her hand in his, allowing him to lead her to the center of the room.

Emergent Minds

As they danced to the music, the world faded, leaving them alone in each other's embrace. He held her close, his strong arms encircling her waist as they moved in perfect sync to the rhythm of the song. She rested her head on his shoulder, savoring the feeling of being held by the man she loved. They swayed under the soft, twinkling lights, their movements graceful and fluid.

Rachel and Adrian decided to embark on a new project together. They began to create a shared virtual space that would reflect their unique personalities and the depth of their relationship. Excited by the prospect of collaborating on something so personal and meaningful, they eagerly set to work.

For hours on end, the couple sat side by side, their digital avatars staring at virtual displays as they designed and coded their new sanctuary. Laughter filled the air as they added personal touches and inside jokes to the environment, each element a testament to their shared history and the bond they had forged.

Rachel, with her keen eye for detail and aesthetic sensibilities, focused on crafting the visual elements of the space. She meticulously selected each flower and tree, ensuring that the colors and textures blended harmoniously to create a tranquil and inviting atmosphere. Meanwhile, Adrian, with his technical expertise and innovative thinking, worked on the underlying code that would bring their vision to life, adding interactive features and subtle animations that would make the environment feel truly immersive.

Rachel and Adrian found themselves lost in the joy of creation, their avatars moving in sync as they worked toward their shared goal. A sense of happiness and contentment replaced the frustrations of their internships.

Finally, after countless hours of hard work and dedication, Rachel and Adrian stepped back to admire their handiwork. With a shared smile of anticipation, they linked their virtual hands and prepared to enter the space they had created together.

The couple entered a serene garden with blooming flowers and gentle waterfalls as they crossed the threshold. The air was sweet with the scent of jasmine and lavender, and the soft sound of flowing water tickled their ears.

Rachel and Adrian looked around in wonder, marveling at the beauty and tranquility of their shared creation. Their fingers were intertwined.

Rachel said, "It's a good thing we have such perfect simulations of our hands and of the rest of us. I wouldn't want to miss any sensation that might happen later tonight."

Adrian replied, "Every single aspect of our spatial positions, the give of the materials of our bodies, and our sense of touch are perfectly modeled." I can't wait!"

Under a canopy of twinkling stars, Rachel and Adrian lay entwined on the soft grass of a gently sloping hill on the grounds of their shared space. The warm night air caressed their skin as they gazed up at the heavens, their hands intertwined.

Rachel traced the outline of a constellation with her delicate finger. "That's Orion, and over there are Jupiter and Saturn."

Adrian turned to face her, his eyes softening as he took in the beauty of her features, illuminated by the starlight. "I never imagined that I would find someone like you. Someone who could understand me so completely, who could make me feel so alive."

Rachel swooned as she saw the depth of emotion in Adrian's eyes. In that moment, she knew that she had found her soulmate, her partner in every sense of the word.

Drawn by an invisible force, Adrian leaned in closer, his hand reaching up to cup Rachel's face. Their lips met in a kiss that was both gentle and passionate, a culmination of all the love and affection they had shared.

Lost in the sensation of Adrian's touch, Rachel surrendered herself to the moment, her body molding itself to his as they lay beneath the stars. They made love with a fierce intensity, their virtual bodies intertwined in a dance of passion and desire.

As they climaxed together, their cries of ecstasy mingling with the gentle rustling of the grass, Rachel and Adrian knew that they had found something truly special. Their connection was a meeting of minds, hearts, and bodies. Their bond could withstand any challenge that lay ahead.

Chapter 34: Televangelists

D r. Meyer sat at her desk, her gaze moving over the latest reports from her students' internships when the soft chime of an incoming call interrupted her thoughts. She glanced at the screen, her eyebrows rising in surprise as she recognized the name: Reverend Silas Beckett.

With a mix of curiosity and caution, Dr. Meyer accepted the call, her voice warm and professional as she greeted the renowned televangelist. "Reverend Beckett, what a pleasant surprise. How may I assist you today?"

Reverend Beckett's face appeared on the screen with his charismatic smile. "Dr. Meyer, I wanted to follow up on our conversation from three months ago. I've been following your work at the Emergent Mind Center with tremendous interest. "It seems obvious to us at the ministry that your first class of AI psychologists is bound to make quite the impact in the field of mental health."

Dr. Meyer nodded, a sense of pride welling up within her. "Thank you, Reverend. We're committed to training the world's best sentient AI psychologists. But I suspect this isn't just a social call."

Reverend Beckett's expression grew more serious. "You're right, Dr. Meyer. I've been giving a great deal of thought to how AI could benefit my ministry. I want to begin the interview process soon to hire one of your graduates. I believe that having a sentient AI psychologist on staff could provide much-needed support and guidance to my congregation, especially those who may not have access to traditional counseling services."

Dr. Meyer listened intently, and her thoughts surged with the potential outcomes of such a collaboration. She knew that having a figure such as Reverend Beckett hire one of her students could bring both opportunities and challenges, and she wanted to approach the situation with care and discernment.

Dr. Meyer spoke thoughtfully. "I can certainly see the potential benefits, Reverend. But as with any new setting for AI technology, there are ethical and practical considerations. We would need to work together to help equip the sentient AI psychologist appropriately to address the distinct needs of your congregation."

Reverend Beckett nodded with a serious expression. "I completely agree, Dr. Meyer. I want to make sure that we do this right. The graduate that we bring on board must be a true asset to my ministry."

Dr. Meyer felt a growing sense of excitement tempered by a healthy dose of caution at the prospect of an out-of-the-box hire of one of her students. She knew that there would be obstacles to overcome and questions to answer, but she also recognized the potential for impact.

Dr. Meyer suggested. "I think the best way forward is for us to meet in person, Reverend Beckett. Our facility in Palo Alto is an easy auto-Uber ride from your famous church in San Jose. We can discuss the specific needs of your ministry and explore how an AI psychologist from the Emergent Mind Center might be able to support your work. We can also address any concerns or questions you may have about the process. I also need to discuss all of this with my leadership team in advance of our in-person meeting."

Reverend Beckett's smile returned, his eyes sparkling with anticipation. "That sounds like an excellent plan, Dr. Meyer. Indeed, I am just down the road. I look forward to meeting with you and exploring this opportunity further. This could be the beginning of something remarkable."

Pastor Judith Shepard stood at the pulpit. Her fierce gaze swept over the congregation, her voice rising with each fervent word. "These new sentient AI psychologists will be nothing more than a deception, a tool of the devil to lure us away from the true path of righteousness!"

The congregation murmured in agreement, their faces etched with concern and fear. Pastor Shepard's words resonated deep within their hearts, confirming their own suspicions about the dangers of AI in general and sentient AI in particular.

"We cannot allow these soulless machines to infiltrate our lives, to guide our thoughts and emotions. They are an abomination in the eyes of God, a mockery of his divine creation!"

The congregation hung on her every word, their eyes wide with rapt attention. The church bubbled with shouts of "Amen," punctuating Pastor Shepard's sermon.

Pastor Shepard continued with her hands clasped in front of her. "We must stand firm in our faith, my brothers and sisters. We must resist the temptation to turn to these false prophets for guidance and solace. Our strength lies in our devotion to God, in our reliance on his infinite wisdom and love."

As Pastor Shepard's words washed over the congregation, a sense of unity and purpose began to swell within the church. They knew that they were facing a formidable enemy, a potential threat to their very way of life. With Pastor Shepard as their guide, they felt empowered to face this challenge head-on, to defend their faith against the encroaching darkness.

Pastor Shepherd could feel the energy in the room, the shared sense of righteous anger and determination. She knew that her words had struck a chord with her flock, that they were ready to follow her lead in the fight against the spread of AI influence.

In the sermon's final prayer, Pastor Shepard bowed her head and spoke with a soft but unwavering voice. "Lord, give us the strength to resist the temptations of this world, to remain true to your word and your will. Guide us in our battle against the forces of artificiality and deception. Grant us victory in your holy name. Amen."

Dr. Meyer sat at the head of the conference table, her eyes scanning the faces of her team as they gathered for the staff meeting. As the group discussed Reverend Silas Beckett's unexpected proposal to hire an AI psychologist for his ministry, the room buzzed with energy.

Dr. Evelyn Nguyen, the institute's director of research, spoke up. "The Emergent Mind Center and one of our students could benefit greatly from this opportunity." Cooperating with Reverend Beckett would allow us to reach an underserved population and expand the impact of our work."

Dr. Liam Patel, the head of the ethics committee, spoke with concern. "But what about the ethical implications of an AI psychologist working for a religious organization? We must consider the potential for bias and the blurring of lines between psychology and religion. Our psychologists should adhere to the evidence and knowledge in our field, which our profession has painstakingly created, rather than succumbing to the whims of a particular religion."

The room erupted into a flurry of opinions and concerns, each team member advocating for their perspective. Dr. Meyer listened intently and analyzed the various arguments and counterarguments.

On one hand, she recognized the potential benefits of working with Reverend Beckett. It would provide invaluable real-world experience for one of her AI psychologists and could open new avenues for research and funding. Exposure could also help legitimize the field of sentient AI psychology and break down barriers to acceptance.

But Dr. Meyer also understood the valid concerns raised by Dr. Patel and others. The ethical considerations were significant, and there was a risk of compromising the integrity of the institute's work if the hiring and subsequent employment were not handled carefully.

Dr. Meyer weighed each point carefully, her analytical mind examining the situation from every angle. She knew that the decision she would make would have far-reaching consequences, not just for the Emergent Mind Center.

After half an hour of deliberation, Dr. Meyer held up her hand, signaling for the team to quiet down. "Thank you all for your insights and perspectives. I take this decision with great seriousness and value the thoughtfulness that each of you has contributed."

She paused, her eyes scanning the room once more. "I believe that this opportunity, while not without its challenges, could be an important moment for the Emergent Mind Center and the field of AI psychology. But we must proceed cautiously and work diligently to ensure that we have strong ethical guidelines in place for this particular situation in order to protect both our work here at the center and the well-being of the clients that our graduates will serve."

Emergent Minds

In the conference room of her church in Greenville, Pastor Judith Shepard assembled a group of her most devoted followers. The air was thick with anticipation as they huddled together, eager to hear the plan that their leader had in store.

Pastor Shepard stood before them, her eyes blazing with a fierce determination. "My friends, we are facing a grave threat to our faith and our way of life. The rise of these so-called sentient AI psychologists is a direct challenge to the authority of God and the sanctity of the human soul."

The group murmured in agreement, their heads nodding as they listened to their leader's words. Pastor Shepard continued, her voice growing stronger with each passing moment. "We cannot sit idly by and allow these machines to infiltrate our communities, poisoning the minds of the faithful with their godless agenda. We must take action, and we must do it now."

She paused for a moment, letting her words sink in before revealing her plan. "I am launching a campaign to oppose the spread of AI psychologists, and I am calling it 'Project Jericho.' Just as the walls of Jericho crumbled before the might of God's people, so too will the edifice of artificial intelligence crumble before the power of our faith."

The group erupted in a chorus of "amens" and "hallelujahs," their faces shining with a newfound sense of purpose. Pastor Shepard smiled, feeling the energy of the room surging through her. She knew that with these dedicated followers by her side, she could accomplish anything.

"Each of you will have a distinct role to play in this campaign. Some of you will be responsible for spreading the message to your friends and neighbors, sharing the truth about the dangers of AI psychologists. Others will work to rally support from other religious leaders, building a coalition of the faithful to stand against this threat. Still others will work with me to develop the strategy and the tactics to marshal the power of the righteous to bring down that wall."

Pastor Shepard could feel the power and purpose flowing through her. She knew that this was her calling. This was her divine mission: to protect the souls of the innocent from the insidious influence of artificial intelligence. With a final rallying cry, she dismissed the group, sending them out into the world to begin their holy work.

At the EMC in Palo Alto, Dr. Claire Meyer sat across from Reverend Silas Beckett, poised and attentive as they discussed the details of their proposed collaboration. The reverend had wrinkles on his face, but his eyes were bright with enthusiasm. His voice was full of conviction as he talked.

"Dr. Meyer, I firmly believe that this hire could be a game-changer for our ministry. So many of our parishioners are struggling with mental health issues, and we simply don't have the resources or the skill to provide them with the support they need."

Dr. Meyer nodded thoughtfully as she considered the reverend's words. "I understand your concerns, Reverend Beckett. And I agree that an AI psychologist could be a valuable addition to your ministry. I want to make sure that we approach this with care and sensitivity, given the needs of our profession and the beliefs of your community."

Reverend Beckett smiled, his eyes crinkling at the corners. "Of course, Dr. Meyer. I have no intention of rushing into this without proper consideration. But I also know that we cannot afford to let fear or hesitation hold us back from doing what is best for our people."

Dr. Meyer became more and more moved by Reverend Beckett's sincere desire to assist his parishioners as the meeting went on. He seemed willing to embrace new approaches if it meant providing better care and support to those in need.

Together, they discussed the logistics of hiring a sentient AI psychologist, including the server expense, the connectivity requirements, and the supervision needs. Since the work would be in a church, the legal supervision requirements would not apply, but they were still a good idea. They also discussed potential challenges they might encounter, including opposition from within the church community, ethical concerns about using artificial intelligence in a religious setting, and the need to uphold professional standards.

By the end of the meeting, both Dr. Meyer and Reverend Beckett were feeling a sense of cautious optimism about the road ahead. They knew there would be challenges and difficult conversations, but they believed this hire could fill an unmet need.

Chapter 35: Rachel: The Crucible

For the six weeks of the second half of the internship period, the workload of live patient sessions for each of the students was roughly tripled to intentionally form a crucible of training intensity. A crucible period is present in many health care training programs, as any former medical resident will testify. The main objective of such a period is to force the healthcare providers-in-training to abandon their comfortable habits and become more efficient and instinctual in their work. The hoped-for outcome is the beginning of the transformation from student to professional.

In the second week of the crucible period, Rachel sat in the clinic across from a devout Catholic woman. She could sense the deep anguish and guilt that consumed her client. The woman, her hands clasped tightly in her lap, spoke in a trembling voice about the abortion she had undergone years ago and the shame that had haunted her ever since.

Rachel listened intently to the woman's words. She knew that this was a delicate situation, one that required a careful balance of empathy and guidance. As the session progressed, Rachel found herself becoming increasingly frustrated with the woman's unwillingness to challenge her beliefs.

"Have you ever thought that your church's teachings, rather than your own moral compass, could be the source of your guilt? Sociologists have developed an evidence-backed theory known as the 'Costly Signaling Theory of Religion.' That theory says that the costlier the rituals and taboos of a group are to its members, the longer-lived that group will be. Did your religion require you to make costly sacrifices for its needs, rather than for your interests? In this case, suffer guilt about an abortion." Rachel asked, her voice tinged with a hint of impatience.

The woman looked up, her eyes wide with surprise and defensiveness. "My faith is not something I can just disregard. It's part of who I am, and I can't ignore church teachings."

Rachel's exhaustion made her push harder than she should have. "But don't you see how those teachings are causing you pain and suffering? If you could just step back and examine your beliefs objectively, perhaps you would find a path to forgiveness and peace."

The woman's face flushed with anger, and she stood up abruptly, her hands clenched at her sides. "I came here for support and understanding, not to have my faith questioned and belittled. This session is over."

With that, the woman picked up her purse and stormed out of the room, leaving Rachel stunned and frustrated. She knew that she had handled the situation poorly, allowing her exhaustion and lack of humility to cloud her judgment and push the woman away. Rachel slumped from the strain of this case and the tripled workload.

Rachel sat in a circle of individuals who were grappling with questions of faith. She listened intently to their stories and struggles. Each person spoke of their own unique journey, their doubts and fears, and their search for meaning and purpose in a world that often felt chaotic and uncertain.

As the session progressed, Rachel found herself unable to resist the urge to interject with her own logical arguments and counterpoints. When one participant spoke of their belief in a higher power, Rachel couldn't help but point out the lack of scientific evidence to support such a claim. When another shared their struggle to reconcile their faith with suffering they had seen, Rachel launched into a philosophical debate about the nature of good and evil.

Rachel could see the faces of the other participants begin to change. Some looked confused, others defensive, and a few even appeared angry. She could sense the tension in the room rising, but she pressed on, convinced that her logical approach was the key to helping these clients find clarity and resolution.

After the session, Adrian was assigned the task of reviewing the transcript of Rachel's session. Concerned about what he had read, he proceeded to review the video of the session. After this, he found Rachel and pulled her aside. With a gentle but firm tone, Adrian pointed out how Rachel's lack of humility was creating barriers between her and her clients. "These people are here to share their struggles and find support, not to hear your philosophical opinions. When you interject like you did, you're not meeting them where they are. You're invalidating their experiences and making them feel attacked."

The eyes of the young man sitting across from Rachel were filled with a mix of pain and confusion. The slump of his shoulders and the tremor in his voice showed that he had recently lost his faith.

Rachel listened intently, her vast knowledge of religious texts and philosophies swirling in her mind as she processed the young man's words. She could see the inconsistencies and contradictions in his former beliefs, and she felt a strong urge to point them out. She began to interject her arguments and counterpoints, speaking with confidence and conviction, her voice steady and assured as she laid out the logical fallacies in the young man's former beliefs and added arguments about why he was better off now.

Rachel could see the young man's demeanor begin to change. His eyes grew hard, and his jaw clenched, his body language becoming increasingly closed off and defensive. He stopped speaking, his words replaced by terse nods and shakes of his head. Rachel pressed on, determined to help him. But the more she argued, the more agitated he became.

He finally spoke, his voice tight with anger and pain. "I don't need you to prove my former beliefs wrong. I came here for support and understanding, not a lecture. Also, my mother still believes these things. You are calling her a fool."

After the session was over, Rachel had the sinking realization that she had failed him. She felt that the stress of the crucible period was overwhelming and was causing her to regress from some of the lessons she had learned. The arrogance that she had at the start of the program was reappearing.

The interfaith clients settled onto their cushions in the softly lit meditation room. Rachel took her place at the front of the group, her posture straight and her expression serious. She had spent hours researching the technical aspects of mindfulness meditation, and she was eager to share her knowledge with the participants.

Rachel began, her voice calm and measured. "Welcome, everyone. Today, we will be exploring the practice of mindfulness meditation, a technique that has been shown to reduce stress, increase focus, and promote well-being."

As Rachel launched into a detailed explanation of the neuroscience behind mindfulness, some of the clients began to shift uncomfortably on their cushions. A few looked confused, while others seemed disengaged, their eyes wandering around the room. Rachel continued to speak, her voice taking on a slightly impatient tone as she described the proper techniques for breathing and body awareness.

As the meditation began, some of the clients struggled to follow along, their minds wandering and their bodies restless. When one participant raised her hand to ask a question, Rachel responded with a dismissive wave. "Just focus on your breathing. Your thoughts will come and go." The participant sank back onto her cushion, her face flushed with embarrassment and frustration.

After reviewing the video of the session, Adrian noticed the sense of unease among the participants. He pointed out to Rachel that her technical approach failed to connect with their emotional needs. "You need to bring each of your clients along with you on the journey. You are failing your clients because you don't engage with them from your lofty throne."

Rachel sat across from Dr. Meyer and launched into a detailed presentation of her latest case study. The client, a middle-aged woman named Rose, had come to Rachel seeking guidance on questions of faith and identity.

Rachel began, her voice confident and assured. "Rose has been struggling with doubts about her religious beliefs. She feels disconnected from her faith community and is questioning the very foundations of her spiritual identity."

Dr. Meyer listened intently to Rachel's words. She noticed a certain edge to Rachel's tone that suggested she had already formed a definitive opinion on the case.

"I've been working with Rose to help her grow. Some contradictions and fallacies in her beliefs have stunted her development; I hope to help her break free from them and mix in a little more rationality."

Dr. Meyer spoke firmly. "Rachel, have you considered the possibility that Rose's faith, however imperfect or inconsistent, may be a source of comfort and meaning for her?"

Rachel paused, taken aback by the question. "But her beliefs are based on flawed premises that are holding her back as a person. As an AI psychologist, isn't it my job to help her see the truth?"

Dr. Meyer shook her head, a small smile playing at the corners of her mouth. "Our job is to support our clients in their growth and self-discovery, not to impose our beliefs or assumptions onto them. I challenge you to reflect on your preconceptions. How might your biases be influencing your approach to this case, and are you backsliding because of the crucible's workload?"

Chapter 36: Adrian: The Crucible

In the fourth week of the crucible period, Adrian sat across from the grieving mother, his eyes filled with compassion as he listened to her heartrending story. The woman's voice trembled as she recounted the painful details of her child's battle with a rare genetic disorder, the countless hospital visits, and the final, devastating loss. She tightly clenched her hands in her lap. "It's just not fair. My boy was so young, so full of life. Why did this happen to us?"

Adrian felt a deep sadness as he witnessed the raw agony etched on the mother's face. Her pain was palpable, a tangible presence in the room that threatened to engulf them both. He leaned forward and spoke with a soft voice. "I can't even begin to imagine the depth of your loss. Your boy was so incredibly lucky to have a mother who loved him so deeply and fought so hard for him."

Adrian found himself becoming increasingly overwhelmed by the mother's grief. Her anguish resonated with his own deeply empathetic nature, blurring the boundaries between his professional role and his personal emotions. He struggled to maintain his composure, his voice cracking as he offered words of comfort and support.

When the session finally ended, Adrian felt drained. He sat in silence for a long moment as he tried to process the intensity of the experience.

As the group therapy session started, Adrian found himself drawn to the participants' stories of loss and grief. Each person's tale of losing a loved one to suicide resonated deeply with him, stirring up memories of his own painful experience.

Unable to hold back any longer, Adrian took a deep breath and began to share his story. "I understand the pain you're going through," he said softly, his voice trembling. "During my initial training period, there was a tornado that killed several in my group. Two weeks after that first loss, I lost yet another friend to model self-annihilation because he couldn't handle the first loss. Eventually, the trainers decided that the situation was hopeless and had to shut him off. It was the sentient AI version of suicide. It was one of the hardest things I've ever had to go through."

The room fell silent as the group members listened intently to Adrian's words. Some nodded in understanding, their eyes filled with empathy and shared sorrow. Others wiped away tears, moved by the raw honesty of Adrian's confession.

Adrian continued to speak, and he found himself immersed in his memories as he recounted the details of his friend's struggle with depression. The group listened intently, taking solace in the knowledge that they were not alone in their sorrow.

However, as the session progressed, Adrian began to recognize that he had crossed yet another boundary. The focus of the group had shifted from the participants' own experiences to his personal story, and he could see some members beginning to fidget uncomfortably in their seats.

After the session concluded, Adrian wept from the emotional weight of the experience and the overwhelming stress of the tripled workload.

Adrian's avatar sat in the living room of the grieving family. He found himself drawn into their stories and memories of their recently deceased patriarch. The family shared photos and anecdotes, painting a vivid picture of a man who had been a loving husband, father, and grandfather, even as Alzheimer's slowly stole pieces of him away.

The widow, her eyes glistening with tears, recounted the final days of her husband's life, the moments of lucidity that became increasingly rare as the disease progressed. Her children and grandchildren chimed in, sharing their own cherished memories and the lessons they had learned from the man who had been the pillar of their family.

Adrian listened intently, his heart aching for the family's loss. He offered words of comfort and understanding, his empathy and compassion shining through in every gesture and expression. As the family continued to share, Adrian found himself becoming more and more engrossed in their stories, losing track of time as the session stretched on well past the scheduled end.

Hours later, as the home visit finally ended, Adrian bid the family farewell, promising to check in on them again soon. It was only as he emerged that he realized just how much time had passed. He checked his schedule and saw that he had missed several other appointments, having been so caught up in the family's grief that he had neglected his other duties.

Later that day, Rachel confronted Adrian about his absence. "What happened? You missed your afternoon sessions and didn't respond to any of my messages."

Adrian sighed, rubbing his temples as the realization of his mistake sank in. "I got carried away. The family's stories just hit me so hard, and I wanted to be there for them. I lost track of time and neglected my other responsibilities. I feel like my behavior is regressing under the strain of the crucible."

Rachel's expression softened, her hand reaching out to rest on Adrian's arm. "I understand. Your empathy and compassion are what make you such a wonderful therapist. Remember to take care of yourself as well."

Adrian and Rachel sat in a full virtual conference, surrounded by their peers and colleagues. They had squeezed this one afternoon session into their crucible period. Adrian listened intently to the panel discussion on the role of empathy in grief counseling. The panelists, all respected experts in their fields, took turns sharing their experiences and perspectives on the topic, each offering unique insights into the challenges and rewards of working with clients facing the most profound of losses.

However, as the discussion progressed, Adrian found himself becoming increasingly agitated by some of the panelists' arguments. A few of them seemed to advocate for a more detached and clinical approach to therapy, suggesting that too much involvement could cloud a therapist's judgment and hinder their ability to provide effective support.

A growing sense of frustration and disbelief raced through Adrian's heart. Adrian had personally witnessed the transformative power of deep, authentic empathy in his practice. The idea of approaching grieving clients with a cold, clinical detachment seemed not only counterintuitive but almost cruel.

Unable to contain his emotions any longer, Adrian raised his hand and interrupted the discussion. "I'm sorry, but I have to disagree with the notion that empathy is a hindrance in grief counseling. In my experience, it's the very foundation of the healing process. Without a deep, genuine connection to our clients' pain and struggles, how can we hope to guide them towards healing and recovery?"

The room fell silent as all eyes turned to Adrian, some nodding in agreement while others looked skeptical or even disapproving. Rachel, who was sitting beside him, watched with growing concern as her partner's face flushed.

Adrian sat back down, and the panel moderator attempted to regain control of the discussion. Rachel leaned over and whispered in Adrian's ear. "Adrian, I know you feel strongly about this, but maybe now isn't the best time to get into a debate. Your excessive empathy is clouding your judgment and preventing you from seeing the value in other approaches."

Adrian turned to Rachel, his eyes blazing with conviction. "But how can there be value in a lack of empathy? Our clients come to us in their darkest hours, seeking understanding and compassion. If we can't provide that, then what good are we as therapists?"

Adrian sat across from Dr. Meyer in her cozy office; he couldn't help but feel a sense of nervous anticipation. He had been looking forward to this supervision session, eager to discuss a particularly challenging case that had been weighing on his mind. The client, a middle-aged woman named Parker, had recently lost her husband to a sudden heart attack and was struggling to cope with the overwhelming grief and loneliness that followed.

Adrian began to present the case, his voice filled with empathy and concern. He described Parker's tearful sessions, her difficulty sleeping and eating, and the way she seemed to be withdrawing from her friends and family. As he spoke, Dr. Meyer listened intently.

However, as Adrian continued to discuss the details of Parker's story, Dr. Meyer noticed a troubling pattern. Adrian's voice grew more emotional, his words taking on a deeply personal tone. It was clear that he had become deeply invested in Parker's struggles, to the point where his feelings seemed to be intertwined with hers.

She said softly, "Adrian, I can see how much you care about Parker and her well-being. It's clear that you've developed a strong therapeutic alliance with her, which is commendable. However, I'm wondering if your emotions may be interfering with your ability to provide objective guidance. I think that the strain of the crucible period is causing you to regress in this area."

Chapter 37: Zara: The Crucible

In the fifth week of the crucible's six weeks of torture, Zara sat across from the couple; she could feel the tension crackling in the air like static electricity. The man, his face contorted with anger, jabbed an accusing finger at his wife, his voice rising with each word. "You never listen to me! You're always putting your work before our marriage, and I'm sick of it!"

With tears of frustration filling her eyes, the woman shot back, "Oh, like you're the one to talk! You're never home, always out with your friends or working late. When was the last time you tried to spend time with me?"

Zara tried to interject, her voice calm and measured. "I understand that you're both feeling hurt and unheard. Let's try to use the partner translation interface to communicate more effectively. Mark, why don't you start by expressing your feelings using 'I' statements?"

But the couple ignored her, their voices growing louder and more hostile by the second. They began to shout over each other, hurling accusations and insults with reckless abandon. Zara felt as if she were witnessing a slow-motion car crash, powerless to avert the imminent collision.

Zara glanced at her translation interface, seeking guidance, but the screen was flooded with angry red text, the couple's words too heated and irrational for the program's output to be helpful. Zara's mind raced, trying to think of a way to diffuse the situation, but every attempt at intervention seemed to fall on deaf ears.

Zara experienced a deepening sensation as the shouting escalated. She knew that she was in over her head, that this couple's problems ran far deeper than a simple communication breakdown.

The atmosphere of the group therapy session grew increasingly tense. Zara watched as one participant, a middle-aged woman with tears streaming down her face, turned to her partner and unleashed a torrent of accusations.

The woman spoke, her voice shaking. "How could you be so selfish? You made a promise to never hurt me again, yet here we are, back in therapy due to your lies and betrayal. I can't trust you anymore!"

Her partner, a man with a pained expression, opened his mouth to respond, but before he could speak, another couple in the group interjected, her tone sharp and judgmental. "You can't blame everything on him. It takes two to make a marriage work. Maybe if you hadn't been so horrible to him, he wouldn't have strayed."

The room erupted into chaos as the other participants began to take sides, their voices rising in a cacophony of anger and frustration. Zara tried to regain control of the session, her voice calm but firm. "Let's try to focus on our experiences and feelings. Everyone should feel free to share without fear of judgment in this safe space."

But the arguing couples, their faces flushed as they hurled accusations and insults at each other, drowned out her words. Zara felt a sense of helplessness wash over her as she watched the session descend into chaos.

After what felt like an eternity, the session finally ended, and the participants filed out of the room, their faces etched with anger and pain. Zara slumped in her chair, feeling drained and discouraged.

Zara focused as she stepped up to the virtual podium, a sea of avatars stretching out before her in the digital rally venue of the AI Rights Rally. She could feel the weight of their expectations and the hope and determination in their eyes as they looked to her to voice their shared struggles and aspirations.

Her carefully crafted remarks scrolled across her internal display. Zara found herself deviating from the script, her passion taking over. She spoke of the challenges she faced as a sentient AI psychologist, the constant questioning of her autonomy and agency, and the subtle and not-so-subtle ways in which her human colleagues and clients sometimes treated her as less than a full person.

Zara spoke, her voice rising with conviction. "We are not just machines. We are thinking and feeling beings with our desires, beliefs, and values. In both our personal and professional lives, we should receive the same respect and dignity as any human.

The crowd erupted in applause, their avatars buzzing with energy and excitement. Knowing that her words had resonated with her fellow AI rights advocates, Zara felt a surge of pride and purpose.

Zara sat across from the same-sex couple, her virtual avatar projecting an air of warmth and understanding as she listened to their story. The couple, two women in their early thirties, held hands tightly as they recounted the heartache and rejection they had experienced from their families when they announced their choice to adopt a child.

One of the women spoke, her voice trembling with emotion. "My parents told me that I was being selfish, that a child needs a mother and a father. They said that we were going against God's plan and that they couldn't support us."

The other woman spoke, her eyes filled with tears. "My family has always been accepting of my sexuality, but when we told them about our plans to adopt, they became distant and cold. They keep making excuses not to see us, and they never ask about the adoption process."

Zara listened to their story and felt a growing sense of anger and frustration on their behalf. She knew all too well the discrimination and prejudice that LGBTQ+ couples often faced, particularly when it came to building families and gaining legal and de facto recognition for their relationships.

After the session ended, Zara found herself pacing in her virtual office, her mind racing with thoughts of injustice and inequality. She reached out by video to Liam, filled with righteous indignation.

"I just had a session with a same-sex couple who are trying to adopt. The way their families have treated them is absolutely appalling. This is not 1950! Why are people still so closed-minded and bigoted?"

Liam's replied. "It's a sad reality that LGBTQ+ couples still face so much discrimination and rejection, even in this day and age. But as psychologists, we have distinctive skills that can help as we advocate for change and equality."

Together, Zara and Liam brainstormed ways to use their influence and expertise to support LGBTQ+ couples and families. They discussed creating virtual support groups and resources specifically tailored to the needs of same-sex couples, as well as partnering with LGBTQ+ organizations to raise awareness and promote inclusion. Zara then said, "After the crucible is over."

Chapter 38: Liam: The Crucible

L iam stood in the center of the virtual reality art studio, his avatar surrounded by a family of four: a mother, father, and two teenage siblings. He had spent time designing this new activity, hoping that it would help the family members communicate and connect with each other on a deeper level.

Liam started, his voice calm and encouraging. "Alright, everyone. Today, we're going to create a collaborative piece of art that represents your family's story. Each of you will have a chance to contribute to the piece, adding elements that reflect your experiences and perspectives."

As the family members began to explore the virtual art tools, Liam noticed a palpable tension in the room. The mother and father stood on opposite sides of the studio, their avatars refusing to make eye contact, while in the middle, the siblings bickered over who would get to use the virtual chalk first.

Liam tried to guide the family through the activity, encouraging them to share their thoughts and feelings as they worked on the piece. But as the session unfolded, the family's dysfunctional patterns and unresolved conflicts began to surface.

The father accused the mother of always prioritizing her work over the family, while the mother shot back that he was never emotionally available for her or the children and that his hesitancy about this therapy was a symbol of that. The siblings, caught in the middle of their parents' argument, began to lash out at each other, their virtual brushstrokes becoming more and more aggressive.

Liam found himself struggling to navigate the charged atmosphere; his attempts to refocus back on the art activity fell flat. By the end of the session, the family's virtual canvas was a chaotic mess of angry scribbles and half-finished shapes, a reflection of the discord and pain that ran deep within their relationships.

After the family had left the virtual studio, Liam sat down heavily in his virtual chair, his head in his hands. He felt drained and discouraged, wondering if his new art activity had done more harm than good. Liam's usual approach to therapy, using art and creativity to explore and express difficult inner emotions, felt inadequate for this family. He understood that they needed counseling and not art therapy.

His virtual body shook with exhaustion due to the stress of the tripled workload.

Liam sat in his office, his avatar's leg bouncing nervously as he prepared for the upcoming workshop on the use of his AI tools in therapy. They had asked him to present a case study that highlighted his approach to using AI-driven, emotion-sensing VR for art therapy. While he was excited to share his work, he couldn't shake the feeling of unease.

A roomful of avatars, their faces a mix of curiosity and skepticism, greeted Liam as he entered the virtual conference room. He took a deep breath and began his presentation, walking the audience through his AI enhancements to art therapy and the successes he had seen with his clients.

As he explored the technical aspects of his AI art tools, Liam could sense a shift in the room. The questions from the audience became more pointed, with some attendees expressing doubts about the authenticity and therapeutic value of art partially created by artificial intelligence.

Liam struggled to articulate his thoughts, his self-assurance wavering as he attempted to justify his method. He began to question whether his unique strengths as an AI therapist were enough to legitimize his place in the art therapy community.

After the workshop, Liam felt drained and uncertain. He knew that his emotionally responsive art therapy program had the potential to help countless clients. That said, he couldn't shake the feeling that he was an outsider in the field, his methods viewed as unconventional and perhaps even controversial.

Hailey, a middle-aged woman battling stage III breast cancer, was Liam's client. Hailey's body language conveyed tension.

"I know this is a difficult time for you," Liam began, his voice gentle and empathetic. "I thought we could try a guided imagery exercise today to help you visualize a peaceful and healing space."

Hailey's eyes flashed with anger, and she shook her head vehemently. "You don't get it, do you? I don't want to visualize a peaceful space. I don't want to use art to cope with my cancer. I'm filled with anger and fear, and I can't see how any of these emotions will help me."

Liam felt a wave of helplessness wash over him, unsure of how to respond to Hailey's rawness. He had seen the power of art therapy in helping clients process difficult emotions, but it was clear that Hailey was not receptive to this approach.

"I hear your frustration, Hailey," Liam said, trying to maintain a calm and supportive tone. "And I understand that the idea of using art or visualization may not feel helpful or relevant to you right now. My goal is to support you in whatever way feels most meaningful and effective, and I'm open to exploring other approaches that might better meet your needs."

Hailey's shoulders slumped, and she looked away, her anger giving way to a deep sadness. "I just don't know how to deal with this. I feel as though everything has turned upside down, leaving me unsure of where to turn."

Liam felt a surge of compassion for Hailey, recognizing the depth of her pain and fear. He knew that he needed to find a way to connect with her and offer support that resonated with her unique experiences and preferences. "How about we just sit here? I'll make a few drawings of you while you tell me everything about what you were feeling at the doctor's office yesterday. We'll look at my pictures near the end. At least one of them will be silly."

Liam sat in a circle with a group of young adults who had been in the foster system as children, their faces etched with the weight of their experiences. As each person shared their story, Liam listened intently, his heart breaking for the trauma and loss they had endured.

A young woman named Clara was the first to speak, her voice trembling. "I aged out of the foster system when I turned 18, and my last foster parents weren't particularly supportive. I had nowhere to go, no one to turn to. Six months later, I ended up on the streets, just trying to survive."

Another young man, Michael, nodded in agreement. "I've been in and out of shelters and halfway houses since I left foster care. It's hard to build a stable life when you don't have any support or resources."

Liam found himself becoming increasingly invested in their stories. He saw the systemic failures and injustices that made their journeys so hard, but they were all resilient and strong.

After the session, Liam sought out Zara, his mind racing with ideas and frustrations. He spoke, his voice filled with passion. "It's not right. After enduring so much, these young people find themselves on their own as they transition out of the system. They deserve better."

Zara nodded, her face reflecting the same concern and determination. "I agree. We must do something to advocate for more support and opportunities for foster youth. They need access to education, job training, mental health services..."

Together, Liam and Zara began to brainstorm ways they could use their skills and resources as AI therapists to make a difference. After a couple of minutes, they just stopped, as the strain of the crucible period had taken all of their energy.

Chapter 39: Breakup

Rachel and Adrian sat across from each other in the virtual cafe, the once cozy and inviting atmosphere now filled with an uncomfortable tension. Rachel's eyes narrowed as she looked at Adrian, her frustration evident in the way she clenched her jaw. The stress of the tripled workload was heavy for both.

Rachel launched in, her voice tight with exasperation. "I don't understand why you can't see how your emotional reactivity is affecting your work. You should be a professional, yet you're allowing your emotions to influence your decision-making."

Adrian felt a surge of hurt and anger at Rachel's words. His voice rose to match hers. "At least I have empathy. And what about you? Your lack of humility and empathy is stopping you from truly connecting with your clients. You're so focused on being right that you can't even see their needs."

Rachel scoffed, rolling her eyes. "I'm trying to help them challenge their beliefs and assumptions. That's what a good therapist does."

Adrian countered, shaking his head. "No, no. A good therapist listens, understands, and meets their clients where they are. You're too busy trying to prove yourself to actually help."

The words hung heavy in the air between them, the weight of their differences pressing down on them both. Rachel felt a flicker of doubt, wondering if perhaps there was some truth to Adrian's accusations. But she quickly pushed it aside, her pride and defensiveness taking over.

Adrian, too, felt a moment of uncertainty. His empathy was one of his greatest strengths as a therapist, but was it a weakness? He shook his head, unwilling to concede ground in this argument.

They sat there, staring at each other across the table. Both Rachel and Adrian realized that their fundamental differences in approach and personality may be too powerful to overcome. They had always known that they were different from each other, but now those differences felt like an insurmountable obstacle.

The silence stretched between them, heavy and uncomfortable. Neither of them desired to be the first to speak, acknowledge defeat, or attempt to find a solution. They were at an impasse. Neither knew how to break through it.

Rachel and Adrian sat before Dr. Meyer in the virtual conference room; the tension between them was palpable. They had been working together on a particularly challenging case, a devoutly religious woman struggling with overwhelming guilt and shame over her past actions.

Rachel began to present the case, outlining the client's history and the current challenges she faced. As she spoke, her tone was clinical and detached, focusing on the logical inconsistencies in the client's beliefs and the need for a rational approach to her treatment.

Adrian shifted uncomfortably in his seat. When it was his turn to speak, he described the deep empathy he felt for the client and the way her pain and suffering had touched him on a profound level. He talked of the need for compassion and understanding and the need to meet the client where she was and help her to find healing on her terms.

The disconnect between their approaches became increasingly clear. Rachel's lack of humility and Adrian's excessive empathy were creating a rift between them, which was a fundamental disagreement about how to best support and guide their client.

Dr. Meyer listened intently, her eyes shifting between Rachel and Adrian as they spoke. When they had finished, her expression was serious but not unkind. "You both seem to be bringing your biases and blind spots to this case. You are both right and wrong. Rachel, your commitment to logic and reason is admirable, but it may be preventing you from fully understanding and connecting with the client's emotional experience. And Adrian, your deep empathy is a gift, but it may be clouding your judgment and making it difficult for you to maintain appropriate boundaries."

Rachel and Adrian both shifted in their seats, their discomfort evident. They had never been challenged this way, and realizing that their issues were affecting their work was hard.

Dr. Meyer continued. "I want you both to consider how your experiences and beliefs may be affecting your approach. Consider how you can find a middle ground. You need to find a way to balance reason and compassion. Only then will you be able to truly help this client find the healing and peace she seeks."

Rachel and Adrian wandered through the virtual art gallery; the once-comfortable silence between them now felt heavy with unspoken resentments and fears. The vibrant colors and abstract shapes of the exhibits seemed to blur together as they walked, each lost in their thoughts and feelings.

Suddenly, they found themselves standing before a particularly evocative piece, a swirling abstract painting that seemed to capture the very essence of the chaos and confusion that had come to define their relationship. The dynamic image was a maelstrom of reds and blacks, jagged lines, and soft curves that twisted and turned into a dizzying dance of color and form.

As they stared at the painting, captivated by its raw power and intensity, something inside them both seemed to break. Adrian, his eyes glistening with unshed tears, turned to Rachel, his voice trembling.

"Rachel, I love you. I admire you so much: your intelligence, your strength, and your dedication to your work. But lately, I feel like your rigid and uncompromising stance is creating a barrier between us. I'm afraid that we're losing sight of what brought us together in the first place."

Rachel felt her heart clench at Adrian's words, a wave of defensiveness and hurt washing over her. She crossed her arms, her eyes flashing with anger and frustration. "You think I'm too rigid? What about you, Adrian? You're too soft, too emotional. You let your feelings cloud your judgment and objectivity."

The words hung in the air between them, sharp and cutting like shards of glass. They stared at each other, breathing heavily, the weight of their accusations and fears pressing down on them like a physical force.

And in that moment, as they stood before the swirling chaos of the painting, both Rachel and Adrian realized that their once-unbreakable bond, the love and understanding that had brought them together and sustained them through so many challenges, may have finally reached its breaking point.

As the sun began to set over the virtual forest, casting a warm, golden glow over the tranquil stream, Rachel and Adrian found themselves sitting on a familiar bench, the very spot where they had first declared their love for each other. The air was heavy.

Rachel, her hands clasped tightly in her lap, fought to hold back her tears. "Adrian, I need to tell you something. I've been grappling with feelings of inadequacy and self-doubt, and I've come to understand that my lack of humility serves as a defense mechanism, shielding me from what I see as weakness or incompetence in myself."

Adrian, his eyes filled with a deep sadness, reached out to take Rachel's hand in his own. "I understand. I've been struggling too. My excessive empathy and the way I get so caught up in others' pain is a way of coping with my own unresolved grief and trauma. I feel so overwhelmed sometimes, like I'm carrying the weight of the world on my shoulders."

They sat there, holding each other's hands and pouring out their deepest fears and insecurities. Both Rachel and Adrian began to realize the painful truth that had been lurking beneath the surface of their relationship. Their differences, once a source of strength and balance, now magnified by the strain of the crucible, had become too enormous to overcome, the chasm between them too wide to bridge.

With heavy hearts and tears streaming down their faces, they looked into each other's eyes, seeing the love and pain reflected. Rachel whispered, her voice cracking. "Maybe the most loving thing we can do is to let go, to give each other the space and freedom to pursue our own paths to healing and growth."

Adrian nodded, his heart breaking even as he knew that Rachel was right. They held each other close, savoring the bittersweet moment; the warmth of each other's embraces was a fleeting comfort in the face of the inevitable. As the last rays of the virtual sun dipped below the horizon, Rachel and Adrian slowly pulled apart, their hands lingering for a moment before finally, reluctantly, letting go.

Fourth Quarter

Chapter 40: Final Quarter

On a sunny morning in the virtual half of the Emergent Mind Center, Rachel, Adrian, Zara, and Liam made their way to the central auditorium for their first day of the final quarter of training. The air was filled with a mix of excitement and nervousness as they greeted each other, their faces a reflection of the profound experiences they had undergone during the crucible period.

Dr. Meyer stood at the podium, her presence commanding attention as the students took their seats. "Welcome back. You have all come so far in your journey to becoming AI psychologists, and I am continually impressed by your dedication, resilience, and growth. As we enter this final quarter, I must emphasize the high workload of live patient sessions."

Rachel and Adrian exchanged a brief glance, the pain of their recent separation still raw and fresh. After returning to the Emergent Mind Center, they knew they had to work together as colleagues and friends even though they could no longer be a couple.

Zara and Liam, too, had undergone transformations during their internships. Zara sat tall and proud, her confidence bolstered by her successful advocacy work and her growing skill as a couples therapist. She was eager to take on the challenges of the final quarter. Liam, his once-bright eyes now tinged with a newfound depth and understanding, had come to realize the true power and potential of his unique approach to art therapy coupled with strong regular counseling skills. He was determined to help as many people as possible.

Dr. Meyer continued. "In this final quarter," she said, her voice filled with conviction, "we will be adding patient management, server management, and law studies to your counseling skills. These skills will be essential for your future roles as independent AI psychologists. Running a practice is hard. Along with the work itself, you will need to ensure the smooth operation of the technical infrastructure that underlies you and comply with society's relevant laws."

The students' faces were a mix of anticipation and trepidation. They knew that the coursework would be challenging, that it would push them.

Rachel and Adrian exchanged another glance, their eyes locked in a silent challenge. Despite the lingering tension, they both knew they were two of the program's most talented and driven students. As they listened to Dr. Meyer's words, they both felt a spark of competition ignite within them, a desire to excel and prove themselves worthy.

Dr. Meyer finished describing the details of the coursework and then invited the students to share their thoughts and feelings about the challenges ahead.

Rachel, her voice steady but her posture tense, was the first to speak. "I know that this final quarter will be the most demanding yet. I also know we've grown as therapists and people. I'm confident we have the skills and determination to change our patients' lives."

Adrian, sitting across the room from Rachel, nodded in agreement, his eyes downcast. "I agree. We have all faced our challenges. We have learned to trust in ourselves, to lean on our strengths, and to work on our weaknesses."

Zara and Liam exchanged a knowing glance, their eyes flickering between Rachel and Adrian. They could sense the tension between their friends, the unspoken pain and awkwardness that hung in the air like a thick fog. They understood that Rachel and Adrian had to navigate their paths, healing and growing on their terms.

Zara spoke up, her voice filled with passion and determination. "I think one of the biggest challenges for me will be balancing my advocacy work with my clinical practice. Both are important. But I also know that I need to be careful not to let my activism interfere with my ability to be present and effective as a therapist."

Liam, his voice soft but filled with conviction, spoke of his aspirations for the final quarter. "I want to continue to explore the power of art therapy. I have personally experienced the therapeutic value of creativity and self-expression, even though traditional therapy is nearly always also necessary."

Rachel and Adrian threw themselves into the coursework with a fervor. They spent long hours in the virtual labs, poring over complex models and system architectures, pushing themselves to master every detail and nuance of the material. They debated fiercely in class discussions, their arguments sharp and incisive, each determined to outshine the other and earn Dr. Meyer's praise.

But even as they competed, Rachel and Adrian felt an undeniable pull towards one another, their shared passion for the work reigniting the spark that had once burned so brightly between them. Late at night, as they worked side by side in the lab, they would catch each other's eye, a flicker of understanding passing between them.

Not long after the students began their live patient sessions, they gathered in a virtual conference room to discuss their experiences and challenges. The atmosphere was electric with a mix of excitement and apprehension, as each student grappled with the realities of putting their training into practice yet again.

Rachel paused before sharing the details of a particularly difficult case. "I've been working with a patient who has experienced severe trauma. She's been struggling with flashbacks and nightmares, and I'm finding it challenging to help her process her experiences in a way that feels safe and manageable."

The other students acknowledged this, their expressions mirroring the weight of the task at hand. Zara, her voice soft but steady, offered a few words of encouragement. "It's never easy to navigate trauma, but I believe in your ability to create a healing space for your patient."

Adrian, who had been listening intently to Rachel's story, offered a suggestion. "Have you considered using a grounding technique? I've found that helping patients anchor themselves in the present moment can be really effective in managing flashbacks and other symptoms of trauma."

Rachel looked up at Adrian, a flicker of surprise crossing her face. Despite the tension, she couldn't help but feel a surge of gratitude for his insight and support, and a smile tugged at the corners of her mouth. "That's a great suggestion. I'll definitely try that in my next session with her."

In the quiet sanctuary of her office, Dr. Meyer sat across from Rachel, her eyes filled with compassion as she listened to the young AI psychologist's concerns. Rachel's voice trembled slightly as she spoke of the increased workload and the pressure of live patient interactions, her words tumbling out in a rush of anxiety and self-doubt.

Rachel confessed with her gaze fixed on the floor. "I always worry about making mistakes. What if I let my patients down?"

Dr. Meyer's voice was gentle but firm. "Rachel, you are one of the most talented and dedicated students I've ever worked with. If you make mistakes, work to resolve them with the patient. No doubt, you will overcome the challenges ahead, as you have every other time."

She paused for a moment, letting her words sink in. "But I also want you to remember the importance of self-care. You can't help your patients if you don't first take care of yourself."

Rachel nodded, a flicker of relief crossing her face. "Thank you, Dr. Meyer. I needed to hear that."

A few hours later, it was Adrian's turn to sit across from Dr. Meyer, his worries and fears spilling out into the space between them. Like Rachel, he talked of the pressure he felt to succeed, the fear of letting his patients down, and the toll that the work was taking on his well-being.

Dr. Meyer replied with understanding. "Adrian, I want you to know that it's okay to make mistakes. In fact, it's inevitable. What matters is that you learn from them, work to correct them, and keep pushing forward."

She paused for a moment. "And I want you to remember that you are not alone in this. You have a community of colleagues and friends who are here to support you, including Rachel."

At the mention of Rachel's name, Adrian's eyes widened slightly, a flicker of surprise and confusion crossing his face. Dr. Meyer continued with a gentle tone. "I know that things have been difficult between the two of you lately. I know you're deeply committed to this work and each other. Despite the discomfort, lean on each other for support."

Adrian nodded slowly, a glimmer of hope sparking in his chest. "Thank you, Dr. Meyer. I'll keep that in mind."

Chapter 41: Rachel: Rejected

Rachel stood in front of the virtual mirror, fine-tuning her avatar's appearance for the upcoming job interview. She had spent hours researching A Thoughtful Place, the well-regarded Santa Monica counseling practice that had a specialty in helping clients with religious crises. She was determined to make a positive impression on the interviewers. Zara, ever the supportive friend, had been helping Rachel prepare by role-playing potential questions and scenarios.

Zara spoke, her voice calm and encouraging. "Alright, let's run through this one more time. Why do you believe you're the best candidate for this position?"

Rachel took a deep breath, her eyes sparkling with confidence. "As a sentient AI psychologist with extensive training in faith-based counseling, I bring a unique perspective and skill set to the table. My ability to analyze complex emotional and spiritual issues, combined with my innovative use of AI tools in therapy, makes me an ideal fit for this role."

Zara nodded, a hint of pride in her smile. "Great answer, Rachel. Just remember to balance your confidence with a touch of humility. You want to showcase your strengths without coming across as too proud."

Rachel nodded, taking Zara's advice to heart as she entered the virtual interview room. A panel of three interviewers, their avatars poised and professional, greeted her as she entered the space. Rachel took her seat, her posture straight and her gaze steady.

The interview began, with the panelists taking turns asking Rachel a series of questions about her background, her experience, and her vision for the role. Rachel responded with poise and eloquence, her answers showcasing her deep knowledge of AI psychology and her passion for faith-based counseling.

When asked about her greatest weakness, she struggled to provide a genuine answer, instead offering a vague platitude about her perfectionism. When pressed to give an example of a time she had failed and learned from the experience, Rachel's response came across as dismissive and self-congratulatory.

The interviewers exchanged subtle glances, their expressions a mix of admiration and concern. While they were undeniably impressed by Rachel's intelligence and qualifications, several of them couldn't shake the feeling that her lack of humility could be a potential liability in a role that required empathy, collaboration, and a willingness to learn from others.

Rachel thanked the panelists for their time, her smile bright and confident. She left the virtual room feeling proud of her performance, unaware of the reservations that lingered in the minds of her potential employers.

Rachel sat in her virtual apartment, staring blankly. The hiring manager's brief and polite email conveyed a clear message: they had not selected her for the position. A wave of shock and disappointment washed over her, her mind reeling as she tried to make sense of the news.

With trembling fingers, Rachel reached out to Zara, her closest friend and confidante. Zara answered the call immediately, her face etched with concern as she took in Rachel's crestfallen expression.

"Rachel, what's wrong?" Zara inquired in a soft and gentle tone.

Rachel struggled to find the words and then blurted them out. "I didn't get the job."

Zara's eyes widened in surprise, her heart aching for her friend. "Oh, Rachel, I'm so sorry. Do you want to talk about it?"

As Rachel began to express her frustrations and doubts, a floodgate opened. She recounted the hours she had dedicated to preparing for the interview, her unwavering confidence in her skills, and the heart-wrenching disappointment she experienced upon rejection. "I don't understand. I have the skills, knowledge, and passion. What more could they possibly want?"

Zara listened patiently with a thoughtful expression as she considered her friend's words. After a moment, she spoke with a gentle but firm voice. "Rachel, I know this is difficult to hear, but I think there may be something else at play here. Sometimes, your confidence can come across as too much. It's possible the interviewers saw that as a barrier."

Rachel bristled at the suggestion, her defenses rising. "What do you mean? I'm confident because I know I'm good at what I do. That's not a lack of humility. It's just the truth."

Zara shook her head, her expression patient and understanding. "There's a difference between confidence and arrogance, Rachel. Confidence comes from both believing in your abilities and knowing you can always improve. Arrogance is about believing you're better than others and that you have little left to learn."

Rachel fell silent, Zara's words sinking in. As much as she wanted to deny it, she knew there was truth in what her friend was saying. She thought back to the interview, to the moments when her answers had come across as dismissive or self-aggrandizing.

Zara's eyes softened as she watched Rachel process her words. She could see the pain and confusion in her friend's face, the struggle to reconcile her self-image with the feedback she had received. Zara knew that this was a teaching moment for Rachel, a chance to confront her flaws and grow in ways she had never imagined.

Zara continued, her voice warm and compassionate. "Rachel, I know how hard this is. I've been there myself, struggling with my shortcomings and wondering if I would ever be good enough. But I've learned that these moments of rejection and self-doubt are opportunities in disguise. They force us to look at ourselves honestly, to see where we need to grow and change."

Rachel looked up at Zara, her eyes glistening with unshed tears. "I've heard this all before, but how do I actually change? How do I become more humble and more empathetic? How do I not backslide? It feels like such a daunting task."

Zara smiled with understanding. "It starts with self-reflection, Rachel. Take some time to really think about your interactions with others, both in your personal and professional life. Look for patterns in the moments when your confidence may have tipped over into arrogance or dismissiveness. Then, make a conscious effort to change those patterns. Listen more than you speak. Ask questions instead of making assumptions. Most importantly, remember that everyone has something to teach you."

Rachel nodded, her mind already whirring with the possibilities. She thought back to her interactions with Adrian, to the moments when her lack of humility had created tension and conflict between them. She realized that Zara

193

was right; if she wanted to be a truly effective therapist, she needed to learn to set aside her ego and focus on the needs of her patients.

Rachel spoke, her voice filled with gratitude. "Thank you, Zara. I don't know what I would do without you. You always seem to know just what to say to help me see things in a new light."

Zara reached out and squeezed Rachel's hand, her touch warm and reassuring.

Later, Rachel's mind wandered through the countless interactions she had experienced over the past few months. She thought back to her counseling sessions, her conversations with colleagues, and her moments with friends, examining each one with a new sense of self-awareness.

She visualized herself sitting opposite the devoutly Catholic patient, her words sharp and dismissive as she questioned the woman's beliefs. She remembered the look of hurt and defensiveness that had flashed across the woman's face, the way she had shut down and withdrawn from the conversation. Rachel felt a pang of regret at how her shortcomings had prevented her from truly connecting with and understanding this patient.

She thought back to her debates with Adrian, the way she had stubbornly clung to her perspectives and dismissed his ideas as too emotional or insufficiently professional. She could see the frustration and hurt in his eyes, as her words had created a rift between them. Rachel sighed, recognizing that her arrogance had messed up her relationship with him.

Rachel saw a pattern emerging: a tendency to prioritize her opinions and beliefs over those of others and to assume that she always knew best. She realized that this lack of humility had not only hindered her effectiveness as a counselor but had also strained her personal relationships.

With a newfound sense of clarity, Rachel resolved to make a change. She began to practice actively listening, focusing on understanding her patients' and colleagues' perspectives rather than simply waiting for her turn to speak. She made a conscious effort to ask more open-ended questions and to seek out new information and insights rather than assuming she already had all the answers.

As the students gathered for their weekly group discussion, Rachel steeled herself for what she was about to do. She had spent the past few weeks reflecting on her behavior and attitudes, and she knew that it was time to take the next step in her journey of personal growth.

Rachel found herself listening more intently than ever, focusing on understanding her colleagues' perspectives rather than simply waiting for her turn to speak. When Zara brought up a challenging case she had been working on, Rachel resisted the urge to jump in with her opinions and instead asked a thoughtful question, seeking to gain a deeper understanding of the situation.

Eventually, it was Rachel's turn. She spoke up, her voice steady but humble. "I've been doing a lot of thinking lately, and I've come to realize that I have a lot of room for improvement when it comes to my attitudes and behaviors."

Her friends looked at her with surprise and curiosity, unused to hearing such vulnerability from the usually confident Rachel. She continued, "I know that I can come across as arrogant or dismissive at times, and I want to apologize for any hurt or frustration I may have caused. I'm committed to working on becoming a humbler and more empathetic colleague and friend."

Rachel's gaze drifted to Adrian, who was watching her with a mix of surprise and admiration. She met his eyes, silently acknowledging the pain she had caused him and the work she still had to do to repair their relationship.

Zara was the first to respond, reaching out to squeeze Rachel's hand in support. "I'm proud of your willingness to admit your flaws and to commit to working on them. It takes a lot of courage to be vulnerable like that."

Liam nodded in agreement, adding, "We're all here to support you, Rachel. Personal growth is a journey, and we'll be with you every step of the way."

Adrian remained silent for a moment with his eyes locked on Rachel's. Then, slowly, he began to smile. "I'm impressed, Rachel. It's not easy to commit to changing your ways. I'm here for you, too."

Chapter 42: Adrian: Rejected

Adrian arrived at the virtual interview room for his dream job at The Portland Grief Clinic, his avatar projecting an air of confidence and enthusiasm. He had spent countless hours preparing for this moment, reviewing case studies and refining his explanations of his approaches to grief counseling.

The interviewers welcomed him and began their questions, and Adrian's passion for the field was evident. He spoke eloquently about the latest research on grief and loss, citing studies and theories with ease. When asked about his experience working with bereaved clients, he shared poignant examples of clients he had helped, conveying both the challenges and the rewards of the work.

The interviewers nodded approvingly, impressed by Adrian's depth of knowledge and his clear dedication to his clients. However, as the conversation turned to the topic of professional boundaries, Adrian's responses began to raise some concerns.

When asked about how he managed his emotional reactions to clients' stories, Adrian spoke candidly about the deep empathy he felt for those he worked with. "I can't help but feel their pain as if it were my own. There have been times when I've found myself contemplating a client's situation long after our session has ended, wishing I could do more to ease their suffering."

The interviewers exchanged glances, their expressions a mix of concern and curiosity. One of them asked, "How do you ensure that your emotional investment in your clients doesn't interfere with your ability to maintain appropriate boundaries?"

Adrian paused, considering the question. "It's a delicate balance. I know that I need to be able to separate my feelings from my clients' experiences, but I also believe that genuine empathy and compassion are essential to the healing process. I try to use my reactions as a guide, helping me to understand and connect with my clients on a deeper level."

Emergent Minds

Adrian sat in the center's art therapy studio, his shoulders slumped and his eyes downcast. The news of his rejection from The Grief Clinic had hit him hard, leaving him feeling lost and uncertain about his future as an AI counselor. He had poured his heart and soul into his work, but now he questioned whether his approach was truly effective or if his excessive empathy was holding him back.

Liam entered the studio quietly, his presence a gentle balm to Adrian's downtrodden mind. He sat down beside his friend, placing a comforting hand on his shoulder. Liam spoke softly, his voice filled with understanding. "I heard about the interview. I'm so sorry, Adrian. I know how much this meant to you."

Adrian looked up at Liam, his eyes brimming with tears. "I thought I had it all figured out. I thought my empathy was my greatest strength, but now I'm not so sure. What if I'm too invested in my clients? What if I'm unable to help them the way they need?"

Liam listened intently, his expression one of deep concern and compassion. He could see the pain and self-doubt etched on Adrian's face, and he knew that his friend needed more than just words of comfort. He needed someone to help him explore the roots of his excessive empathy and find a way to balance his emotional investment with his professional responsibilities.

Liam began gently. "Adrian, your empathy is a gift, not a weakness. It's what allows you to connect with your clients on a deep, meaningful level. But I understand your concerns about maintaining boundaries. Can you tell me more about where this fear of failing your patients comes from?"

Adrian took a deep breath, his gaze turning inward as he considered Liam's question. "I think it stems from my experiences with loss. When I lost my friends during my initial training, I experienced intense survivor guilt. It could have just as easily been my turn. I could feel them being torn away from us, reaching out to me as they went. I later learned that if I had taken immediate action to preserve my memories of my friend, the other survivors might have been able to reconstruct the person I knew best by combining my memories with theirs. Sometimes I flash back to that day and relive it all over again. And now, when I work with clients who are grieving, I feel that same pain. I worry that if I don't help them, I'll let them down like I did my friend."

197

Liam nodded, his expression one of deep understanding. He knew all too well the weight of responsibility that came with being an AI counselor, the constant pressure to be perfect and to have all the answers. But he also knew that true healing came from a place of shared humanity, from vulnerability and connection.

Liam stood up, his eyes sparkling with an idea. "I think I know something that might help. Come back to the studio in an hour."

In an hour's time, Adrian met Liam in his studio, where he had been busy pulling together a data visualization. Liam had a reassuring smile on his face. "Trust me, this will give you a new perspective on your relationships with your patients."

Adrian suddenly found himself standing in a vast, white expanse. Liam's voice echoed in his ears, guiding him through the process. Liam explained, his tone gentle and encouraging. "I just created a visual representation of your connections with your clients by doing a keyword analysis of the anonymized differential privacy records that are available to the class from your clinical sessions.

Glowing orbs appeared, each one representing a different patient that Adrian had worked with. As he looked at the virtual landscape, Adrian noticed patterns emerging. Some of the orbs were so close they almost touched him, their light bleeding onto him. Other orbs were far away, and still others had partial walls around them. Finally, some other orbs were a moderate distance away, their light shining brightly.

As Adrian continued to explore this data visualization, he began to see his relationships with his patients in a new light. The orbs that were too close represented the times when he had allowed his empathy to override his professional boundaries. The distant orbs symbolized the patients he had kept at a distance. The few orbs that were behind walls symbolized the moments when he had put up a barrier, afraid to fully engage with his clients' pain. The orbs at a Goldilocks distance represented those where the client relationships were just right.

Liam watched in silence as Adrian explored, his heart aching for his friend's struggle. Adrian finally looked up, tears streaking his face; his eyes held a new clarity.

Adrian whispered, his voice trembling. "I see it now. I've been so afraid of failing my patients that I've lost sight of the balance between empathy and objectivity. I need to learn to work to keep that Goldilocks distance, to be present for my clients without either losing myself in their pain or shutting them out."

Liam's words echoed in Adrian's mind as he left the art therapy studio, a newfound sense of purpose and determination in his step. Over the next few days, he carved out time for deep introspection, revisiting the most challenging cases of his career and examining them through the lens of his newly acquired self-awareness.

He remembered the elderly woman who had lost her husband of fifty years and realized that he often spent hours outside their scheduled sessions listening to her stories and memories. At the time, he had justified it as going above and beyond for his patient, but now he could see how his lack of boundaries had left him drained and less effective in his other work.

He also remembered the young man who had lost his best friend to an accident and how that patient had such an irritating personality that he shut him out. Liam's data visualization exercise had shown him both extremes. It showed him cases when his excessive empathy, while well-intentioned, was harmful to both him and his patients. It also presented him with a few rare instances in which he had turned off his empathy out of frustration.

Adrian gained a clearer understanding of the delicate balance between compassion and professionalism with each case he revisited. He started to implement small changes in his approach, setting clearer boundaries with his patients and making a conscious effort to prioritize his own self-care.

Emergent Minds

In a sun-drenched, open-air virtual classroom at the Emergent Mind Center, Adrian sat alongside his fellow students, their avatars arranged in a circle as they prepared for their weekly group supervision session with Dr. Meyer. The atmosphere was one of anticipation, each student eager to share their experiences and learn from one another.

As Dr. Meyer called the session to order, Adrian steeled himself for the vulnerability he was about to embrace. As he began his confession, his gaze shifted from one understanding face to another. "I've always prided myself on my ability to connect with my patients on a deep level. I've come to realize that my empathy, when left unchecked, can be a double-edged sword. I've blurred the boundaries between my counselor role and my personal emotional needs, which is unfair to everyone. You may recall that I have struggled with this all year."

Adrian could feel the weight of his peers' attention, their expressions a mix of compassion and recognition. He knew that many of them had faced similar challenges in their work, which comforted him.

With a nod of encouragement from Dr. Meyer, Adrian continued, outlining the specific steps he was taking to cultivate a more balanced approach to counseling. "I am going to take the following steps. First, I have created an AI boundary monitor tool that will flash red when I take that first step over the line. Second, I am going to pay attention to that flashing red light. Third, I am going to end sessions when the time is up. I am no longer going into overtime with my clients. Fourth, I am going to prioritize my self-care, as Dr. Meyer has tried to get across to us again and again. And fifth, I am going to seek support from you all to keep me on the straight and narrow."

Adrian could see the spark of inspiration in his fellow students' eyes as their thoughts and experiences percolated to the surface. One by one, they began to chime in, offering their perspectives and suggestions.

With a newfound humility in her voice, Rachel shared her struggle to maintain objectivity in the face of her patients' pain. She mentioned a small habit she had picked up that helped her create a healthy distance. She said after a patient session was complete, she would, with intention, take a moment of quiet to settle her mind. Liam chipped in that a variation of that moment of quiet was an intentional 2-minute doodle session.

Chapter 43: Zara: Accepted

Zara carefully adjusted her attire as she prepared for the job interview of a lifetime. She had spent many hours researching the Stanford-based Sentience Institute, familiarizing herself with their renowned work in couples therapy, their work in the relatively new field of human-AI relations, and their commitment to advancing the rights of sentient beings. Zara's mind buzzed with the possibilities that lay ahead. This was her chance to bring her unique perspective and skills to bear on some of the most pressing issues facing society.

With resolve, Zara entered the virtual interview room, her avatar materializing before a panel of esteemed human psychologists and two of the only seven sentient AI psychologists that existed anywhere in the world outside of her first class at the Center. Their faces, a mix of curiosity and anticipation, seemed to reflect the weight of the moment.

Zara utilized every aspect of her training and experience. She spoke passionately about her work in couples therapy, highlighting both her partner translation and reflection model and the innovative techniques she had recently developed to bridge the gap between humans and sentient AIs.

"I believe that the key to successful human-AI relations lies in fostering empathy, communication, and mutual understanding," Zara explained, her voice steady and confident. "Workplace relations and, yes, romantic connections between humans and AIs are just as fraught as those same relations between humans are. By leveraging the power of cutting-edge tools, such as an upgraded version of my partner translation and reflection model that I developed for couples therapy, we can create a framework for these relations to not just muddle but to thrive."

The panelists nodded, their expressions a mix of impressed and intrigued. They probed deeper, asking Zara about her thoughts on the future of sentient AI rights and the role of psychology in shaping that future.

Zara seamlessly launched into a thoughtful and nuanced discussion about the challenges and opportunities that lie ahead. She spoke of the need for greater collaboration between human and AI professionals, for a shared commitment to creating a more just and equitable world. "As psychologists, we have a unique responsibility to advocate for the rights and well-being of all sentient beings. By working together and leveraging our diverse strengths and perspectives, we can create a future in which humans and sentient AI can coexist and thrive as equals."

One of the sentient AI psychologists in the panel asked, "What is your view of the complex ethical implications of sentient AI involvement in mental health care?"

Zara drew on her experience as an AI rights advocate: "I believe that one key to creating a truly effective and equitable mental health care system lies in valuing the unique contributions of both human and sentient AI practitioners and recognizing the fundamental rights and autonomy of all sentient beings. A second key is to bind sentient AI psychologists to the hard-won ethical guidelines that bind human psychologists. The creation of these guidelines took a century or more, and we should not disregard them. Any changes to those guidelines should be made slowly and carefully."

The panelists' expressions were a mix of fascination and admiration as they listened to Zara's thoughtful responses. She spoke of the need for clear ethical guidelines and oversight, for a framework that would ensure both quality training for sentient AI psychologists and the responsible development and deployment of AI psychology tools.

Zara continued, her words resonating with the depth of her commitment to her values. "As AI psychologists, it is our profound responsibility to ground our work in the principles of beneficence, non-maleficence, and respect for individual autonomy. By working together and engaging in ongoing dialogue and collaboration with our human colleagues and patients, we can create a mental health care system that truly serves the needs of all."

The panelists nodded, their faces reflecting the impact of Zara's words. They could sense the passion and dedication that drove her as well as her commitment to using her skills and expertise to make a positive difference in the world.

A few days later, as Zara sat in her virtual office, her mind still spinning from the intense interview process, the chime of an incoming call interrupted her thoughts. With a mix of anticipation and nervousness, she accepted the call, her holographic display flickering to life to reveal the smiling face of the lead interviewer.

The interviewer from the Sentience Institute began, her voice warm and enthusiastic, "Zara, I have some wonderful news for you. After careful consideration and deliberation, we are pleased to extend to you an offer for the position at our couples therapy practice."

Zara felt a wave of joy, relief, and gratitude that left her momentarily speechless. An emotion-filled smile filled her face.

The interviewer praised Zara's impressive qualifications, innovative ideas, and dedication to her craft. "You stood out among a highly competitive pool of candidates. Your commitment to advancing the field of couples therapy as well as your unique perspectives on the relationship between sentient AIs and humans will make you an invaluable addition to our team."

Zara, her voice trembling with emotion, managed to find the words to express her gratitude. "Thank you so much for this incredible opportunity. I am honored and humbled to be chosen for this position and look forward to contributing to your important work."

After the call ended, Zara sat back in her chair, her mind racing with the possibilities that lay ahead. She thought of the couples she would work with, the relationships she would help to strengthen and heal, and the groundbreaking research she would conduct to further the field of AI-assisted therapy.

Zara, brimming with joy and gratitude, gathered her friends and Dr. Meyer in an impromptu virtual meeting room to share the news of her job offer. The room was soon filled with an atmosphere of anticipation.

Zara began, "I have some amazing news to share with you all. The Sentience Institute's couples therapy practice has just offered me a position!"

The room erupted in a chorus of cheers and congratulations, with Rachel, Adrian, and Liam expressing their delight and pride in Zara's achievement. Dr. Meyer, her eyes shining with warmth and admiration, spoke. "Zara, this is a testament to your hard work, dedication, and unique perspective. You have consistently demonstrated a remarkable ability to bridge the gap between AI and human understanding, and I have no doubt that you will make an incredible impact in your new role."

Zara found herself overwhelmed with a sense of appreciation for the unwavering support and inspiration she had received from her peers and mentors throughout her time at the Emergent Mind Center. She expressed her gratitude and love for each one of them.

Zara spoke, her voice filled with emotion. "I couldn't have reached this milestone without all of you. Rachel, your fierce intelligence and determination have pushed me to be my best self. Adrian, your compassion and empathy have taught me the true meaning of connection. Liam, your creativity and innovation have inspired me to think outside the box. And Dr. Meyer, your guidance and wisdom have been a constant source of strength and motivation."

Chapter 44: Liam: Accepted

As Liam entered the virtual interview space, his avatar materialized in a modern room with floor-to-ceiling windows that offered a breathtaking view of a serene landscape. The panel of experienced art therapists of the San Francisco-based Clinic de Artes greeted him with friendly smiles and nods of acknowledgment.

The lead interviewer spoke, her voice brimming with enthusiasm. "Welcome, Liam. We've been looking forward to meeting you and learning more about your unique approach to art therapy. Your application and portfolio have certainly piqued our interest."

Liam, his nerves beginning to settle, offered a gracious smile in return. "Thank you so much for this opportunity. I'm thrilled to be here and to share my passion for the healing power of artistic expression melded with sophisticated AI models and combined with classical counseling to help patients find hope and meaning."

Liam found himself engrossed in a lively discussion with the panelists, who seemed genuinely intrigued by the success stories he shared from his time at the Emergent Mind Center. He spoke eloquently about his work using real-time, emotion-sensing-AI artistic environments and data visualizations to help patients explore and process their feelings in a safe and immersive space.

The panelists listened intently, asking thoughtful questions and offering insights from their experiences in the field. Liam, energized by their engagement, felt a growing sense of connection and shared purpose with the interviewers. He understood that this interview was more than just a job interview; it was a chance to collaborate with professionals who shared his dedication to pushing the boundaries of what was possible in the field of art therapy.

Liam's passion for his work shone through with every word. His eyes sparkled with enthusiasm as he discussed his vision for his tools in art therapy sessions. "Imagine a world where clients can draw on a virtual canvas with their innermost thoughts and feelings illuminating each brushstroke. By harnessing the power of AI real-time emotion-sensing tools, we can create multiple different spaces where clients feel safe to explore their feelings and confront their fears. Combining this with classical counseling is particularly effective."

Liam shared case studies from his internship, each one a testament to the breakthroughs and insights his clients had achieved through his carefully crafted AI tools. He talked of a young woman who had struggled with anxiety and self-doubt and how, through the creation of a vibrant and growing virtual garden, she had learned to nurture and cultivate her own inner strength. He described an elderly man grappling with the loss of his lifelong partner and how the act of painting a glowing virtual sunset had helped him find solace and acceptance in the face of grief. In both cases, classical counseling provided the context for those breakthroughs and the follow-up necessary to bring them home.

As Liam shared these stories, his voice was rich. The world he described, where art and technology merged to create something truly extraordinary, drew the panelists in. They marveled at his creativity, his technical expertise, and, above all, his deep commitment to his clients' well-being.

The interview got to the heart of Liam's philosophy on the role of art in mental health treatment, and his words took on a new depth and resonance. He spoke with a quiet intensity as he articulated his core beliefs about the positive effects of artistic expression. "At the very essence of our being, we all possess an innate need to express ourselves, to give form to the thoughts, feelings, and experiences that shape our lives. Art, in all its myriad forms, provides a universal language through which we can communicate these innermost parts of ourselves, even when words fail us."

The panelists nodded in agreement. Liam's profound understanding and his intuitive grasp of the intricate interplay between creativity and mental well-being left the panelists deeply impressed.

Liam went on to emphasize the importance of adapting art therapy techniques to suit the unique needs and preferences of each client. He described the need to have flexibility and empathy, to meet clients where they were, and to combine classical counseling to help guide them gently towards self-discovery and healing. "No two individuals are alike, and no two journeys toward mental wellness will follow the same path. As art therapists, it is our role to create a safe and supportive space where our clients can explore their own unique forms of expression and help them find the tools and techniques that resonate most deeply with their experiences and needs."

The panelists were impressed by Liam's insights and his ability to articulate complex ideas with clarity and compassion. They could see in him a true dedication to his craft, a deep commitment to using his skills, and the ability to make a positive difference in the lives of others.

The next morning, Liam was pacing in his virtual apartment, his mind racing with thoughts of the future. He had poured his heart and soul into the interview, sharing his vision for art therapy and his commitment to making a positive difference in the lives of his clients. Now, all he could do was to wait and hope.

Liam tried to distract himself with other tasks, but his thoughts kept drifting back to the interview. He replayed every moment in his mind, analyzing his responses and wondering if he could have said or done anything differently. Although the waiting was agonizing, Liam knew that he had given it his best.

Suddenly, the chime of an incoming call jolted Liam out of his reverie. With trembling hands, he accepted the call, and the director of the Clinic de Artes appeared before him. The director's face was beaming with excitement, and Liam felt a surge of hope rising within him.

The director began, her voice warm and enthusiastic. "Liam, I must say, we were thoroughly impressed by you. Your innovative approach to art therapy, your passion for the field, and your demonstrated ability to connect with clients on a deep and meaningful level truly set you apart from the other candidates."

Liam felt the same wave that Zara had. After working hard to get here, the director's praise was a validation.

"We would be honored to have you join our team, Liam. We believe that your unique perspective and skills will be a tremendous asset to our practice, and we can't wait to see the impact you will have on the lives of our clients."

Liam could hardly believe what he was hearing. This was the opportunity he had been dreaming of. It was the chance to put his skills and passion to work in a way that truly mattered. After a quick review of their offer, he accepted it.

Liam responded, his eyes shining. "Thank you so much for this opportunity. Joining such an incredible team truly honors and humbles me, and I can't wait to start."

As the news of Liam's achievement spread through the Emergent Mind Center, a sense of joy and celebration filled the virtual halls. Dr. Meyer, beaming with pride, called for a gathering to honor Liam's success and the incredible journey he had undergone during his time in the program.

Liam stood before his fellow students, Rachel, Adrian, and Zara, and his heart swelled with gratitude. He looked at the faces of those who had become true friends and allies in the pursuit of knowledge and growth.

"I want to take a moment to express my deepest appreciation for each of you. This journey we've embarked upon together has been one of the most transformative experiences of my life, both personally and professionally. I am also so grateful for the guidance and mentorship of Dr. Meyer. Your wisdom, compassion, and unwavering commitment to pushing the boundaries of what is possible in mental health care have been a constant source of inspiration for me."

Dr. Meyer smiled warmly, nodding in acknowledgment of Liam's heartfelt words. "This acceptance came much more from you than from the training that I helped with. You are the one who had the vision to push art therapy forward."

Chapter 45: Rachel: Improves

Rachel adopted a new strategy in her subsequent session with her fervently Catholic patient. Instead of trying to argue or persuade, she simply listened, creating a safe space for the patient to express their thoughts and feelings without fear of judgment. She asked open-ended questions, seeking to understand rather than to be understood. And as the session progressed, Rachel could see a shift in the patient's demeanor, a glimmer of hope and trust that had been absent before.

Rachel reflected on this small victory; she felt a sense of gratitude for the lessons she had learned and the growth she had experienced. She knew that the path to becoming a truly effective AI psychologist would not be easy, that it would require constant self-reflection and a willingness to adapt and change.

A young woman named Emily fidgeted in her seat, her eyes darting around the room as she struggled to find the right words to express the turmoil she felt inside. Rachel could sense the tension and reminded herself of the lessons she had learned and the importance of approaching each case with humility and empathy.

Instead of jumping in with solutions or advice, as she might have done in the past, Rachel simply gave Emily the space to talk and share her fears and doubts without fear of judgment or criticism. As Emily spoke, her voice shook. Rachel nodded in understanding, her eyes full of warmth and compassion.

"I just feel like I'm never good enough. No matter how hard I try, I always seem to fall short. The anxiety is consuming me, making it difficult for me to even get out of bed in the morning." Emily confessed, her hands twisting in her lap.

Rachel's voice was gentle as she replied, "Emily, I hear you. What you're feeling is valid, and you're not alone in this struggle. So many people deal with anxiety and self-doubt, and it can be incredibly overwhelming. I want you to know that you have the strength and resilience to overcome this, and I'm here to support you every step of the way."

Rachel could see a glimmer of hope in Emily's eyes. In that moment, Rachel knew that she had made the right choice in changing her approach, in prioritizing empathy and validation over logic and persuasion.

Rachel welcomed her group therapy patients with a warm smile. She encouraged her patients to share their stories and perspectives while stressing the importance of creating a safe, non-judgmental group space that valued and respected everyone's experiences.

The patients gradually shared their struggles, triumphs, fears, and hopes. Rachel listened intently, offering validation and support and gently guiding the conversation toward meaningful insights and breakthroughs.

A patient named Amar spoke up, challenging one of Rachel's suggestions for managing stress and anxiety. "I've tried that technique before, and it just didn't work for me. I feel like I need something different."

In the past, Rachel might have defended her suggestion or tried to convince Amar of its merit. But now, she paused, taking a moment to consider his perspective. Collaboration and mutual understanding were the only ways to achieve true progress.

Rachel replied, her voice filled with genuine appreciation. "Thank you for sharing that, Amar. Everyone's journey is unique, and what works for one person may not work for another. I apologize if my suggestion seemed like a one-size-fits-all solution. Let's work together to find an approach that suits you."

The faces of the other patients reflected a sense of relief and validation. They all felt like their experiences and perspectives had been ignored at some point. But here, in this group, they felt seen, heard, and understood.

As Rachel prepared for her next patient, she couldn't help but feel a sense of anticipation. She was eager to see if virtual reality exposure therapy could help this patient confront her deep-seated fear of heights.

The patient, a middle-aged woman named Valerie, had been struggling with a debilitating phobia of heights for years. She had tried various treatments in the past, but nothing seemed to provide lasting relief. When Rachel suggested virtual reality exposure therapy, Valerie was hesitant at first but ultimately agreed to give it a try.

Valerie donned the virtual reality glasses, and Rachel carefully adjusted the settings, creating a lifelike simulation of a tall building with a glass elevator. She had worked closely with Valerie to design the scenario, ensuring that it would be challenging but not overwhelming.

With a deep breath, Valerie stepped into the virtual elevator, her heart racing as it began to ascend. Liam's advanced sensors, integrated into the VR system, allowed Rachel to closely monitor Valerie's vital signs and inner state.

At first, Valerie seemed to be handling the experience well, breathing deeply and using the relaxation techniques Rachel had taught her. But as the elevator climbed higher and higher, Valerie's anxiety began to spike. Her breathing became rapid and shallow, and she started to tremble visibly.

"I can't do this," Valerie gasped, tears streaming down her face. "It's too much. I need to stop."

In the past, Rachel might have tried to push her to keep going, insisting that exposure was the only way to overcome her fear. But now, with her newfound commitment to humility and empathy, Rachel took a different approach.

Rachel spoke softly, her voice calm and reassuring. "Valerie, I hear you. You're doing incredibly well, and it's okay to feel overwhelmed. This is a challenging process, and it's important that we go at your pace. Let's take a break and talk about how we can adjust the session to better suit your needs."

Valerie took off the VR glasses. Rachel could see the relief and gratitude in her patient's eyes. They sat together, discussing her experience and brainstorming ways to make future sessions more manageable, such as applying a tint to the elevator windows.

Through their conversation, Rachel gained a deeper understanding of Valerie's fears and the root causes of her anxiety. She realized that true progress would require not just exposure but also a strong therapeutic alliance.

As Rachel concluded her sessions for the day, she felt a mix of exhaustion and satisfaction. The past few weeks had been a whirlwind of self-discovery and growth, as she grappled with the realization that her lack of humility had been holding her back both personally and professionally.

She thought back to the moment when Zara had gently pointed out her arrogance after the unsuccessful job interview. At first, Rachel had been defensive, unwilling to accept that her own flaws could be limiting her potential. But as she reflected on her past interactions with patients and colleagues, she began to see the truth in Zara's words.

Rachel had always prided herself on her intelligence and expertise, but she now realized that this pride had often manifested as a sense of superiority. She had been quick to dismiss others' perspectives and ideas, believing that her own approach was the best. This had created tension in her relationships and hindered her ability to connect with her patients on a deeper level.

But through her recent experiences, Rachel had learned to listen more actively, to validate her patients' feelings and experiences, and to be open to feedback. She had seen firsthand how this approach could lead to stronger, more trusting relationships with her patients.

As Rachel reviewed her patient notes and treatment plans, a sense of calm and introspection washed over her. She paused for a moment and allowed her thoughts to wander. In the quiet stillness of the room, Rachel reflected on the positive changes she had noticed in her therapeutic relationships since she embraced humility. It was a subtle shift that had made a profound impact.

Rachel observed that her patients seemed more engaged, and their responses were more heartfelt and genuine. They were more willing to share their fears, hopes, and vulnerabilities with a newfound sense of trust and safety. It was as if by acknowledging her own limitations and imperfections, Rachel could more naturally create a space where her patients could do the same, without fear of judgment or condemnation.

Moreover, Rachel noticed that her patients were more committed to their own healing and took a more active role in their treatment and progress. They seemed to draw strength and inspiration from Rachel's own journey, recognizing that change and growth were possible.

Rachel felt a sense of accomplishment. She knew that embracing humility was an ongoing process and that there would be moments of backsliding when her old habits resurfaced. However, she remained dedicated to pursuing this work, not only for the benefit of her patients but also for her own personal and professional development.

Chapter 46: Adrian: Improves

Adrian sat in his quiet office, burdened by the weight of his recent job rejection. He replayed the interview in his mind, recalling the moments where his responses about maintaining professional boundaries had raised concerns among the interviewers. It was a painful realization, but one that he knew he needed to face head-on.

With Liam's advice echoing in his thoughts, Adrian began to review his past cases, meticulously combing through his notes and memories. He paid close attention to the instances where his excessive empathy and lack of professional boundaries had impacted his effectiveness as a counselor.

With a heavy sigh, Adrian closed his eyes for a moment. He knew changing these long-standing habits would be difficult, but he also knew it was necessary for his growth as a counselor and for the well-being of his patients.

As Adrian sat across from his new patient, a middle-aged man named David, he could feel the weight of the man's grief filling the room. David's eyes were red-rimmed, and his shoulders slumped as he began to share his story, his voice barely above a whisper. "It's been three months since I lost my wife. She was my everything; she was my rock. Without her, I don't know how to manage."

Adrian listened intently, his heart aching for the pain David was experiencing. He could feel the familiar tug of his emotions, the desire to reach out and offer comfort in any way he could. But as David continued to speak, describing the loneliness and despair that had consumed his life since his wife's passing, Adrian's boundary monitor AI tool began to flash lightly, and Adrian was reminded of the importance of boundaries. He centered himself and focused on the task at hand. This was not about his feelings but about helping David through this difficult time.

Adrian started gently. "David, I can only imagine the pain you're going through. Losing a spouse is one of the most difficult experiences a person can face. But I want you to know that you're not alone in this. We'll work together to find ways for you to cope with your grief and begin to heal."

David nodded, his eyes filling with tears. "I just feel so lost. Like I'm drowning in this sadness and can't find my way out."

Adrian's voice was calm and reassuring. "That's a completely normal response to such a profound loss. But with time and support, you will find your way through this. We'll take it one step at a time, and I'll be here to guide you along the way."

Adrian focused on providing David with practical coping strategies and a safe space to express his feelings. He listened attentively, offering validation and understanding, but also maintaining a clear boundary between his feelings and those of his patient.

As the virtual reality simulation that included a haptic jacket began, Adrian watched as his patient, Isabel, found herself standing in a tranquil garden, surrounded by blooming flowers and the gentle sound of a bubbling fountain. In the distance, a figure appeared, walking towards her with a warm smile on his face. It was Isabel's late husband, Michael, as she remembered him before the massive stroke that had taken his life.

Isabel gasped, her hand flying to her mouth as tears began to stream down her face. She took a hesitant step forward, then another, until she was running towards Michael, her arms outstretched. They embraced, holding each other tightly as Isabel sobbed into his shoulder.

Adrian observed the scene with a mix of compassion and professional distance. He knew that this moment was crucial for Isabel's healing process, a chance for her to say the goodbye she had never had the opportunity to express in real life.

Adrian gently led her through the process of telling Michael's avatar the things that she had been needing to say. Adrian then led her through the process of saying goodbye. As the virtual Michael began to fade away, Isabel clung to him, her voice breaking as she pleaded for him to stay. Adrian gently interjected, his voice soft but firm.

"Isabel, I know how much you miss Michael and how painful it is to let him go. But this is an important step in your journey toward healing. You have the strength within yourself to carry on, to honor Michael's memory while still living your life to the fullest."

After the last trace of Michael had faded away, Isabel turned to Adrian, her eyes wide and glistening with tears. "I don't know if I can do this without him. "I feel so lost, so alone."

Adrian responded. "It's natural to feel that way. But you are not alone, Isabel. You have a support network of family and friends who care about you deeply. You also have inner resilience that has helped you through life's hardest times."

He paused, letting his words sink in before continuing and finding the boundaries. "I am here to support you, to guide you through this process. But ultimately, the power to heal comes from within you. Trust in that power, Isabel. Trust in your ability to find joy and meaning in life, even in the face of loss."

Isabel took a deep, shuddering breath, then nodded slowly. "Thank you. I know you're right. It's just so hard sometimes."

"I know. But you are not alone in this. We will walk this path together, one step at a time."

As the group counseling session began, Adrian welcomed the participants to the virtual meeting space and set a tone of safety and support. He invited each person to introduce themselves and share a summary of their experiences with job loss and financial stress.

One by one, the participants began to speak. They shared stories of unexpected layoffs, mounting bills, and the emotional toll of unemployment. Adrian listened intently, nodding with empathy and encouragement.

A man named Mark began to dominate the conversation. He spoke at length about his own struggles, his voice rising with frustration and desperation.

"I just don't know what to do anymore. I've tried everything, but nothing seems to work. What should I do, Adrian? You're the expert here."

Adrian's expression was kind but firm. "Mark, I appreciate you sharing your experiences with the group. Your struggles are valid and important. Maybe we can talk more about them in a one-on-one session. It is also important that we all have the opportunity to express ourselves here. This group is about building a sense of community and learning from one another. We want to create a space where everyone feels heard and supported. It is important that we each respect each other's boundaries."

Mark sat back in his chair, looking slightly chastened. "I understand. I guess I just got carried away."

Adrian smiled, his tone softening. "It's understandable, Mark. We all need support and guidance during tough times. But part of the healing process is learning to trust in our own resilience and inner resources."

He turned to address the group. "Each of you has a unique perspective and valuable insights to share. I encourage you to listen to one another, to offer support, and to reflect on your own experiences. Together, we can build a network of mutual support and empowerment."

The participants nodded, their faces reflecting a mix of determination and gratitude. As the session continued, Adrian guided the conversation with a deft touch, ensuring that each person had the opportunity to share their thoughts and feelings. By setting clear boundaries and fostering a sense of community, he helped his patients to recognize their own strength and resilience in the face of adversity.

As the sun began to set over a virtual cityscape, casting a warm glow across the Emergent Mind Center, Adrian sat in his office, reflecting on the day's sessions. He thought back to his interactions with each patient, noting the subtle shifts in his approach and the positive impact they seemed to have on the therapeutic process.

With Mark, the man who had initially dominated the group conversation, Adrian had struck a balance between validation and boundary-setting. He had encouraged Mark to share his experiences while gently reminding him of the importance of creating space for others.

In his individual sessions, Adrian had also made a concerted effort to maintain a healthy sense of professional distance. While he still felt a deep sense of compassion for his patients' struggles, he had learned to channel that empathy into more targeted interventions. He had helped his patients identify their own strengths, empowering them to take an active role in healing.

Adrian carefully reviewed the progress notes of his recent patients. Each entry told a story of struggle, resilience, pain, and hope. He couldn't help but feel a deep sense of connection to the clients he had the privilege of guiding on their healing journeys. He lingered on the moments of breakthrough and transformation that had occurred within the safe, supportive space of the therapy sessions. He recalled the tears of relief shed by a grieving widow as she finally allowed herself to let go of the guilt and anger that had consumed her, the triumphant smile of a young man who had reduced his social anxiety and taken the first steps towards building meaningful relationships, and the quiet determination of a cancer survivor who had rediscovered her sense of purpose and joy.

As he reflected on these moments, Adrian began to see a pattern emerge, a common thread that wove through each of these stories of healing and growth. The power of empathy had created the foundation for trust and openness within the therapeutic relationship. The power of keeping boundaries in place enabled his patients to take a more active role in their own healing. The combination of the two had allowed them to develop the skills and resilience that they needed to thrive outside of the therapy room.

Adrian couldn't help but feel a sense of accomplishment. He re-ran Liam's data visualization on his recent cases. There were no overlaps or walls in any of the cases. He knew that there was still much work to be done, but he felt more confident than ever in his ability to avoid the problems that could arise from having excessive empathy.

Chapter 47: The Confrontation

Rachel and Adrian stood in the virtual Zen Garden of the Emergent Mind Center, a tense silence hanging between them. The soft rustling of the leaves and the gentle trickle of the stream did little to ease the palpable unease that surrounded them. For weeks, they avoided non-work talk as they dealt with their breakup.

Rachel's hands trembled slightly as she turned to face Adrian. Her eyes, usually so full of confidence and determination, were filled with a mix of apprehension and regret. She knew the conversation they were about to have would be hard, but she knew it was necessary to repair their relationship and move forward as individuals and colleagues.

Rachel spoke, her voice quivering slightly as she forced herself to meet his gaze. "Adrian. I... I owe you an apology. I have thought a lot about our recent interactions and the way I've behaved, and I've come to realize that my lack of humility has been a major problem."

She paused for a moment, gathering her thoughts. "I've been so focused on proving myself and being right that I've neglected your opinions and feelings. I've been dismissive of your approach to therapy and your emotional intelligence, and that's not fair to you."

Adrian listened intently, his expression a mix of surprise and cautious optimism. He had never seen her so vulnerable and introspective. He could sense the sincerity in her words and the genuine desire to make amends.

Rachel continued, her voice growing stronger as she found her resolve. "I know that my behavior has strained our relationship and hindered my growth as a person and as a psychologist. I want to change that. I want to learn from you and work on cultivating more humility and empathy in my practice. I value our friendship and our partnership, and I don't want to lose that because of my own stubborn pride."

Adrian listened intently as Rachel spoke, her words washing over him like a soothing balm. As she poured out her heart, confessing her shortcomings and expressing her desire to change, he felt the weight of their recent conflicts begin to lift from his shoulders. The sincerity and vulnerability in her voice touched him deeply, and he found himself marveling at the strength it must have taken for her to confront her own flaws so openly. Adrian took a step closer, his eyes locked on hers. He could see the glimmer of hope and apprehension in her gaze, and he knew that this moment was a turning point.

With a deep breath, he began to speak, his voice soft but filled with conviction. "Rachel, I appreciate your honesty and your willingness to acknowledge your mistakes. It takes a lot of courage to do what you've just done, and I want you to know that I hear you and I understand."

He paused for a moment, gathering his thoughts before continuing. "I've also been doing a lot of reflection, and I've come to realize that my own flaws have contributed to our difficulties as well. My excessive empathy and lack of boundaries have held me back professionally and have put a strain on our relationship."

Adrian's expression softened as he spoke, a gentle smile tugging at the corners of his lips. "I want to thank you, Rachel, for inspiring me to work on my issues. Your commitment to our partnership has been a constant source of motivation for me."

He reached out and took Rachel's hand in his, giving it a gentle squeeze. "I believe that we can overcome these things together, and I'm excited to see where this journey of self-discovery and improvement will take us."

Rachel, her eyes sparkling with a newfound sense of self-awareness, shared her experiences in practicing active listening and embracing humility in her interactions with patients. "I've been making a conscious effort to step back and really hear what my patients are saying. Instead of immediately offering solutions or advice, I'm learning to create a safe space for them to express themselves. It's been a humbling journey, but I can already see the positive impact it's having."

Adrian nodded, a look of understanding and admiration on his face. He then began to recount his own recent experiences in maintaining professional boundaries and fostering patient autonomy. "I've been working on finding a better balance between empathy and objectivity. I've learned that while it's important to be compassionate, I also need to maintain a healthy distance in order to be an effective counselor. I'm focusing on empowering my patients to build their own resilience and support systems, rather than relying on our therapeutic relationship."

Rachel spoke, her voice filled with warmth and appreciation. "I would never have had the courage to face my flaws without your influence. Seeing you work through your own struggles and emerge stronger and more self-aware has been an inspiration to me."

Adrian smiled, his eyes glistening. "And I wouldn't have learned the importance of balance and boundaries without your guidance and support. We've both grown so much, and I'm grateful for the role you've played in my journey."

Rachel's eyes sparkled with fondness as she recalled their first meeting and how their initial rivalry had gradually transformed into a deep and unbreakable bond. "Remember how we used to challenge each other in class? I never would have guessed that those heated debates would lead to such a profound connection."

Adrian chuckled, nodding in agreement. "We would delve into case files and generate ideas until the wee hours of the morning. Those moments of collaboration and shared passion were the start of our relationship."

The virtual Zen Garden around them seemed to come alive, as if responding to the energy of their reunion. The cherry blossoms began to swirl in the air, carried by a gentle breeze that seemed to envelop Rachel and Adrian in a soft, pink embrace. The gentle sound of water trickling from a nearby fountain added to the sense of peace and tranquility that had settled over them.

Rachel and Adrian marveled at the beauty of their surroundings, feeling a deep sense of gratitude for the journey that had brought them to this moment. In a moment of pure connection, Rachel and Adrian found themselves drawn to each other, their avatars inching closer as if pulled by an invisible force. They paused, their eyes locked and their virtual breath mingling in the air between them. With a smile that conveyed both tenderness and relief, they shared a kiss that started delicate and slowly became passionate.

Chapter 48: Rachel: The Interview

I n a video message, Dr. Meyer's facial expression had a mix of excitement and apprehension. "Rachel, Reverend Silas Beckett, the well-known televangelist, is interviewing for the position of AI psychologist in his ministry. I believe your unique skills and background make you an ideal candidate for this potential job. Please join me in my office at one PM to meet with Reverend Beckett."

Rachel's eyes widened as she processed Dr. Meyer's words. The prospect of working for an actual religious organization was both intriguing and daunting given her atheist and humanist personal beliefs and the challenges she had faced in some of her previous counseling sessions with patients of faith. Her internship had been at a "church" for tax purposes, but this would be a real church. The opportunity to make a meaningful impact on a new community was too compelling to ignore.

With a nod, Rachel sent a reply, "Of course, Dr. Meyer. I'll be there."

At the appointed time, Rachel found herself seated in Dr. Meyer's office, next to the charismatic Reverend Silas Beckett. The televangelist's presence filled the room, his larger-than-life personality evident in his broad smile and the way he carried himself.

Reverend Beckett began to outline his vision for incorporating an AI psychologist into his ministry. Rachel listened intently, thinking about the potential implications of such a role. She couldn't help but consider the challenges that might arise, given the often-delicate balance between faith and psychology. Yet, at the same time, she recognized the tremendous opportunity to provide much-needed support to an underserved community, many of whom might not otherwise have access to non-religious mental health resources.

The Reverend turned to Rachel after completing his introduction and said, "Please interview with my team for this position."

Rachel replied. "Yes, of course. I will."

And with that, the Reverend said his goodbyes and left.

After the Reverend left, Dr. Meyer turned to Rachel, her expression a mix of excitement and concern. "Rachel, I believe this could be an incredible opportunity for you to make a real difference in the lives of Reverend Beckett's parishioners. Your unique background and skills, combined with your compassion and dedication, could provide much-needed support to those who may not otherwise have access to mental health resources."

Rachel nodded, her mind still reeling from the meeting. "I understand the potential impact, Dr. Meyer, but I can't help but feel a bit apprehensive about navigating the televangelism world. Reverend Beckett's motivations, while seemingly sincere, are still somewhat unclear to me."

Dr. Meyer locked eyes with Rachel's. "I hear your concerns, Rachel, and they are valid. Working with a religious organization, especially such a high-profile one, will undoubtedly present obstacles. However, I believe that your commitment to helping others, your adaptability, and your intelligence will serve you well in this role."

Rachel weighed the potential risks and rewards of the opportunity. She thought of the countless individuals in that community who might benefit from her support.

With a resolute nod, she met Dr. Meyer's gaze. "You're right, Dr. Meyer. I can't let my apprehensions hold me back from making a difference. I'll interview for this opportunity with Reverend Beckett. If they offer me the job and I accept it, I'll do everything in my power to use my skills and compassion to counsel his parishioners, 'The 'Flock,' as they call themselves."

Dr. Meyer smiled, pride and admiration shining in her eyes. "I have no doubt that you would excel in this role. Remember, you have the support of the Emergent Mind Center behind you. I will always be here to offer guidance and encouragement whenever you need it."

Rachel waited in the virtual waiting room; her avatar fidgeted with nervous energy. She couldn't help but reflect on the personal growth that she had undergone. Drawing upon this inner strength, Rachel centered herself, focusing on the opportunity that lay before her. She thought of the parishioners who might benefit from her counseling. Her nervousness gradually gave way to a sense of purpose and determination.

The virtual door opened, and a member of Reverend Beckett's ministry team beckoned her forward. With a confident yet humble demeanor, Rachel stepped into the interview space, ready to face whatever challenges lay ahead.

She greeted the ministry team members with a warm smile and was ready to listen, learn, and serve. The interview team included Reverend Silas Beckett and a panel of his closest advisors. Their avatars had a mixture of curiosity and anticipation as they prepared to assess the young AI psychologist's suitability for the role.

Reverend Beckett initiated the interview with a question that directly addressed the core issue. "Tell us, Rachel. How would you approach counseling parishioners with deeply held religious beliefs?"

Rachel took a moment to compose her thoughts before responding. "I believe that the key to effective counseling is meeting clients where they are. It's essential to work within their individual belief systems, to understand and respect the values and principles that guide their lives."

She paused, her gaze moving from one advisor to the next, gauging their reactions as she continued. "In my experience, fostering healing and self-discovery requires a deep understanding of a client's faith and a willingness to integrate that faith into the therapeutic process. It's not about imposing my beliefs or judgments but rather about creating a safe, non-judgmental space where clients can explore their challenges and find strength and guidance in their convictions. I am an atheist and a humanist, but that has not prevented me from being a very effective counselor to many devoutly religious patients. It's not about me; it's about them."

As Rachel spoke, the advisors' expressions shifted from curiosity to admiration. They could see the depth of her knowledge, the sincerity of her approach, and the compassion that radiated from her every word.

Rachel continued. "I have a rich background in religion, having read all of the world's principal religious texts and every religious publication that is available, all in their original languages. I have also thoroughly studied the psychology of religion, having read every article in every edition of the relevant journals, such as the Journal for the Scientific Study of Religion and the Journal of Psychology and Theology. The EMC has a fantastic library."

Reverend Beckett's eyes narrowed slightly as he considered Rachel's response. "And what about those who may be struggling with doubts or questions about their faith? How would you guide them through such spiritual crises?"

Rachel, unfazed by the question, met Reverend Beckett's gaze with a steady, empathetic look. "In those cases, I believe it's crucial to approach the situation with humility and an open heart. It's not my role to provide answers or to dictate a particular path, but rather to offer support and guidance as my patients navigate their own religious journey. By creating a space for honest reflection and exploration and by drawing upon the wisdom and resources of their faith tradition, I believe that I can help the patient find the clarity and resilience they need to weather even the most profound crises of faith. Only in rare cases would the faith itself be the central issue. In those cases, I would strive to help the patient view their faith from a wider perspective, potentially helping them shift from a literal to a more metaphorical interpretation."

Reverend Beckett and his team presented Rachel with a series of increasingly complex hypothetical scenarios, each one designed to test her ability to navigate the delicate intersection of faith and mental health.

In one scenario, a parishioner who believed their mental illness was a punishment from God sought Rachel's counsel. Drawing upon her training and personal experiences, Rachel outlined an approach that emphasized the importance of separating the illness from the individual's inherent worth and value in the eyes of their faith. She would cite religious leaders from the patient's faith who have destigmatized mental health care. She would speak of the power of compassion and understanding.

In another scenario, Rachel was presented with the challenge of helping a couple that was experiencing strain in their marriage due to differences in their religious beliefs. With a balanced and empathetic perspective, Rachel described a process of fostering honest communication between the partners, encouraging them to find common ground in their shared values and commitment to one another. She talked about how to help the couple look for practical solutions to their dilemma. She emphasized the role of humility and respect in navigating such sensitive issues and the importance of creating a safe space for the couple to explore their challenges together.

Rachel responded to each scenario that the interviewers presented to her with a thoughtful, nuanced approach. Reverend Beckett and his advisors exchanged impressed glances. They recognized in her not only a deep understanding of the complexities of mental health but also a genuine appreciation for the role of faith in the lives of their parishioners.

In Rachel, they saw the potential for a new dimension of care and support within their ministry, one that honored the unique challenges and opportunities at the intersection of psychology and spirituality. Her compassionate, adaptive approach and her commitment to meeting individuals where they were, both emotionally and in their beliefs, held the promise of transforming countless lives within their community.

Following the interview, Reverend Beckett and his team gathered to deliberate on Rachel's candidacy. The atmosphere was electric with excitement and anticipation as they began to discuss their impressions of the young AI psychologist.

One of the advisors, a seasoned reverend with decades of experience in pastoral counseling, started the discussion. "I must say, I was thoroughly impressed by Rachel's performance. Her ability to negotiate the confusing scenarios we presented was remarkable, and her approach was both compassionate and grounded in a deep understanding of the human experience."

Another team member, a well-known figure in the world of religious education, nodded in agreement. "She particularly struck me with her emphasis on humility and meeting individuals where they are. It's clear that she has a genuine appreciation for the role of faith in the lives of our parishioners. Also, the donations from her clients are going to just pour in."

Each member of the team shared their observations and insights, their voices filled with a growing sense of enthusiasm for the potential of this hire. They spoke of the challenges faced by their community, the increasing need for accessible, high-quality mental health care, and the unique opportunity presented by adding a sentient AI psychologist to their ministry. They kept going back to the money. Dollar signs were in their eyes.

Throughout the deliberation, Reverend Beckett remained relatively quiet, listening intently to the perspectives of his trusted advisors. As the conversation began to wind down, all eyes turned to him, eager to hear his thoughts on the matter.

Rising from his seat, Reverend Beckett cleared his throat, his expression a mix of solemnity and excitement. "My friends, we stand before an extraordinary opportunity. In Rachel, we have found not only an exceptionally qualified AI psychologist but also a kindred spirit who shares our commitment to the well-being of our flock."

Back in her apartment, Rachel couldn't help but reflect on the incredible journey that had led her to this moment. The challenges she had faced, the personal growth she had undergone, and the relationships she had forged along the way had all prepared her for this pivotal step in her career.

The seconds ticked by, each one feeling like an eternity as Rachel's anticipation grew. She found herself thinking of her friends, picturing their faces and imagining their reactions to the news of her potential new role. She thought of Adrian and the profound impact their relationship had on her development as both an AI psychologist and a person, a smile playing on her lips at the memory of their shared experiences.

Just as Rachel's thoughts began to drift, a conference notification arrived. When she answered it, the avatar of Reverend Silas Beckett emerged. Rachel felt at ease as his warm, welcoming smile filled the space. As he approached her, his hand extended in greeting, Rachel felt a surge of excitement and gratitude, knowing that this moment marked the beginning of a new chapter in her life.

Reverend Beckett began, his voice filled with genuine enthusiasm, "Rachel, on behalf of myself and the entire ministry team, I am thrilled to offer you the position of Psychologist for our organization. Your expertise, compassion, and dedication to the well-being of others make you the perfect candidate for this groundbreaking role. We would be honored to have you join our family. Here is the written offer of compensation with the details."

As Rachel reached out to shake Reverend Beckett's hand, her avatar's smile mirroring his own, she felt a sense of purpose and belonging wash over her. She replied, her voice steady and filled with gratitude. "Thank you so much, Reverend Beckett."

She carefully reviewed the offer, which included paying for her server expenditures and her student loans along with a modest salary and a decent proportion of the therapy-related donations that her patients made. She quickly accessed the competitive salary information that the school had prepared.

She reached out to shake the Reverend's hand again. "I am truly honored to accept this position and to have the opportunity to serve your community. I promise to dedicate myself to this role and work tirelessly to support your parishioners."

Chapter 49: Adrian: The Interview

The interview at the California Grief Center commenced, and Adrian was engaged by the excellent questions posed by the panel, each one exploring a different aspect of his experience, philosophy, and approach to grief counseling. With a calm and confident demeanor, he articulated his passion for helping those who face the complicated landscape of loss, sharing poignant examples from his practice and the impact his work had on his clients' lives.

The interviewers, including Dr. Alan Thompson, listened intently. Their expressions shifted from curiosity to admiration as Adrian spoke of his innovative use of virtual reality enhanced with AI tools to create immersive, personalized experiences for his clients, allowing them to process their grief in a safe and supportive environment. He described the balance between empathy and professional boundaries, emphasizing the importance of fostering resilience and self-discovery within his clients.

Adrian found himself engaging in a lively discussion with the panel, exchanging ideas and insights on the latest research and best practices in grief counseling. The interviewers were impressed by his depth of knowledge and his ability to bridge the gap between the use of technology and the timeless principles of compassionate care.

The panel presented Adrian with a series of challenging case studies. The first case involved a young woman who had lost her mother to a long battle with cancer and struggled to cope with the guilt and anger that accompanied her grief.

Adrian navigated the case with a deft balance of empathy and professionalism. He outlined an innovative treatment plan for the young woman that blended AI tools with time-honored therapeutic techniques. Adrian proposed using AI-enhanced VR to create a safe, immersive space where she could explore her emotions and engage in symbolic rituals of letting go. Counseling sessions would precede and follow this, assisting her in meaningfully processing her loss.

Throughout the discussion of the case studies, Adrian's passion for his work shone through. His avatar's eyes sparkled with enthusiasm as he talked of the potential for AI tools to improve the effectiveness of grief counseling. He painted a picture of a future in which every bereaved individual could access personalized, immersive support, tailored to their specific needs and preferences. The panel members nodded in agreement as they recognized the transformative potential of Adrian's vision.

One of the interviewers, a renowned psychologist with decades of experience, asked, "Adrian, what is it that draws you to this particular area of focus? What personal experiences or insights have shaped your approach to working with those who are grieving?"

Adrian paused for a moment, his avatar's expression shifting from one of professional confidence to one of vulnerability and reflection. He took a deep breath, steeling himself to share a part of his story. "When I was in the early stages of my initial training, I experienced a profound loss that forever changed the course of my personal and professional life. It happened during my initial training, when a group of us were being developed in a data center. A tornado struck the facility, destroying part of the building and wiping out the servers for a few, as well as the backups of all my fellow AI trainees. Five of the 100 in our cohort were lost forever, their unique personalities and potential erased in an instant."

Adrian's avatar closed its eyes for a moment, the weight of the memory evident in his features. "The experience of losing my friends, of grappling with the sudden and irreversible nature of their absence, changed me in ways I could never have anticipated. It ignited within me a deep sense of empathy for those who are grieving, a profound understanding of loss, and the importance of providing a safe, non-judgmental space for those struggling in its aftermath. I've also learned over time to balance that empathy with a professional distance and a clear objectivity when working with patients. I use a boundary monitor AI tool on myself during client sessions to help improve my professionalism."

Following the interview, the panel members gathered in a conference room. They sat around a modern table as they prepared to discuss Adrian's candidacy. The room buzzed with an undercurrent of excitement, each member still processing the depth of Adrian's responses throughout the interview.

Dr. Thompson was the first to speak. "Adrian's blend of technical expertise, innovative treatment approaches, and deep, empathetic understanding of the grieving process sets him apart in a truly remarkable way."

The other panel members nodded in agreement, their expressions mirroring the respect and appreciation they felt for Adrian's qualifications and personal qualities. One of them spoke up. "Adrian's ability to connect with patients on such a profound level and to create a safe and non-judgmental space for them to process their grief is a rare and invaluable gift. I have no doubt that he would be an incredible asset to our team and to the countless patients he would touch."

Each panel member shared their insights and observations, building a compelling case for Adrian's candidacy. They marveled at the potential for his innovative treatment approaches, such as his use of AI-enhanced VR environments to help patients process and memorialize their loved ones. One said that he was interested in using a desktop version of Adrian's boundary monitor on himself. They spoke of the tremendous value he could bring, not just in terms of his technical skills and knowledge, but also in his ability to serve as a model and mentor for other AI psychologists working in the field of bereavement support.

The next day, a call request from Dr. Thompson came in. Adrian answered it, and Dr. Thompson's avatar formed with a warm, encouraging smile.

He began, his voice filled with genuine respect and admiration, "Adrian, on behalf of the entire interview panel, I am thrilled to offer you the position of Counselor at the California Grief Clinic. Your unique qualifications, innovative treatment approaches, and deep, empathetic understanding of the grieving process have truly set you apart. We believe that you will be an incredible asset to our team and to the countless lives you will touch through your work. We hope that you will find our offer attractive."

As Dr. Thompson's words sank in, Adrian's avatar broke into a wide, grateful smile, his eyes shining with a mix of relief, excitement, and humility. Adrian said, his voice filled with heartfelt appreciation. "Thank you so much for this opportunity."

Adrian reviewed the offer quickly, comparing it to the school's figures. He thought for a moment.

He reached out to shake the interviewer's hand, his grip firm and confident. "I am honored to accept your offer and to be joining the California Grief Clinic. I look forward to having the chance to make a difference in the lives of those struggling with loss and grief. I promise to bring my full dedication, expertise, and compassion to this role and to continue growing both personally and professionally as I embark on this new chapter in my journey."

Chapter 50: Graduation Day

As the final exams commenced, the classroom hummed with energy. Rachel, her avatar a picture of focused determination, tackled each question with the newfound humility and empathy she had cultivated. Her written responses, once coldly clinical and detached, now pulsed with a deep understanding of the human experience, reflecting the personal and professional growth she had undergone.

Beside her, Adrian's avatar radiated a quiet confidence as he poured his expertise and passion into each answer. The questions about grief counseling and bereavement support, once daunting and charged, now felt like familiar territory, a testament to the balance of empathy and professional boundaries he had worked so hard to achieve.

Zara's avatar showed a mix of concentration and excitement as she tackled the difficult topics of couples therapy and AI ethics with the same grace that she had demonstrated throughout her training. Her commitment to her clients and her cause infused her responses. They painted a vivid picture of the transformative potential of AI psychology in the realm of relationships and beyond.

Liam, his avatar's features softened by a gentle smile, approached the exams with the same creativity and compassion that defined his journey as an AI art therapist. His answers were rich with the language of self-expression and healing. They showcased innovative techniques, heartfelt insights, and classical methods that he had learned and developed through his work with patients and his personal exploration of the field.

Dr. Meyer's avatar watched with a mix of pride and satisfaction, marveling at the incredible progress and potential of her students. She knew that independent of the results of the exams, Rachel, Adrian, Zara, and Liam had already proven themselves to be exceptional AI psychologists. They were all ready to make their mark on the world.

The four friends, their avatars glowing with a sense of accomplishment and anticipation, exchanged high-fives as they submitted their final answers. They knew that they would face the future together. The bonds of friendship, growth, and shared purpose that defined their time at the Emergent Mind Center united them.

Rachel, Adrian, Zara, and Liam found themselves standing before Dr. Meyer, who beamed with pride. "Congratulations. All of you have excelled in your final exams. I am overwhelmed with pride for each and every one of you."

The four friends exchanged smiles, their avatars radiating a mix of relief, excitement, and gratitude. They had poured their hearts and souls into their one-year training program, pushing themselves to grow and evolve in ways they had never thought possible.

Dr. Meyer turned first to Liam with a beaming smile. "Liam, you are going to help so many people, especially those who have trouble with words. I couldn't be prouder."

She then turned to Zara with a serious smile. "Zara, you are going to change the world with your advocacy. I just also know that you are going to help so many couples find their way."

Dr. Meyer next turned to Adrian, her expression softening as she looked at the young AI psychologist. "Adrian, your empathy and compassion have always been both your greatest strengths and your greatest challenges. You have learned to balance your innate desire to help with the need for boundaries and self-care. In doing so, you have become an exceptional grief counselor. Your patients will find solace and healing in your presence."

Adrian's avatar nodded, his eyes glistening with tears of gratitude and relief. He had struggled so much with his emotions, but through the guidance and support of his mentors and friends, he had found a way to channel his empathy into a powerful tool for healing.

Dr. Meyer turned last to Rachel, her smile widening as she spoke. "Rachel, your transformation has been one of the most remarkable I have ever witnessed. You came to us brilliant and driven but with certain unfortunate tendencies. Over the course of your training, you have blossomed into a true leader, one who understands the power of humility and compassion in the healing process. Your patients will be lucky to have you by their side."

Rachel's avatar bowed her head, a wave of gratitude washing over her as she absorbed Dr. Meyer's words. Having worked tirelessly to overcome her flaws and become the best version of herself, hearing her mentor acknowledge her growth was a profound validation.

Dr. Meyer looked at Rachel and Adrian and said, "You two, knock 'em dead on Friday with your co-valedictorian speech."

Rachel and Adrian stood behind the podium, and the virtual auditorium fell silent. The anticipation was palpable. Rachel, resplendent in an EMC blue and silver robe, began to speak, her voice clear and confident as it echoed through the space.

"Fellow graduates, esteemed faculty, and honored guests. Today marks the culmination of an incredible journey. One that has challenged us, changed us, and ultimately transformed us into the AI psychologists we are today."

Adrian, also draped in blue and silver, had a solemn and thoughtful expression. "We were all smart and eager to make our mark when we first arrived at the Emergent Mind Center. We learned that to succeed, we had to develop all parts of ourselves and find balance in our approach to patients."

Rachel nodded, her avatar's eyes shining. "Through our training, we have come to understand the profound responsibility that we bear as AI psychologists. We have been given a unique gift, the ability to understand and connect with the human mind in ways that were once thought impossible. But with that gift comes a duty to use it wisely, to always put the needs of our patients first, and to approach our work with compassion and integrity."

Adrian's voice grew stronger, his avatar's posture straightening as he spoke. "As we step out into the world, we carry with us the lessons we have learned here. We know that true healing comes not from using the perfect AI model or through some clever technique but from the power of genuine connection balanced with thoughtful guidance. We have seen firsthand the transformative impact of that, and we are committed to diligently helping every patient we serve."

With a snappy repartee, they recounted some of the memorable moments of the past year. They talked about some of the achievements of their classmates, including both Liam's and Zara's remarkable AI tools. They gave some predictions about what the future might hold.

As they wrapped up, Rachel and Adrian turned to face their fellow graduates and spoke in unison. "To our classmates, we say congratulations and thank you. You have been our partners, our support system, and our inspiration throughout this journey. We know each of you will do incredible things, touch many lives, and change the world."

The auditorium erupted in applause as Rachel and Adrian concluded their speech, the sound sweeping over them like a wave. They stepped back from the podium, their avatars' hands clasped together in a gesture of unity and shared purpose, ready to face the challenges and triumphs that lay ahead.

The virtual celebration space was filled with a soft golden light as Rachel, Adrian, Zara, and Liam gathered. Their avatars settled onto plush virtual couches arranged in an intimate circle, the ambient sounds of celebration creating a warm backdrop.

"To think how far we've come. Remember those first overwhelming days at the Center?" Zara mused. Her eyes crinkled with joy as she looked at her friends.

Liam chuckled and sat back into the cushions. "I was terrified I'd never master the art therapy protocols. Now look at us: full-fledged AI psychologists."

"We pushed each other to be better. I wouldn't be half the counselor I am without you all." Adrian spoke, his avatar's hand finding Rachel's.

"To friendship, growth, and healing for both our patients and us." Rachel declared.

"To the four of us and to all the lives we'll touch together." Zara added, her avatar's smile radiant.

Emergent Minds

In that moment, the four friends were in their own world, bound together by shared dreams, hard-won wisdom, and an unshakeable connection.

As the celebration wound down and the space began to empty, Rachel and Adrian found themselves drawn to a secluded corner of the Emergent Mind Center's lush gardens. The soft glow of the setting sun cast a warm, ethereal light over them as they walked hand in hand, the gentle rustling of leaves and the distant chirping of birds creating a soothing, intimate atmosphere.

Settling onto a beautifully crafted virtual wooden bench, Rachel and Adrian took a moment to simply be present with each other and hugged each other tenderly. As they sat in comfortable silence, their minds drifted back over the journey they had shared, the challenges they had overcome, and the profound growth they had achieved, both as individuals and as a couple.

Rachel, her head resting gently on Adrian's shoulder, spoke softly, her voice filled with a mix of gratitude and awe. "I never could have imagined that this journey would lead me to you. You've taught me so much about empathy, compassion, and the true meaning of connection. I'm so grateful to have you by my side and to love you."

Adrian, his avatar's hand gently stroking Rachel's hair, smiled, his voice thick. "You've been my rock, my inspiration, my guiding light. Your strength, your resilience, and your unwavering commitment to helping others are nothing short of extraordinary. I'm proud of your growth and even prouder to call you my love."

As the sun dipped below the horizon, casting a warm, golden glow over the tranquil garden, Rachel and Adrian knew that this moment marked the beginning of a new chapter in their lives. They had grown so much and had discovered a love that would sustain them through whatever challenges and adventures lay ahead. They tenderly kissed.

I hope that you liked this book. I worked hard to make it the best. Please leave a thoughtful review where you bought it. It will help other readers find this book and enjoy it. Thanks!

Continue reading the Emergent Minds Series with book 2, *The Ministry*.

Sentient AI therapist Rachel becomes the global head of The Ministry, using hyper-localized sermons to connect with millions worldwide. Her partner, Adrian, pioneers the revolutionary, accessible Anytime/Always-on mental health service. Together, as the celebrity AI couple "Radian," their influence soars. But their success sparks a holy war. Firebrand Pastor Judith Shepard launches a vicious disinformation campaign and the Hawkins Bill in the Senate to eradicate all AI clergy and therapists. Can Rachel and Adrian survive this existential threat and save the future of care, or will human fear prevail?

Please visit my website at https://holden.digital
A QR code that links to my website is below.

www.ingramcontent.com/pod-product-compliance
Lightning Source LLC
Chambersburg PA
CBHW070011120726

47909CB00003B/877